P9-CMX-194

EMERALD WINDOWS

Terri Blackstock

ZONDERVAN™

GRAND RAPIDS, MICHIGAN 49530

Books by Terri Blackstock

Cape Refuge (Book 1 in series)
Emerald Windows

Newpointe 911
Private Justice
Shadow of Doubt
Trial by Fire
Word of Honor

Sun Coast Chronicles
Evidence of Mercy
Justifiable Means
Ulterior Motives
Presumption of Guilt

Second Chances
Never Again Good-bye
When Dreams Cross
Blind Trust
Broken Wings

With Beverly LaHaye
Seasons Under Heaven
Showers in Season
Times and Seasons
Season of Blessing

Novellas
Seaside

DEDICATION

This book is lovingly dedicated to the Nazarene.

ACKNOWLEDGMENTS

*C*hrist is the author and finisher of my faith, and the power and provider of my books. He is the One who gifts me with ideas that often keep me awake in the night. And it is He who grants a shared vision to those who play crucial roles in the publication of my work: Greg Johnson, Dave Lambert, Lori VandenBosch, Bob Hudson, Sue Brower, and so many others who have come to mean so much in my life. God has blessed me more than I could ever have hoped or imagined, and so often, these precious people are instruments of those blessings. I thank them for allowing me to dig through the layers of worldliness, youth, and misunderstanding originally written into this book so many years ago, and get to the heart of what the Lord intended for this story. And no words can ever express the depth of gratitude I have for my Lord, who is in the merciful business of granting second chances to those of us who long ago ran out of first ones.

We want to hear from you. Please send your comments about this
book to us in care of the address below. Thank you.

ZONDERVAN™

GRAND RAPIDS, MICHIGAN 49530

WWW.ZONDERVAN.COM

ZONDERVAN™

Emerald Windows
Copyright © 2001 by Terri Blackstock

Requests for information should be addressed to:
Zondervan, *Grand Rapids, Michigan 49530*

Library of Congress Cataloging-in-Publication Data

Blackstock, Terri, 1957–
    Emerald windows / Terri Blackstock.
      p. cm.
    ISBN 0-310-22807-7
    1. Glass painting and staining—Fiction.   I. Title.
PS3552.L34285 E5 2001
813'.54—dc21   2001045382

All Scripture quotations, unless otherwise indicated, are taken from the *Holy Bible: New
International Version*®. NIV®. Copyright © 1973, 1978, 1984 by International Bible Society.
Used by permission of Zondervan. All rights reserved.

All rights reserved. No part of this publication may be reproduced, stored in a retrieval system, or transmitted in any form or by any means—electronic, mechanical, photocopy,
recording, or any other—except for brief quotations in printed reviews, without the prior
permission of the publisher.

Published in association with the literary agency of Alive Communications, Inc.,
7680 Goddard Street, Suite 200, Colorado Springs, CO 80920.

Interior design by Beth Shagene

Printed in the United States of America

04 05 06 07 08 /❖ DC/ 10 9 8 7

EMERALD
WINDOWS

CHAPTER

$\mathcal{T}$HE WINDOWS OF HAYDEN'S landmark church—St. Mary's—were caked with dust, and from outside Brooke Martin could see web-shaped cracks that had already been evident seven years earlier when she'd last seen the place. It surprised her that the congregation of Hayden Bible Church—usually much tighter with their purse strings than they were with their gossip—had decided to allocate funds to buy the building and renovate it. It surprised her even more that they had hired her to design the stained-glass windows that would replace the broken-out glass. There had been a time when the people of Hayden, Missouri, wouldn't have hired her to mop their floors. Apparently, things had changed. And it was about time.

She left her car and walked around the building to the small employee parking lot in the rear, skirted by pine trees and one sprawling oak that shaded the pavement from the early spring sun. Only one car occupied a space there—a 1980 Buick with a rusty back fender and a dent in the driver's door. She stopped at the sight of it, and for a split second gave serious thought to running back to her own car and out of Hayden in the time it would take to say "not again . . ."

Her hands began to tremble, and she dropped her portfolio to her side. Inhaling deeply, she let her troubled gaze drift to the church door. Anger swelled migraine—like in her temples. Had crucial details been left out of this job offer?

A March breeze whispered through her hair, as if trying to calm her, and she paused at the door and told herself that it wasn't facing Nick Marcello now that bothered her so. It was that she hadn't faced him before. She had simply run away. But what else could she have done? With the town rejoicing over the juiciest piece of gossip they'd ever scavenged, she had gotten out of town as fast as she could, hoping to spare her family any more shame.

But this time, Brooke reminded herself with a grim lift of her chin, she had made a pact with herself. She had vowed that when she came back to take this job, she would face the town with dignity and integrity, and then, by creating a work of art that would send them all reeling, she would redeem herself. She had assumed that process would involve facing Nick Marcello again. She just hadn't expected to do it so soon.

She opened the door and stepped into the musty old sanctuary. The door creaked behind her, then slammed with an echoing thud. She stood quietly for a moment, listening, looking.

"Deliveries go back here!"

That familiar voice came from just inside the darkened corridor at the back, and she forced herself to move. Stepping over a beam on the old wood floor and around a dusty pew lying on its back, she made her way to the only doorway with light. She saw him standing at a table, bent over a blueprint, studying it intently.

He seemed younger than he had when she was in high school. But maybe it was just that she was older. She recalled the dress shirts and ties he'd always worn, the freshly pressed trousers, the shiny loafers. Now he wore an old flannel shirt, paint-stained jeans, and tennis shoes.

"No delivery," she said. "Just me."

He looked up, then slowly straightened. "Brooke."

Brooke tried to smile, but the effort was too much for her. "I . . . I didn't know you would be here. Pastor Anderson said—"

"If you'd known, you wouldn't have come." He crossed the room, still keeping distance between them. "That's why I asked him to call for me."

"He should have told me."

He nodded, as if he'd already given that a lot of thought.

"I'm in charge of artistic development in the renovation," he said. "But to be perfectly honest, that consists mainly of those windows. I'm going to be helping you design them. The church is counting on them being a new point of interest in the sanctuary. *I'm* counting on them being a masterpiece."

Brooke set her jaw and walked to the table, processing the information that changed everything. "I don't know, Mr. Marcello."

"Brooke, I haven't taught in seven years, and you're still calling me Mr. Marcello? It's Nick, okay? Say it. Nick."

She looked down at her feet. "Okay, I don't know, *Nick.*"

Nick stepped toward her, and reluctantly, she brought her eyes up to his. "You don't know what, Brooke?" he asked. "If you can create a masterpiece, or if you can work with me?"

"Both. It's nice seeing you. But I can't stay."

She turned and walked back into the darkness of the corridor, down the hall, and back into the old sanctuary.

Nick followed. "Look, I didn't hire you for this job because of any of that mess. I hired you because you're talented. I've kept up with your work since you left."

She kept walking

"I saw the windows in the church you did in Columbia. And the door you did at that restaurant in Kansas City." She stopped, her hand on the door. "You're doing well, but you could do so much more. My decision to hire you was a business decision; I needed someone with your talent."

Turning back, Brooke looked up at the old broken glass that skirted the circumference of the ceiling. "I've never done anything of this caliber, though."

"You've done plenty of this caliber," he said. "Maybe just not this size."

She regarded him with questioning—almost suspicious—eyes. It wasn't often that she was recognized as an artist. Most people viewed her as an interior decorator of sorts, someone who added life to dull rooms.

"I've always wanted to work with you," Nick said quietly. "Ever since you were in high school and I saw the talent you had. I know we could do something really amazing with these windows."

"This is the first time I've been back to Hayden since—" She glanced up at him, steadied her voice. "Since I graduated. The gossip has had seven years to die down. I don't know if I can stand to have it start back up again."

Nick crossed his arms, and she saw him stiffen visibly, as if the subject was growing tedious. "Brooke, seven years can heal a lot of wounds. It's past time to move on."

She loathed the fact that her own wounds had not healed. "I need time to think about this," she said.

He turned away from her, slid his fingers into his front pockets and seemed to consider the wood grain on the dirty pew in front of him. "How much time do you need?" he asked. "I wanted to get started this week. It'll take months to do this job right, and we haven't got a day to waste."

Brooke looked up at the windows again. She had pinned so many hopes on them. A job like this could establish her as a serious stained-glass artist. Her boss and mentor, Mr. Gonzales, had encouraged her to take this job, even though it meant she would be out of the shop for months. He was close to retirement. When he closed the shop she'd worked in since graduating from college, she would have to open her own or work for someone else. These windows might mean the difference between being on her own and being under someone else's thumb.

Coming back to Hayden had been hard enough. She had rolled into town, bracing herself for the debilitating reminders of what had driven her away. Working with her old art teacher would only open those wounds. "I don't know," she said again. "Maybe I can give you an answer tomorrow."

Nick looked at her for a moment, then shrugged. "All right."

She started back to the door.

"Brooke?" His voice resonated in the old, dusty sanctuary.

Brooke turned around and saw that the tension in his expression was gone. "Uh-huh?"

"It was good to see you."

"Yeah," she said. "It was good to see you too, Nick."

And that was exactly why she couldn't take the job.

CHAPTER

2

$\mathcal{N}$ICK WENT BACK TO THE OFFICE he had taken over for the duration of the renovation and sat down at the desk. Maybe this *was* a mistake. Maybe he was fooling himself to think that hiring her was strictly a professional decision. It *had* been good to see her. She seemed to have grown; in the few minutes their conversation had lasted, she had shown a quiet strength and unwavering will that hadn't been there before. But she still had that unique, creative style of dressing, with the chains and bracelets that added an artist's flair to her thrift-shop clothes. He'd watched the rich girls clamor to imitate Brooke in high school, and wealthy women probably envied her style now. Her hair was a little darker, and her eyes still said things she would never have expressed openly.

She'd been seventeen when he'd first seen her, sitting in the front row of his class, working on a sketch of the mangled bicycle he'd placed at the front of the room. The project had been deliberately difficult, and he'd used it to test the students' skills and talents. Slowly he had walked up and down the aisles between work stations, commenting on each student's crude progress ... when he had come to her.

It was her work that caught his attention first. The lines of her sketch had been so precise, so accurate, that he doubted he could have captured the bicycle better himself. But something about the drawing had reached out to him. It was the uniqueness of the image ... the vision of something fresh in something so used up.

He remembered the way she had looked up at him, embarrassed that he'd been watching her.

"It's not finished," she had said, and he'd recognized the apology in her voice.

"It's good," he told her. "Have you been studying art for long?"

"Just two years," she said, meeting his eyes directly. "Mr. Jasper taught me last year, but he didn't let us get very creative. He was really into precision."

"You can get as creative as you want in my class."

Brooke laughed under her breath. "Yeah, I kind of thought you'd feel that way when I saw you," she said. "Most stuffed shirts don't own antique hot rods."

If there was anything that made a friend of Nick, it was complimenting the classic Duesenberg he only brought out of his garage for antique car shows. "You saw my car?"

"I went to the Autofest Car Show last summer," she said. "I wanted to draw some of the vintage cars. Yours was my favorite."

He had laughed then, not really caring that others in the room were beginning to listen in. "I'm proud of that car," he said. "My grandpa left it to me, and there aren't many like it. It's a real work of art."

"Yeah, it is," Brooke had agreed. "And you've taken good care of it. That's how I knew I'd like your class."

There had been a lot of pretty young students in his classes that year he'd taught at Hayden High School, and not all had been there because of a burning interest in art. Some of them saw art as an "easy A." Others competed for the interest of the new young teacher. But Brooke had been different. Her passion for art had been evident in every assignment she'd completed for him. She had fast become his favorite student.

He'd grown even more amazed when she brought in the sculpture she'd worked on at home for a year, to finish it as her final project for the class. The stone sculpture intrigued him so much that he found himself watching, mesmerized, as the piece came to life. It was the sculpture of two hands—a man's and a woman's—joining in a gentle embrace. There was something so tentative about the touch that it had tapped an emotion deep within him. That was what great art did, he'd taught his students. It grabbed you by the heart and didn't let you go. He hadn't expected one of his students to have talent that surpassed his own. Captivated by that talent, he'd offered her extra advice, extra lessons, extra help. When they reached the final term of the year, he urged her to enter the sculpture in the statewide competition for an art scholarship at the University of Missouri. The new goal had sent her into a tailspin of nerves and self-doubt.

One day, when she'd stayed after school with another student to work on her project, she had looked up at him with forlorn defeat in her eyes. "I can't do it," she said, setting down her chisel. "It's too ambitious. I should have tried something easier."

"What do you mean you can't do it?" he asked. "You're almost there already."

"With the woman's hand," she said. "But I can't get the man's hand right. I don't know how to capture the texture . . . the strength."

Before he'd realized what he was doing, Nick had sat down beside her and offered her his hand. "Here," he said. "Study mine."

Brooke's hand had trembled as she'd taken his hand, and she had studied it as if it were a fragile piece of china that she had no right to touch. "Feel the texture," he'd said quietly. "Feel the bone structure. The veins. The imperfections. Notice the way the light falls over it, and the contrast of shadows."

Slowly Brooke had begun to study his hand with the most tentative touch he'd ever experienced. He had tried to separate himself from his emotions as she nervously traced the lines in his knuckles. Then she had turned his hand over, and explored the height of the bones and the cracks in the skin. Her touch had grown less tentative as she stared down at the shadows playing across his palm and the way the light from the window moved across it. Her artist's eyes had not missed a thing.

Startled by the realization that the emotion he was feeling was not appropriate between a teacher and a student, he finally withdrew his hand. "Now see if that helps," he'd whispered.

He looked up then and saw the other student staring, as if she'd witnessed something she wasn't supposed to see.

He realized that Sharon Hemphill, the daughter of the school superintendent, who came from old family money and owned half the town, had clearly misinterpreted what had just happened.

He went to her desk and looked at her project. It was an uninspired mosaic of her favorite pop star, but it looked nothing like him.

"Maybe the eyes are too far apart, Sharon," he said, hoping to divert her attention.

The chubby girl looked up at him with round, striking eyes. "It looks more like a caricature than a portrait, doesn't it, Mr. Marcello? Maybe I'm using the wrong medium. My mother saw it the other day and said my talent was more in line with painting on velvet. She suggested Elvis." She said it as if it amused her, but Nick knew from living in Hayden all his life that nothing the girl ever did could please her mother.

Brooke got up and came over to her. "You can do it, Sharon," she said. "Look ... just take out this piece, and move this around ..."

Nick watched with admiration as the piece took on new life. The girl's pale face brightened. "Wow. That made a huge difference. Thanks."

"Sure." Brooke went back to her seat and stared down at her sculpture with deep concentration.

As he might have expected, rumors had begun to fly around the school after that. Sharon Hemphill must have described what she'd seen with an imagination he wished she'd applied to her art work instead. Nick had assured the principal that there was nothing going on—that he'd never even been alone with Brooke, that she was a very gifted student working on the most poignant piece of sculpture he'd seen by an amateur, and that as her teacher, it was his job to guide and encourage her so that she could win the state competition. The principal had chosen to believe Nick.

But that wasn't the end of the rumors.

Brooke had shown up with her sketch pad at another car show an hour from town, and the Hemphills, Sharon's parents, had seen her talking to Nick and assumed they had gone there together.

Another time he'd gone into a coffee shop and found her sipping a latte and working on a charcoal drawing. He had joined her for a few minutes—just enough time for two teachers from the school to see them and draw conclusions. Mr. Hemphill, the superintendent, confronted him the next morning with the threat of firing if there was "one more incident."

Sharon had approached him at lunch, apology dimpled into her face. "Mr. Marcello, I'm so sorry about my parents. Dad was going to fire you today, but I talked him out of it. I know you haven't done anything wrong, but to my mother, you're guilty until proven innocent. With her on the school board and my dad being superintendent, the deck is kind of stacked against you."

He had smiled, set his fork down, and looked at the young girl who seemed too pleasant to have come from such a family. "I appreciate that, Sharon."

"See, my mom has always had a thing about Brooke." She stopped and tugged at her baggy pants. "It's almost like somebody from Brooke's neighborhood . . . you know, blue collar family and all . . . doesn't have a right to be talented and pretty and thin . . ." She looked down at the books she held. "Everything I should be, but I'm not. It really chaps her. And then there's that appearance thing. It doesn't matter how things really are. It's how they *appear*, you know? That's why she's got it in for you. If you were bald and had a fifty-pound paunch, she'd leave you alone."

Nick nodded, seeing Sharon in a new light. "I'm glad you told me."

She stood there in her ill-fitting clothes, as if she didn't know what to do next. "Well . . . guess I'll get back to class."

"Aren't you going to eat lunch?"

"No," she said. "My mother won't let me drive my car until I've lost thirty pounds."

"You're kidding," he said.

"I wish."

That explained why her clothes were so baggy lately, and why she looked so pale. She was probably starving herself. A case of bulimia waiting to happen.

She drew in a deep breath, then hugged her books tighter. "I'll see you sixth period, Mr. Marcello."

She left the room, and Nick realized that if her father and mother would be so unmerciful to their own daughter, they certainly wouldn't go easy on him. He vowed to avoid even the *appearance* of evil.

But just before graduation, Nick got word that Brooke had won first place in the University of Missouri scholarship competition. Because he was her art teacher, Nick had presented the award on graduation night.

Brooke had sprung out of her seat at the announcement and cried as she'd made her way to Nick. He'd wanted to grab her up and hug her, but he knew the rumors would only mushroom if he did. Instead, he shook her hand, congratulated her, and gave her the small statue.

After the ceremony, Nick had gone to stand in the lobby to congratulate each of his graduating students. Brook was one of the last to come out. She held her diploma in one hand and her award in the other, looking as excited and vibrant as he had hoped she would. He had taken a step toward her, but she'd been encircled by her family, swallowed into their hugs and congratulations, and ordered to put her robe back on and pose for an eternity of pictures.

He had thought of waiting to congratulate her, but a surprising melancholy had fallen over him. The school year was over. His star student was going to college. He would have no reason to see her again.

That melancholy had disturbed him, and finally, he had withdrawn from the crowd and headed for the art room. He had turned on one of the easel lights, casting the room in a dim yellow glow, and had stared at the air as he reminded himself that he couldn't get so attached to his students if he was going to make it as a teacher.

When she'd stepped through the doorway, it had startled him. She had her graduation gown draped over her arm, and her award and diploma in her hands.

"I was looking for you," she said with a smile. "I thought I might find you in here. Do you ever go home?"

"Sometimes." Smiling, he nodded down at the statue in her hands. "How does it feel?"

She tried to answer, but the words wouldn't come. Grinning, she just shook her head. "You knew and didn't tell me."

"I wanted you to be surprised," he said. "And I wanted everyone to know about it. Your moment of triumph. You deserved it."

Her eyes misted over. "I couldn't have done it without you."

"Sure, you could have."

She shook her head, insisting that she couldn't. "Where is it?" she asked. "My sculpture, I mean. Did they return it?"

"I have it in the closet. I thought of displaying it in the foyer at graduation, but I was afraid it would get knocked over and chipped in the crowd." He went to the closet and got it out. "Here. You can make it the centerpiece of your first showing. It's really amazing, Brooke."

She took it reverently. "Did you know I named it *Infinity?*" she asked quietly.

"I saw that on the entry form," he said. "Interesting name. Where did it come from?"

"I just thought those hands represented something that lasted. Something that just goes on and on, no matter what." She studied the sculpture, her green eyes sobering. "Mr. Marcello, I want you to have it."

Nick caught his breath. "But, Brooke," he said. "It's the best thing you've ever done. You should keep it . . . or sell it . . ."

"I could never sell this," she whispered, setting the sculpture in his hands. "It means too much."

He took it then, frowning down at it, and tried to think of something eloquent to say. When words failed him, he just reached down to hug her.

Suddenly the lights flashed on, flooding the room in cruel fluorescents. Nick and Brooke jumped apart and turned to the door. There stood the school superintendent, Gerald Hemphill, and his wife, Abby, gaping at them in horror and condemnation, as if they'd caught a teacher molesting a child.

Abby Hemphill looked as if she'd been personally offended. "Apparently we've interrupted something," she said. Then picking up Brooke's graduation gown, she thrust it at her. "I suggest you take this and go home."

"Yes," her husband said. "We have some important matters to discuss with Mr. Marcello."

"I just came to thank him—"

"It's all right, Brooke," Nick said. "I can handle this."

For the rest of his life, Nick was sure he would never forget the look of mortified humiliation on Brooke's face as she left the room.

Mr. Hemphill had fired him on the spot, and the school board had threatened to take legal action. But the thought that kept running through his mind was that Brooke was hurting. As soon as he'd gotten near a telephone that horrible night, he'd called her.

"It's going to be all right," he'd assured her. "We'll get this straightened out."

But the next morning the headlines in the paper read, "Teacher Fired for Rumored Affair with Student," and the article told how rumors had abounded for weeks about twenty-four-year-old Nick Marcello and eighteen-year-old Brooke Martin. It also stated how Mr. and Mrs. Hemphill had discovered them in a compromising position after the commencement ceremony and fired Nick.

Brooke had left town that same day, and as far as Nick knew, she had not returned until today.

Now he had the chance to work with her again, one artist with another. He hoped she didn't turn him down. His interest in her was strictly business, he assured himself. Some lessons were never forgotten. Especially when one learned them the hard way.

CHAPTER 3

*B*ROOKE PULLED HER CAR OUT of the church parking lot and onto the main street that ran through Hayden, past J. C. Penney's, the Phillips 66 gas station owned by Jarrett Plummer and his son, and the old rec hall where she'd had her first art lesson at age five. Everything was the same as when she'd left it. Yet everything was different.

She'd had her down moments since she'd left Hayden, and Brooke was certain she'd have more of them in her life. But there hadn't been a day since that graduation night that she hadn't felt the abysmal humiliation that had begun when she'd looked up, startled, into the shocked faces of Mr. and Mrs. Hemphill. A day hadn't gone by since then that she hadn't closed her eyes at least once in remembrance of that hug and wondered how something so innocent could have had such ugly consequences.

Now, as she drove through the blue-collar section of town to her family's home, she recalled the anger in her father's face the night Mrs. Hemphill called and told him what they'd allegedly caught his daughter doing. For the first time in her life, Brooke had seen in her father's eyes that he was capable of doing harm to another human being. As long as she lived, she would never forget his huge frame bolting across the floor as he'd carried his broken pride like a weapon that would exact the only revenge he understood.

"Daddy, where are you going?" she had shouted.

"I'm going to find Nick Marcello and kill him!" George Martin's voice had shaken the frame house.

She turned to her mother. "Mom, stop him!"

"No!" her mother screamed. "If *he* doesn't kill him, I'll do it myself!"

How could her parents so quickly and easily believe the things the Hemphills said? "But it didn't happen that way! It was just a hug! He was congratulating me! He doesn't feel that way about me, Mom!" she cried. "We never did anything, Daddy. We just hugged. What's wrong with that?"

"He's a grown man, and you're a child!" her father had roared. "He's a teacher!"

"He didn't *do* anything!" Brooke sobbed, but she knew that nothing she said would ever make things right in their eyes. "Nick did *not* take advantage of me."

"That's not the way Abby Hemphill tells it!" her mother said, hysteria cracking her voice. "We've worked all our lives in this town to be known as good people with good children, and it wasn't easy with an income that makes people look down on you, anyway. But now, in one night, it's all ruined. We're reduced to trash, because whatever happened, Abby Hemphill's word is the only word that matters!"

And her mother had been right. As long as she lived, Brooke would never forget the headlines the next morning, the words that implied she and Nick had been having a secret affair for some time. When she read that he had been fired for something he hadn't done, it had been too much to endure.

She had packed her suitcases that morning, withdrawn all the money she'd worked at the local theater box office to save, and driven the little third-hand car she'd bought months earlier out of town before her parents even knew she was gone. The only person who had seen her leave was her little sister, Roxy, only ten years old at the time. Roxy had sat on the porch and waved good-bye, a look of mournful confusion on her face as she tried to understand the events that would change her family forever.

The summer that followed was the loneliest and most miserable of Brooke's life. She had rented a tiny hole-in-the-wall apartment in Columbia, Missouri—three hours from Hayden—and taken a job as a waitress to support herself until school started. There, she had nursed her wounded pride. But she imagined that the blow to her pride was nothing compared with the loss of Nick's livelihood. She doubted that he would ever forgive her.

She had concentrated her time and efforts on school, and had been considered by her professors to be a stellar art student. After graduating, she had gone to work for a stained-glass artist. She had been there ever since, nurtured and trained by one of the finest. Her boss—a jolly old man who treated her like his daughter—always wanted her to stretch and take on new projects, and he'd been thrilled by her opportunity to do the windows at St. Mary's.

If he'd only known what those windows might cost her.

She pulled into the driveway of her family home and sat for a moment, staring at the little house in which she had spent a happy childhood, before she'd known what cruel games adulthood played on people. What would her parents say, now that the black sheep of the family was back in town? Would they count the days until she left, fearing that the longer she stayed, the more gossip she would provoke? And when they learned she would be working with Nick . . .

She reeled the thought back in and told herself just to face what came and not to dwell on the unknown. Slaps in the face were easier to endure when they came as a surprise, she told herself. Dread and anticipation were wasted energy. She knew firsthand.

Brooke grabbed her suitcase from the back seat and got out of the car. For a moment, she peered up at the small house that clearly represented the Martins' modest status, but revealed their stoic pride in what little they had. The house was freshly painted in blue, though it had been white the last time she'd seen it. And they had changed the color of the front door. A large awning hung over the picture window, a new addition in the last few years. Funny that her parents had never mentioned it when they'd visited her in Columbia—but then, it was such a little thing . . . not the kind of thing families talked about when they got together only once or twice each year.

Brooke went up the steps to the porch, set her suitcase down and shook her key chain around until her old house key was in her hand. It jammed in the knob, as if it didn't fit, and she stepped back, frowning.

The door opened from the inside, and her mother smiled at her, as she had when Brooke was a little girl—before she had become the family albatross. Alice Martin's expression gave Brooke's heart a nostalgic twist, making her ache for the simple childhood days when her parents' approval was so easily earned. For a moment, as Brooke smiled at her mother, who still wore her hair in the same frosted bob she'd worn for fifteen years, she wondered whether it could be possible that things hadn't changed that much, after all. "Brooke, we've been waiting for hours. Where have you been?"

"I got tied up." Brooke hugged her mother and stepped over the threshold, dropping her keys back into her purse. "The key . . . it didn't fit . . ."

"We had the locks changed a few years ago," her mother explained, taking her suitcase out of her hand and setting it against the wall. "Roxy lost her purse, and we were afraid whoever found it would break in." Her mother saw the distraught look on her daughter's face and gently touched Brooke's hair. "I'm sorry, honey. It never occurred to me to tell you. It's been so long since you were here. I guess I thought you'd never come through that door again."

Brooke sighed, and her gaze panned the living room. Her mother had covered the warped hardwood floors with an inexpensive wall-to-wall carpet, and new furniture filled the room.

The old recliner she remembered with its split seams where the stuffing oozed out was gone, as was the old couch with the leg that fell off if you sat on the wrong end. The unfamiliarity and newness made her want to step back outside and focus on her mother's face a little longer. "Everything looks . . . different," she whispered.

Her mother took her hand and drew her toward the kitchen. "Don't look so surprised, Brooke. When you decide to stay away for seven years, you have to expect a few changes."

Brooke rallied and forced a smile, determined not to reveal how difficult this homecoming was. Maybe she should have come home a few days earlier, allowing more time to break the proverbial ice and put the past behind her. But somehow, before today, she hadn't been able to do it.

The swinging door to the kitchen burst open, and her father hurried out, his leather-tanned face sporting the same smile he'd worn when she was his princess.

"There you are!" He swept her up into his arms and swung her around, as if she weighed fifty pounds again. "I took off work early today to see you, but we were beginning to think you'd never show up."

"I'm sorry, Dad," Brooke said, her delight at seeing him fading as he set her down, waiting for an explanation. "I had something to do before I could come home."

"Well, it'd better be good to keep your old man waiting."

Tell them now, Brooke told herself. *Get it over with, so you can relax and enjoy the rest of the night.* Brooke's throat constricted suddenly, and she opened her mouth to tell them about the renovation and the windows and Nick. "I had to—"

The sound of footsteps cut her off, and she turned to see her sister, Roxy, leaning in the doorway, watching the homecoming with an expressionless face. Her baby-blond hair was pulled up in a clip, and loose curls trailed down her back. Her eyes, an almost bronze color that Brooke had never seen on anyone else, seemed distant and guarded. Brooke had begun to notice a change in her sister a couple of years before, during the family's visits in Columbia.

"She's just preoccupied with her job at city hall," her mother had said, trying to explain Roxy's aloofness. Or, "She's got that artist's temperament like you had. Her dancing is about all she cares about." But Brooke had sensed that there was something more in the strain etched on her sister's face and the distance she'd put between them.

"Roxy." Brooke reached for her sister and pulled the stiff young woman into a one-sided hug. Roxy's subtle resistance instantly confirmed that all was not well. Brooke released her and saw that, while Roxy did smile, it didn't appear to be without effort. "Hi, Brooke," she said quietly.

Brooke peered into her eyes, searching for a clue as to what was wrong. "Are you okay?" she asked.

"Sure," Roxy said. "Fine."

Brooke dropped her hands.

Her mother stepped between them before Brooke could analyze her sister's mood further, guiding them both into the kitchen. "I've kept dinner warm for you, Brooke," she said. "So, tell us. What in the world finally convinced you that you wouldn't turn into a pillar of salt if you came home?"

Brooke watched her mother bustle around the stove filling the plates . . . her father, easing into his designated place at the head of the table . . . her sister, still standing slightly away from the table, waiting with grudging interest for Brooke's answer.

"It's a commission," Brooke said. "I had an offer to do the stained-glass windows at St. Mary's. Hayden Bible Church bought the building, and they're renovating—"

Her mother swung around, astounded as she regarded her daughter. "You mean, they asked *you* to do it?" A slow smile spread across her face as she met her husband's eyes.

"Of course they asked," George replied with a characteristic chuckle, puffing up as if the townspeople assigned his daughter to every important job that came along. "Our little girl designs the best windows in the hemisphere. Who else would they have asked?"

"Well, the church members aren't really the ones who picked me," Brooke said tentatively.

Her mother brought two of the plates to the table and set them on their place mats, still listening intently.

"In fact," Brooke went on, "I'm not even sure they know that I was chosen."

Her mother went back for the other two plates, and Roxy sat down. "Then who hired you?" her mother asked.

Brooke stared down at her plate, wishing some miracle would occur to wipe the subject from their minds. They hadn't discussed Nick Marcello in all these years. Why did they have to do it now? She took a deep breath and told herself there was no way to avoid it. "Nick Marcello asked me," she whispered.

Her mother dropped the fork she had just lifted, and it landed on her plate with a loud clatter. Her father didn't move a muscle, but his face hardened to a colorless granite. Even Roxy's eyes seemed to dull in consternation as she stared at the iced tea beside her plate.

"What in the Sam Hill has Nick Marcello got to do with it?" her father bit out.

Brooke met her father's eyes and swallowed hard. "He's in charge of artistic development for the renovation." She turned to her mother, saw that the same expression had altered her face as well. "Mom, I haven't agreed to take the job yet. I didn't even know he was involved until I got into town today, and when I saw him this afternoon, I told him that I'd have to think about it."

"Think about it?" her mother repeated. "You actually have to *think* about it? After all that's happened? After all he's put us through?"

"Don't even think about starting that up again, Brooke," her father said.

Brooke took a deep breath and warned herself that losing her temper would serve no purpose. "Dad, nothing is starting up again. I'm not going to embarrass anybody. I was interested in the job because it's a fantastic career opportunity. My boss, Mr. Gonzales, strongly encouraged me to do it. That's absolutely the only reason."

Her mother leaned toward her in disbelief. "You *can't* be considering taking this job, Brooke." The statement sounded too much like an order, and Brooke's white-knuckled fingers clamped more tightly over the edges of her chair.

"Mom, a job like this could really launch my career. It's the kind of thing stained-glass artists work toward all their lives. That has to be considered."

"She's going to take the job," her mother uttered, shooting a glance back to her father. "She's going to work with him, and it'll all start up again."

"*Nothing* is going to start up!" Brooke said. "I'm a grown woman now, and he's not my teacher anymore. We aren't involved or even interested in each other, and we never have been. Don't you think, after seven years, I ought to have the chance to work in my home town, holding my head up? Haven't I earned that?"

"That's not something you can earn," her father said. "Once your reputation is taken away from you, you can't get it back."

"Dad, that isn't—"

"Just eat," her mother blurted out, her eyes misting with anger. "It's been sitting long enough. We'll talk about this later."

Roxy's chair scraped back from the table and she got to her feet. "I'm not hungry," she said. And before anyone could protest, she left the table.

CHAPTER

4

$\mathcal{T}$HE REMAINDER OF THE MEAL WAS short and stressfully quiet, and Brooke managed to choke down at least half of the dinner that had once been her favorite. She told herself she wouldn't cry and wouldn't engage in a screaming argument with her father and mother, like the one she'd had when she was eighteen.

Without a word she helped her mother clear the table, then went to look for Roxy. What was bothering her? *Surely not the thing with Nick,* Brooke thought. Roxy had been too young to understand when the scandal erupted. Still, Roxy's aloofness troubled her.

She knocked on her sister's bedroom door, and at Roxy's uttered "What?" opened it and stepped inside. Roxy was sitting on the wide bench in front of her window, hugging her knees to her chest.

Brooke looked around the small room that revealed the stages of Roxy's growth: a tattered teddy bear on a shelf next to several ballet trophies, a framed photo of her dancing in *The Nutcracker,* a stack of books on a table ranging from Shakespeare to Pat Conroy, a pair of toe shoes hanging from a hook on the wall. She looked at her sister, wishing that words came more easily and that she knew how to dispense with the awkwardness between them. "Sorry about the scene at the table," Brooke said.

Roxy's gaze drifted out the window. "What did you expect?"

Brooke set a hand on the bedpost. "I don't know. I guess I'd hoped that after seven years it would die down a little. At least among my family. I keep thinking enough time has passed. That we could talk about it . . . make some sense of it all."

Roxy didn't answer. Instead she kept her eyes fixed on some invisible object outside the window.

Brooke sighed. "I like your room," she said, trying to find some common ground. "The last time I was in here, you were mostly into Little Mermaid." She smiled and stepped over to the stereo system, sitting on a cabinet in the corner. "You had this little plastic tape player with a picture of Donald Duck on the top, and you listened to Sesame Street records all the time and made up little dances to them."

"I don't dance anymore," Roxy said.

Brooke turned back to her. "Why? You were good."

Roxy laughed mirthlessly. "How would you know? You never saw me dance. Not since I was ten."

"No, but Mom told me you were the soloist in the ballet company, and that—"

"I quit." Roxy left the window and lifted her toe shoes off their hook. She looked down at them, holding them with a reverence that didn't match the lack of interest in her voice.

Brooke knew she was pushing too hard, but she couldn't keep from asking, "Well, why?"

"Because I got tired of it," Roxy said. "Why the sudden interest?"

Brooke's quiet laugh held no amusement. "Because you're my sister."

Roxy brought her eyes to Brooke's, disgust and resentment narrowing them. "I graduate from high school in June, Brooke. But you probably didn't know that, either, did you?"

Brooke's forced smile faded, and she braced herself for what-ever was coming. "Of course I know. What are you talking about?"

"I'm talking about the fact that I grew up while you were off running from your problems."

Brooke lowered herself to her sister's bed and settled her eyes on Roxy, suddenly aware that the coolness Roxy had displayed earlier had roots much deeper than awkward shyness. "What's the matter, Roxy?" she asked quietly. "Why are you mad at me? Is it Nick?"

Roxy laughed, a sound so cold and heartless that it made Brooke shiver. "Is it Nick?" she repeated harshly. "Hasn't it always been Nick, Brooke? For you, for our family, for me?"

Brooke's patience stretched taut at the vague accusation. She hadn't expected this from Roxy. Emotion welled in her throat, making her voice wobble. "It didn't happen to you, Roxy. It hap-pened to me. You were little, and you probably have no idea what I went through back then. But don't judge me for staying away when you don't know how I felt."

Roxy's eyes were two golden flames dancing with fury as she faced her sister. "You've got a lot of nerve, you know that? Do you think it only affected you? You made headlines in the news-paper, Brooke! I may have been ten years old, but I could read! And if I hadn't, it wouldn't have mattered because everyone else in town was there to tell me about it!"

The outburst made Brooke's face burn. "I'm sorry that you were hurt by it," she said, tears coming to her eyes though she spoke through clenched teeth. "It hurt all of us."

"It didn't hurt you," Roxy charged. "You didn't have to face it. You disappeared, remember? *I'm* the one who had to sit in class and listen to my teachers whisper about you when they thought I didn't know what they were talking about. I'm the one who got in fights with the kids at school because they made fun of me for being your sister. For over half my life, I've been known as the sister of that girl who had an affair with her teacher! There's not a lot to talk about in Hayden, Brooke. They milked that scandal for all it was worth."

Anger pulsated through Brooke's veins, and one hot tear fell onto her cheek. "I didn't have an affair with him, Roxy," she said, clipping each word. "I didn't even kiss him. It was all a lie."

"Not according to the Hemphills," Roxy reminded her. "They set the truths in this town, and they're still here. He's still running the school system, and she's still on the town council, and they still own half the town. Their children are grown, following in the family tradition. And when they hear that you've come back here to work with *him* . . . it's going to start all over!"

Brooke lifted her chin defiantly, and her words came slowly, quietly, through her teeth. "I won't let them dictate my life anymore, Roxy. I'm tired of trying to redeem myself from a bunch of lies."

"Redeem yourself?" Roxy cried. "What have you done to redeem yourself? I'm the one who's tried to redeem you!"

Brooke's tears stole down her face, but she held her posture defiantly stiff, determined not to collapse under the weight being set upon her shoulders. "I'm sorry I hurt you," she whispered.

"It's too late for apologies," Roxy said, the finality in her tone bolting the door to whatever relationship they might have had. "About seven years too late."

Brooke bit her quivering lip, for there was nothing left to say. Finally she pulled herself together enough to leave the room. The loss hit Brooke like the death of someone she had cherished, but she managed to keep the pain from her face until she was hidden in her room, where no one else could see.

Brooke had learned long ago to deal with her pain alone.

She lay on the bed in the bedroom that had been converted into a cold, impersonal guest room. Had this really been her home? The architecture was unaltered, but nothing looked the same . . . and in her soul she could feel the difference, as if she'd been transported back into the wrong family.

She rolled onto her back and looked at the ceiling where long ago she had painted a blue sky and clouds so vivid that one would have thought she was sleeping outside. Roxy used to sneak into her bed at night after their parents were asleep, declaring that she couldn't sleep in her own room because there were no clouds. But the clouds were gone now, and in their place was white latex paint that fit the new practical decor of the room.

Tears rolled down her temples and soaked the roots of her hair. Why did some things change so much, when other things— things like memories and heartaches and humiliations—never changed at all? It all boiled down to those stubborn feelings . . . and Nick Marcello.

She turned onto her stomach and fluffed the pillow, then buried her face in it.

It was out of the question, of course, to take the job he'd offered. She would have to tell him no, because she couldn't stand the looks on her parents' faces or the pain on her sister's. It was too much for one person to endure, yet she had carried the burden of a hateful town for seven long years. She'd simply carry it seven more . . . or however long it took for the feelings to fade. And someday they would, she was certain, if she fought them hard enough and stayed far enough away.

CHAPTER

5

$\mathcal{T}$HE DARKNESS FILLED NICK'S OLD Buick like a comfortable scent. Yes, it was an ugly old clunker, but he needed an everyday car—it would be foolish to subject the valuable Duesenberg parked in his garage to the wear-and-tear of daily traffic.

He felt more lonely tonight than he had in some time, and he found that fact disturbing. Wasn't his aloneness one of the most valuable assets in his life? Wasn't it something he cherished?

Tonight the solitude was a plague, and the loneliness was a punishment. For what, he wasn't sure.

His headlights swept across his front lawn as Nick approached. Behind the house, he could see moonlight playing off the surface of the canal that threaded behind his pier, a parking lot of sorts for the boats his neighbors kept there. On any other night, his artist's eye would have recorded the gentle scene, and he might have rushed into his studio, leaving the house dark, and captured the picture from the massive window that looked out over the water. The power of light in the darkness had always fascinated him. Tonight it only made him feel more alone.

Some unconscious decision compelled him to drive on when he reached his driveway, and without a second thought, he headed back out of his neighborhood. He needed someone to talk to tonight.

Moments later, he idled in the driveway of an older two-story home, full of light spilling out from the first floor and dim night-lights lending faint hues to the windows of the rooms upstairs.

"Nick? What are you doing here?" a woman's voice from the open garage called out into the darkness. "I'll never get the kids to bed now!"

Nick grinned as the woman came out of the garage, hoisting a curly-haired baby on one hip and carrying a basket of laundry on the other. "How's it going, Anna?"

"Not too bad," she said, the sound of the washing machine in the garage muffling her words.

Nick took the baby and pressed a kiss on her fat cheek. She beamed up at him. "What's this kid doing up so late?"

"She's spoiled rotten, that's what," Anna said, as if that answered the question. "Controls the whole house. Me, Ma, Vinnie, everybody."

Nick carried the baby into the house, and at the sight of him, his mother got off the couch, worry animating her face. "Nicky! What's the matter? You never come over here this late!"

"Uncle Nicky!" Two of the children flung themselves at him, and he greeted them each by turning them upside down, then blowing on their stomachs until they squealed with laughter. Then he planted a kiss on his mother's cheek and offered a wave to his brother-in-law, who sat at the dining room table with a calculator and a stack of bills.

"Nothing's the matter, Ma. Can't a guy come by to see how his ma's doing once in a while?"

"Well, that's nice," his mother said. "Come watch Bogart with me. I have popcorn."

"Bogart?" he asked. "I will, Ma. But first I need to talk to Sonny. Where is he?"

"In his room over the garage," Anna said, flopping the baby down on the floor and beginning to change her diaper. "Nineteen-year-olds hang out with their family as little as possible."

"He's working on some project for his shop class at Vo-Tech," Vinnie said. "Kid's great with his hands."

"I think I'll go up and say hello," Nick said, then turned back to his mother. "Here's lookin' at you, Kid."

"Wrong movie," his mother said. "Hurry back."

Nick left the house through the back door and climbed the stairs to the garage apartment Sonny had moved into when the baby—number four in his sister's family—was born. He knocked on the door and heard something in the room fall. Then, in a voice a little too loud, Sonny called, "Just a minute!"

"Hey, Sonny," Nick said through the door. "What are you doing in there? You hiding a girl or something?"

The door opened, and his nephew, every bit as tall as Nick and with the same black hair, faced him with a mischievous grin. "Picasso!" he said, waving Nick into a room that looked as if it had been ransacked by a gang of thieves. "I thought you were Pop."

"So you had to hide the evidence before you could open the door?" Nick asked, looking around for a sign of the culprit. "Where is she?"

Sonny laughed and cleared off a chair for Nick to sit down. "No, I was just working on something. A . . . project for school."

"Oh, yeah?" Nick asked, still suspicious. The strong scent of oil paints wafted through the air, and he saw a palette lying on a table, blotted with various colors of fresh paint. "I didn't know they did home projects in electrician school."

Still wearing a wry smile, Sonny straddled a chair backward and propped his hands on the back. He evaluated Nick with a critical eye, then sighed. "If I tell you something, do you promise you won't tell nobody? Pop would bust a gut, and Grandma would fake a heart attack or something. Ma would just martyr up like Joan of Arc."

Nick laughed. "Come on, I can't stand the suspense."

Sonny took a deep breath, apparently struggling with some monumental confession. "Well, I've been, sort of . . . playing around with paints and stuff."

The confession was uttered with as much shame and guilt as if he'd admitted to a drug addiction. "You mean, you've been painting? Like I do?"

Sonny stood up, running his fingers, blotched with dried paint, through his hair. "Yeah, just like you, Picasso. Only not as good. Not anywhere near as good."

A glint of pleasure and surprise illuminated Nick's eyes, and he sat up straighter and scanned the room. "Well, let me see."

"No, I can't," Sonny said, suddenly wilting. "It's pretty terrible, really."

"Sonny, let me see," Nick told him. "I'm not a critic."

A self-conscious smile tugged at Sonny's lips, and he crossed his arms and stared at Nick for a long moment. Finally, he went to his bed, got down on one knee and pulled a wet canvas out from under it, along with the collapsible easel he'd hidden there. Mechanically, he set it up.

In vivid color, Sonny had captured the house he lived in, stroking its character and history in every line and hue, from the crooked mailbox on the front corner to the laundry line strung up on the side. His chin propped on two fingers, Nick studied the painting with a lump of emotion in his throat, then turned back to his nephew. "Why didn't you tell me you could do this?"

Sonny gave a half laugh. "Guess I thought if I didn't tell nobody, I'd get tired of it after a while and lose interest. No harm done."

Nick knew that feeling. "It doesn't go away, though, does it?"

Sonny sank back down to his chair. "Pop thinks I'm gonna finish Vo-Tech and keep working with him as ⸻ pride's all caught up in it. I don't really have a ch⸻

"No," Nick said. "I *don't* know. Everybo⸻

"Aw, man, that's easy for you to say. You'r⸻ Nobody's ridin' you about it."

Nick's laughter came as a surprise to them both, for nothing about the subject was funny. "You think my pop liked what I did? When I went to college to study art, he swore I was just loafing. I was supposed to work in the shoe store with him. The family business. He was going to rename it Marcello and Son Shoes, just for me. To this day Ma says she's glad he didn't live to see what I've done with my life. Like I've gone to work for the Mob or something."

"No," Sonny said with a wicked grin. "In this family, that would be a lot more respectable than being an artist."

"You're right." Nick looked back at the painting, wondering at the raw talent smoldering just below his nephew's tough-guy façade. "Look, have you had lessons or anything? Any kind of training?"

"Just what I learn from books," Sonny said. "But what I wouldn't give to learn more." His eyes lit up, as if sharing his secret with Nick had set him free, and he'd just discovered the power to ask for help. "Nick, you could teach me, couldn't you? I mean, you were a teacher."

"You got it," Nick said without hesitation. "Only problem is, I'm about to be working long hours for a while at the church. But if you want, you can use my studio anytime you want. I'll give you a key."

"You mean it?" Sonny asked, his eyes as wide as a kid's half his age.

"Yeah. And the reason I came up is to ask you if you'd want to work with me this summer on the windows. If Brooke agrees to work with me, she and I are needed for the most complicated part of designing. There're a lot of things that we need help with."

Sonny's eyes sparkled with surprise and a touch of amusement. "Brooke? Not the one . . ."

Nick swallowed and held out a hand to stem Sonny's question. "She's an artist too, Sonny. The best I've run across in stained ' ss. It's strictly business."

"I know. I didn't mean nothin'." Sonny's voice faded, and he ⌐ his gaze to the floor. "Stained glass," he whispered with awe. "Man, if you think you can use me, I'll be there. Pop'll kill me if I quit helpin' him in the afternoons, but I could help at night until school's out. But I'll never convince him to let me do it in the summer. He was counting on my working full-time for him."

"Try," Nick said with a grin. "Maybe he'll change his mind. Now, you get back to work on that. I have to go watch Bogart with Ma."

Sonny smiled with a new sparkle of excitement in his eyes that Nick hadn't seen before. "Thanks, Picasso. If Pop says yes, I won't let you down."

"Yeah, well," Nick muttered as he started out the door. "You're not the one I'm worried about."

CHAPTER

6

*I*T WAS EARLY MORNING WHEN Brooke loaded her suitcase into her car and left the house without saying goodbye. A strange feeling of déjà vu crept over her, but she told herself there was no other way.

She drove through a takeout window at a fast-food restaurant and got a cup of coffee. Staring out the window, she sat in her car to sip it until the cup was empty. She had to tell Nick. She couldn't just leave town without thanking him for the job offer. She had to tell him why she couldn't take it.

With dread, she cranked her car and headed toward St. Mary's.

When she pulled into the back parking lot of the decrepit building, his Buick was already there, along with several pickup trucks, a cement truck, and various other commercial vehicles, indicating that the renovation was already underway. Gathering all her courage, she got out of the car and slid her hands into the pockets of her jeans.

She stepped into the church and saw the activity already beginning. Men were up on ladders, removing the old windows and replacing them with boards covered with plastic in case of rain. Others were stripping the walls, while still others worked on pulling up the old flooring. It would have been exciting had Brooke been a part of it all.

Brooke stepped over some thick electrical cords and around some machinery and headed for the office behind the sanctuary. The light was on, and she knew that he would be there, waiting for her to bring him an answer ... expecting it to be the one he wanted. Dragging in a shaky breath, she forced herself to step through the doorway.

Nick looked up. "Brooke, you're early." His voice, once again, held a tentative note, as though he held back for fear of frightening her away. She hated seeming so fragile.

His eyes swept her baggy T-shirt and old jeans, then rose back to her hair, long and neglectfully straight. "And you're dressed for a hard day's work," he said. "Does that mean you've decided to—?"

"I'm not taking the job, Nick," she cut in quietly. "I'm going back to Columbia today."

Nick's face fell. At first he registered disappointment, then benign nothingness. It was almost as if he'd rehearsed the response he would give if she let him down. He'd expected it, she realized. "I see."

"I think it's best for everyone," she said.

"Everyone?" he asked. "Who is 'everyone'?"

She sighed. "My parents. My sister. You."

"Me?" he asked, raising his eyebrows with the question. "Why is it better for me?"

"You can find someone else to do the windows. Someone who won't bring a dark cloud to the project. Someone who won't start everyone in town talking."

Nick stood up slowly. "Do I look like I care what anyone says?" he asked. "I'm the one who stayed in town, remember? I'm still here, Brooke. They haven't sent me running, yet."

She leaned back against the door's casing. "You don't understand," she whispered. "It wasn't just you and me who were hurt seven years ago. There were other lives affected."

Nick came around his desk and took her shoulders, his eyes trapping her with such force that she couldn't look away. "Listen to me, Brooke. We didn't do anything. I wasn't some dirty old man taking advantage of a child. Neither of us deserved the pain they put us through. And if people were hurt by it, that wasn't our fault."

Those tears that had badgered her all night rushed forward again, and she caught her breath on a sob. "It doesn't matter whose fault it was," she said. "What matters is that it has to stop. And my working here with you isn't going to stop it."

"Wrong, Brooke," he said, not allowing her to look away from him. "Think of yourself for a change. You'll never find peace as long as you keep running away."

"I'll never find peace as long as I keep making the same mistakes," she corrected.

He gazed at her for a moment, processing those words as if they held some hidden meaning. "Maybe you're right," he said finally. "But be sure you know what the mistakes really were. If you don't take the time to figure that out, then you can't help but repeat them. Why can't we put it behind us and go on with our lives? We shared something important back then, Brooke. A love of art. Together we can create something that people will come from miles around to see. This is a career-maker, Brooke. It's too big to pass up."

She turned away again and tried not to let his tone sway her. Anguished, she ran her fingers through her hair. He took a step toward her and gazed down into her face. "There doesn't have to be any intense involvement between us. You're not a kid with a crush on me, and I'm not your teacher. We can be friends and partners. And we can show them all what we're made of."

"What is that, exactly?" she asked. "I'm not sure what I'm made of. That's part of the problem."

"Well, maybe I can help you find out. Come on, Brooke. Say yes."

Suddenly, someone in the doorway cleared her throat, and Nick and Brooke turned to see Abby Hemphill, standing before them just as she had seven years earlier, smiling with I-might-have-known smugness. Her permed, platinum hair was styled in a short bob, and the roots were slightly darker than the rest. Mrs. Hemphill might have been pretty if not for the antagonistic, ready-to-pounce expression she always seemed to wear and the shrewd arch of her pencil-thin brows. Her body was in good shape, though the suit she wore—too severe and authoritative—distracted from her appeal. She smiled now, though Brooke couldn't remember ever seeing a smile so lacking in grace.

Nick crossed his arms. "Hello, Abby."

Mrs. Hemphill pursed her lips and stepped into the small office. "Sorry I interrupted," she said, her silver eyes sweeping critically over Brooke. "If it isn't Brooke Martin. You certainly haven't changed."

Brooke lifted her chin, accepting that with the sting that was intended. "Thank you."

Nick grinned and looked at his feet.

Mrs. Hemphill's mouth grew tighter. "I heard you were back in town," she said. "And that you were going to be working here ... together." She regarded a long, acrylic fingernail, then brought her eyes back to Brooke. "I thought it was only fair to warn you that I intend to oppose the church's commissioning you for this project. I'm going to appeal to them to find another artistic development director."

"It's too late," Nick said. "They've already commissioned me and approved my budget. They gave me authority to hire anyone I choose."

Mrs. Hemphill laughed ... a cold, hollow sound, and she leaned back against the doorway and regarded Nick again. "They may have hired you, Mr. Marcello, but that decision can be reversed. My family's money keeps the church afloat. If we protest, you can rest assured that the committees will listen."

Brooke flashed a furious look to Nick—silently asking if Mrs. Hemphill's threats could be carried out—but Nick only smiled at the woman, undaunted. "Do what you have to do, Abby," he said. "There are plenty of others who support the church."

Her smile was a threat in itself, a promise that things would not go as smoothly as he thought. "We'll see about that, won't we?" she asked, then made her exit, leaving Brooke gaping after her, furious, and Nick only shaking his head in disgust.

Brooke spun around. "You see? I told you! I haven't even taken the job, and already it's started."

Nick dropped to the corner of his desk and gave a helpless shrug. "The way I see it, if it doesn't make any difference *what* we do, we might as well do what we want."

"That's not the answer!" Brooke cried. "You know it."

Nick looked down at the desk, cluttered with papers and blueprints and measurements for the windows. He picked up some of the papers, tossed them up haphazardly and watched them flutter back down to his desk. "What I know is that I can't afford to lose this job. I was counting on this, Brooke. And it's not likely that I'm going to find anyone else to come in here and work under Abby Hemphill's threats to pull the money. And yes, she'd threaten that whether you were here or not, because she has it in for me. I can't do the windows by myself because stained glass isn't my specialty. I guess if you decide to walk away from this, it's over for me too."

The words shattered Brooke's resolve, and she knew that if he lost this job, it would be the second he had lost because of her. Fresh guilt surged through her. Her family would be disgusted and ashamed if she stayed. Nick would be hurt again if she didn't.

Between those two options was a haunting cry in her heart that told her, unequivocally, what she really wanted. She wanted to take the job, create this masterpiece with Nick, and show Mrs. Hemphill and the whole town that they could knock her down, but they couldn't walk on her. It was time she got back up.

Suddenly, her decision seemed clear.

"You won't lose your job," she told Nick finally, glaring out through the door where the woman had stood only moments before. "She won't get away with this again. We're going to fight her tooth-and-nail this time. And I'm going to tell her that right now."

Without saying goodbye, Brooke stormed out of the office.

CHAPTER

7

*I*F BROOKE COULD HAVE SKETCHED the smells of old dust and mildew, she would have drawn Hayden City Hall. She walked down the hall, the heels of her sandals clicking on the cold Formica floor. A small sign on one corner directed her toward the left wing, where the town council members had their offices.

As she passed the office marked *Records,* she wondered if her sister, Roxy, was working yet. Because she only needed three more classes to graduate, the school allowed her to co-op and leave school early each day. If Roxy was already here, Brooke hoped her sister wouldn't see her.

Unfortunately, just as Brooke passed Roxy's office, she stepped out into the hall carrying an armload of papers and looked up in surprise. "What are you doing here?" she asked, her voice echoing in the wide hall. "I thought you had left again."

"You thought wrong," Brooke said, not slowing her step. "Where is Mrs. Hemphill's office?"

"Over there," Roxy said, breaking into a trot to keep up with her. "But Brooke, you can't go in there. You're asking for it if you do."

"Asking for what, Roxy?" Brooke asked. "Gossip? Lies? I get those no matter what I do."

Roxy fell behind as Brooke pushed into the cubicle-like office with Abby Hemphill's name on the door. The woman, sitting behind her desk with the phone to her ear, gasped when Brooke burst in. She dropped the phone and shoved back her chair.

"No need to get up, Mrs. Hemphill," Brooke said, leaning over the woman's desk. "I won't be here long. I just came to tell you that it's open season on Brooke Martin. So go ahead. Take your best shots. I have to warn you, though—it won't be quite as much fun sparring with a grown woman as it was with a high school senior. I'm not as easily intimidated now."

Abby Hemphill bolted out of her chair. "How dare you speak that way to me!"

"I'm going to design the windows for the church because I'm good at what I do," Brooke said, "and because I need the career boost. And no thanks to you, this town will have something to be proud of when I get through. Whether they deserve it is another story. Whether Nick and I do is without question. So I'll be seeing you around, Mrs. Hemphill. The next few months should be interesting."

And before Mrs. Hemphill could catch her breath to reply, Brooke had turned and left the office, pushing past Roxy, who stood stunned and speechless in the hall. But Brooke was sure as she passed her that the tiniest sparkle of admiration shone in her eyes.

For the first time in seven years Brooke felt good about herself.

Abby Hemphill sat paralyzed for a moment after Brooke had gone, trying to contain the raging emotions Brooke had incited. Then her last thread of control snapped, and her arm swept across her desk, knocking off her telephone, her can of pencils, her calendar, her calculator.

"That slithering little tramp!" she bit out through her teeth. She set her face in her hands, felt the heat seething there, and knew that she had to get out of the office before something inside her exploded.

Grabbing her purse, she went to her car, then drove like a maniac to the superintendent's office, adjacent to the high school. There were few cars in the parking lot—it was a school holiday, and only a handful of counselors and teachers were present. Slamming her car door, Abby walked as fast as she could in her high heels.

She stormed into her husband's office. He was on the phone and looked aggravated at the intrusion. "I have to talk to you," she whispered harshly.

Gerald raised his hand to silence her, and continued his conversation.

Abby folded her arms and began to pace across his floor—back and forth, back and forth, like an inmate waiting to be released from confinement.

When her husband finally hung up, she braced both hands on his desk and leaned over. "She's back," she said.

"Who's back?"

"That Brooke Martin. Nick Marcello hired her to work on those windows for *our* church."

Gerald Hemphill distractedly flipped through his Rolodex as his wife railed on, and without looking up at her, he muttered, "Sit down, Abby. I have to make another call."

Abby grabbed his hand to stop him from dialing and forced him to look up at her. "She came to *my* office and chewed me out, Gerald!"

Gerald began dialing again. "Chewed *you* out? That sounds interesting. Abby, what is that on your skirt? For heaven's sake, you look like you've been in a fight."

Abby looked down at her skirt and saw the dust she must have picked up at the old church. She dusted it off with her hand. "Would you listen to me?" she said. "I have to stop this. It isn't right that our building fund is going to be paying those two for having their little affair. If they did that right in the school, what do you think they'll do over there?"

"Yes, is Mr. Hartford in?" Gerald asked into the phone, flipping through some papers on his desk. "Bob, hi. Gerald here. I have those transfer papers you were asking about . . ."

Abby stood back, flabbergasted. "Gerald!" she whispered, but he didn't seem to hear. Instead he lifted one index finger and pointed to the chair.

Abby dropped into it, crossed her legs, and began swinging her foot. The phone call dragged on, and finally she couldn't contain herself any longer. She jumped up and began pacing again.

Gerald hung up and reached for another file, as if he had forgotten his wife was in the room.

"Gerald, I came in here to talk to you!"

"It's not a good time, dear. I'm really swamped today. I'm trying to catch up on a million things while school's out."

"You're always swamped!" she said. "I'm swamped too. But I'm upset about this! It's our responsibility to see that our tithes and offerings are spent well, and I—"

"Could you hand me that phonebook on the table behind you, dear?" he cut in, pointing to the table.

Abby stopped mid-sentence and gaped at him. At times like these, she thought miserably, tears would be a welcome release. But she hadn't been able to cry in years. Anger was the most vivid emotion she knew these days. "Never mind, Gerald," she said. "Just forget it."

She turned and started to leave.

"Good-bye, dear," Gerald replied. "I'll see you at dinner. Lasagna would be nice, with a Caesar salad. Cheesecake, maybe?"

Abby stopped in the hall and leaned back against the wall. Her eyes misted over, but no tears flowed. Lasagna and cheesecake, an immaculate house, a flawless reputation, a trophy wife . . . these were things that mattered to Gerald, and she'd learned long ago how to achieve all of them.

Slowly she left the building and crossed the yard to the high school. She strolled up the corridor, glancing in at the empty classrooms. Occasionally, she passed a room where a teacher worked. There were few familiar faces. It wasn't as easy to get to know the teachers as it had once been. She was so busy now that she rarely came here, and when she and Gerald were invited to faculty parties, she found it harder and harder to laugh and smile and listen to their war stories.

She found herself in the east wing and strolled further to the classroom at the end of the hall, the one that smelled of paint and mineral spirits. She looked inside the door. The teacher wasn't there.

Slowly, Abby stepped inside and looked around at the simplistic drawings on the walls, the crude representations of life. Hayden hadn't had an art teacher in years who really had talent or who was able to inspire creativity in his students. Not since Nick Marcello.

It was too bad he had taken that inspiration one step too far.

She sat down at one of the desks and remembered vividly that night when she and Gerald had seen the light on and had stumbled onto Nick's little fling with that girl. The price for propriety was high. The cost for impropriety, by rights, should be far greater.

And indeed it was. His affair had been nipped in the bud, and Nick Marcello had lost his job. What cut Abby to the quick now was that it hadn't seemed to matter. Over the years he'd done well for himself despite what he'd lost. And now . . .

Abby searched her heart, honestly seeking the reason Brooke grated on her nerves. Perhaps it was the way the girl had always finagled her way into competitions she had no business competing in. She had been chosen as one of the twenty girls to participate in the school's beauty pageant, and Abby's daughter, Sharon, who should have been an obvious choice, had been left out. Brooke wore those distasteful secondhand clothes, and people acted as if she'd bought them on Fifth Avenue. She was thin without trying, and despite her best efforts, Abby hadn't been able to control Sharon's weight until she'd sent her to that fat farm the summer after her senior year. She'd been bone-thin ever since. But was she grateful? No. She had done nothing but embarrass and humiliate the family ever since. Abby hadn't even seen Sharon in almost three years.

But now, to see Brooke prance back into town like some movie star returning to her old haunts, bracelets jangling and hair flying around her shoulders—as if any decent person wore it that way past high school—was just too much to take. She had no right. She should have been put in her place years ago.

She got up and went to the desk at the front of the room, staring sightlessly down at it. It wasn't right that she had chosen the correct path with great sacrifice, while others thumbed their noses at the world and thrived.

Brooke and Nick had not deserved to thrive, she told herself, letting her eyes sweep the room again. He had deserved to lose his job and his respect and his reputation. What he didn't deserve was the opportunity to continue his fling when he began designing those church windows.

After all, the purchase and renovation of the old landmark had been *her* idea to begin with. But then someone else had suggested stained-glass windows, and the pastor had hired Nick, who'd hired that girl, and everything had gotten out of control.

Well, Abby was going to get back in control now, if it killed her. No bracelet-jangler was going to treat her the way she had been treated this morning and get away with it. If she had anything to say about it, Brooke Martin would be out of this town by week's end.

CHAPTER 8

NICK TRIED NOT TO LOOK AS IF HE were waiting for her when Brooke pulled back into the parking lot. He wasn't, after all. He'd merely come outside to take out the garbage.

Well, she was here now, and as he waited for her to get out of her car, he watched her face for a sign of her mood. He couldn't tell from her expression if she was staying or going.

Brooke got out of her car, tossed her hair back with a flip, and faced him squarely. "I told Mrs. Hemphill I was taking the job," she said. "So you win. I'm staying."

A subtle smile gleamed in Nick's eyes, but he didn't let it reach his lips. "I think we both won."

"Not yet, we haven't." She started to go on, stopped, and took a deep breath. The breeze swept her hair back into her face. She pushed it away with one finger as she seemed to struggle with her words. "Look, Nick, I think if we're going to be working together, we should lay down some ground rules. Otherwise I might just be a nervous wreck the whole time, and that won't be productive at all."

Nick leaned back against her car and inclined his head solemnly. "What do you have in mind?"

Brooke looked down at the concrete. Her hair feathered into her face once again. Shoving it back, she met his eyes. Her tone was matter-of-fact when she answered. "It's strictly business, Nick."

Nick nodded. "We're going to be business partners," he said quietly. "What we're going to create together will be very special. But strictly business."

Brooke set her hand on her hip, and for a second Nick thought she was struggling to speak. Instead, she fidgeted with the bracelets on her left wrist. "Okay," she said, her voice a decibel quieter than it had been before. "Then let's get started."

His smile reached his lips then, and he stood up fully. He opened the big church door, and Brooke went in. A committee of well-dressed business people were milling around, dodging the carpenters and contractors. Some women were dragging boxes into the back rooms of the church with strained expressions on their faces, as if they couldn't get away from the contractors fast enough.

"That's the Historical Society," he said. "Even though this is a church project, they're getting involved because the building is a landmark. They're in charge of preserving whatever is salvageable." He stepped over a cord and grabbed Brooke's hand. "Watch your step."

Brooke caught her balance and withdrew her hand at once. She jammed it into her pocket, as if to assure herself that he wouldn't take it again.

Nick let his hand drop to his side. "Anyway, they're all over the place wrapping and packing the pieces that can be moved out. I've got our workroom set up in the back, but I'm afraid we'll have to share it with them for a few days. Just until they're finished moving everything."

Brooke scanned the group again. "Mrs. Hemphill wouldn't be in that group, would she?"

"Of course," he said. "Mrs. Hemphill's in everything. That's why she was here earlier today."

He led her out of the office, through the darkly lit hall, and into the large workroom where he had set up their tables. Several middle-aged women crouched over a box of artifacts, disagreeing about the proper way to wrap each piece.

He knew Brooke recognized some of them. How could she have forgotten the women who'd sat together at town picnics, picking away at the juiciest grapevine morsels. She jammed her hands back into her pockets.

"What do you think?" Nick asked her, drawing her attention from the women back to their work space. "Is this going to be okay?"

Brooke surveyed the large worktable, just tall enough to stand up at without putting strain on the back. To the left of it was a light table made of several pieces of frosted glass with fluorescent bulbs beneath to simulate sunlight through the stained glass. On the wall hung a large pegboard with Nick's tools hooked neatly from it, and beneath that sat a stack of storage bins of various sizes for glass. "It'll work," Brooke said. "Might need a few modifications."

"The thing is," Nick said, "we really need to work onsite to keep from having to move the panels much. They'll be too big."

Her face tightened again, and he wondered if the project would overwhelm her. "There's so much to be done," she said. "It'll take weeks to do the cartoons, and then all the cutting and leading . . . I don't see how we can do this without help."

"Oh, we won't be doing it alone," Nick said, pulling out a drawer of the worktable and removing a stack of sketches. "We'll have to hire more people experienced in cutting glass. I was going to ask if you knew of anyone who might be interested in helping us out when we get to that point."

Brooke sat on a tall stool and thought for a moment. "I know a few people we could subcontract. But do we have enough in our budget to pay them?"

Nick shrugged and began to spread his sketches out across the table. "We have plenty, unless Abby Hemphill pulls the rug out from under us. I don't know for sure what our budget's going to be yet. Abby Hemphill was right. It hasn't completely been approved. But, yeah, they'll have to put it in the budget. If we did this ourselves, it would take years."

"Maybe we could hire some high school kids to help with some of the other things," she said. "Like tracing the patterns, coloring them, cutting them out . . ."

"My nephew has agreed to help," Nick said. "And I'll call the high school and see if we could get some help from the art department."

The chattering women got quiet behind them, and Nick knew at once what they were thinking. Brooke only voiced it. "Do you think they'd really let some of their students work here with you—us?" she asked, barely above a whisper.

Nick glanced back at the women, noting the distasteful looks on their faces. He released a heavy sigh. "Well, maybe not," he mumbled. "Maybe we'll have to find help another way."

The women behind them began to whisper again, and Brooke's eyes connected with his, sharing the common bond of regret.

"These are some of my preliminary sketches," Nick said finally. "I don't want it to be something that you see in a thousand other churches. I want it to be more unique. Fresher and more exciting. Are you familiar with the covenants in the Bible, Brooke?"

She looked up at him and shook her head. "No, not really."

Nick reached onto his stack of sketches, crude puzzle-piece drawings that translated well to glass. "Look at this," he said.

It was a picture of an old, wizened man, holding a child on his bony lap.

"That's beautiful," she whispered. "But what's your theme? Age? Family? Love?"

The sound of activity behind them ceased, and she knew that the women were listening intently, though they couldn't see the drawings. "Covenant," he said. "I want the theme to be God's covenants. This is Abraham holding Isaac. The miracle child born in his old age."

"I like it," Brooke said. She lowered her voice so the ladies couldn't hear, but he could see that they strained to listen. "But I don't know that much about the Bible. I wouldn't know where to begin with a covenant theme."

"I'll teach you about it," he said. "It'll blow your mind, Brooke. Really."

Brooke bit her lip and nodded. "Okay, then give me some Bible references to look up, and I'll do my homework and make some sketches."

"You could start with Adam and Eve. For instance, the curse of God on Eve, where he said he would put enmity between the serpent and Eve, and between his offspring and hers. I'd like to do a window of Christ crushing the head of the serpent."

"Crushing the head of the serpent?" one of the women erupted. "Christ never crushed a serpent."

Nick's face changed. "I'm talking about Genesis 3:5, Mrs. Inglish, when God made a promise. And it was a prophecy about Christ . . ."

Mrs. Inglish's face reddened. "Oh, that."

Nick shook his head and turned back to the table. Slowly he began gathering the sketches. "Why don't we find someplace where we can work without interruptions," he said.

Mrs. Inglish mumbled something to the other women as Nick and Brooke left, something neither of them cared to imagine. The room erupted into a low roar of cackles and chirps.

"Where are we going?" Brooke asked when they were out of earshot.

"Well, there sure isn't any place around here," he said. "I guess we'll go to my house."

Brooke stopped in her tracks. "No."

Nick turned and saw the resolution in her expression. "What, Brooke?"

"It's bad enough that their gossip will be all over town before lunch," she said, "but if we go to your house today while they're looking for something to say about us, we're only feeding it. I won't do that, Nick."

Nick leaned back against a wall, and his shoulders fell as he expelled a long breath. "It isn't that, really, is it, Brooke? You're afraid to go to my house with me for other reasons, aren't you?"

"Of course not."

His eyes were impatient, penetrating, as they locked her in their scrutiny. "Yes, you are. You're afraid to be alone with me."

Brooke's mouth tightened into a thin line; anger flared in her eyes. "I can see now that maybe I was hasty," she said.

"What do you mean?"

"In telling Abby Hemphill I was staying!" she whispered. "I'm not looking forward to rationalizing every decision I make with you, Nick. I'm not interested in explaining myself constantly. Maybe this isn't such a good idea, after all."

Nick pulled her into his office and closed the door behind them. She leaned wearily back against the wall. Nick lifted his hands in apology. "I'm sorry," he said. "Let's just try to work, okay? Don't quit on me just when we've gotten started. We can work in here."

With a look that said it was against her better judgment, she nodded. "All right. Let's work."

Relief drained Nick's face. He turned to the cluttered desk and cleared off a space for her. "We'll each take one side of the desk, and maybe by the afternoon the Hysterical Society will have gone home."

Brooke smiled.

"We're going to get through this, you know," he said. "I promise."

Brooke's smile settled comfortably over her face, despite the sigh unraveling from her lungs.

He only hoped he could keep that promise.

CHAPTER

9

$\mathcal{B}$Y THE END OF THE DAY NICK HAD walked Brooke through a mini-course in God's covenants, and they had divided the circular windows into four panels each and had assigned a different covenant to each group of four. They stayed in the tiny office with the door closed until lunchtime. When they came out, they noticed the members of the "Hysterical Society" nudging each other. They went to a fast-food restaurant and choked down a hamburger in Brooke's car, where they were removed from the stares and gossip they might have encountered inside. Then, feeling refreshed, they braved curious eyes once again and closed themselves back in the office.

By the time they called it a day, the construction crews had left, and all of the women of the Historical Society were safely at home, no doubt lighting up half the telephone lines in Hayden. Still, Brooke felt a sense of accomplishment, a tingling pride that they were on the verge of creating something wonderful.

But when she drove home, that sense of pride sank as she realized that she had yet to face her family. She was certain they'd heard—from someone, if not Roxy—how she had told off Mrs. Hemphill and defied all the town gossips by staying and working with Nick on the windows. And she was right. When she walked in, she saw them all sitting soberly in the living room, still as statues, staring at her as if their silence automatically demanded explanation. Her mother faced her with a hurt, how-could-you-do-this-to-me look, her father wore his stoic that's-gratitude-for-you visage, and Roxy regarded her with a martyred why-don't-you-just-shoot-me-and-put-me-out-of-my-misery expression.

Brooke ignored her emotional pain and told herself to make her explanation cut and dried, hoping to avoid the tears and yelling and scars that never quite healed. She remembered the time her grandmother had died, and her parents had gathered her and Roxy into the living room to break the solemn news. Would her family view this moment as seriously as a death in the family?

"I thought of going straight to a hotel, since I had my suit-case with me," Brooke said, her voice raspy with emotion. "But I decided that I should at least come by and let you hear from my mouth that I'm staying—and I *am* going to be working with Nick on the windows. My work here shouldn't affect any of you. I'll find my own apartment tomorrow, and you won't even have to know I'm in town."

She swallowed and saw that none of them, neither her mother, nor her father, nor Roxy, was about to speak. Their expressions remained unchanged. Heartsick, she started slowly toward the door. Just before opening it, she turned back to them. Tears blurred her vision, and her mouth quivered. The words wobbled with emotion. "I'm truly sorry that my being here embarrasses all of you. But this town has taken enough from me. It owes me this chance to make my mark. And I'm going to do it."

She opened the door and started to walk out.

"Are you going to move in with that man?" Her mother's question stopped her before she'd crossed the threshold.

Brooke turned back to her mother, hardly believing what she'd heard. "No, I am not moving in with Nick. I told you, there is nothing going on between us."

"Then why would you sacrifice all of your dignity, all of the integrity you've worked so hard to rebuild in the last seven years, if he doesn't mean anything to you?"

"Because I'm an artist!" Brooke cried. "A good one. I've never had the opportunity to create anything of this magnitude!"

"Oh, you created something of this magnitude," her mother said. "About seven years ago."

Frustrated beyond control, Brooke pressed her forehead against the edge of the open door and wiped the tears roughly from her face. After a moment she looked at Roxy but found that her sister wasn't glaring at her any longer. Instead she stared despondently at the floor, as if Brooke's very presence exhausted her.

"Look, there's really no point in this," Brooke said as new tears rolled down her face. "I'll never be able to make you believe me. You didn't believe that nothing happened the first time, so why should you believe me now?"

"Because both of you are single and attractive," her father blurted. "And you have a history."

"So what?" she asked. "We're two adults who have made a business decision. It isn't hurting anyone. It isn't betraying anyone."

Her voice broke off, and she felt like a kid again, begging her daddy to let her stay out past ten o'clock. It was ludicrous, and she wasn't going to play the game any longer.

"I'll be at the Bluejay Inn," she said. And then she closed the door and left without looking back.

It was almost eight when Brooke checked in at the Bluejay Inn, the only motel in town. The dirty building stood in a seedy section of town across from a bar where arrests were made nightly. In the neighborhood adjoining the motel, domestic squabbles provided night-time entertainment. At least, that had been the case seven years ago, and it didn't look as if things had changed. The class structure in Hayden was rigid and unforgiving. "Once trapped, always trapped," Brooke's father used to say.

She checked in, then hurried to her room, which was hot and had a musty odor from age and traffic. She realized vaguely that she hadn't eaten, but the motel had no room service and she didn't want to go out.

She lay down on the bed and stared at the ceiling. Even the quiet of her room seemed hostile. It wasn't fair. Nothing that had happened concerning Nick was fair. She was tired of being alone, tired of expecting the worst of people and being right.

The most intense loneliness she had ever experienced coiled in her heart, and she longed for a friend. But Nick was the only friend she had in town.

She sat up on the bed, wiped her eyes, and reached for the telephone book. She found his number and stared at it. She needed to tell him how to reach her. She didn't want him to think she had run again.

With a trembling hand, she picked up the phone and punched out his number.

*N*ick had just finished eating when the phone began to ring. He picked it up mid-ring.

"Hello?"

"Nick?" Brooke's voice sounded hollow.

Nick changed ears and propped one foot on the edge of his bed. "Brooke? Are you all right?"

"Yeah, I'm fine," she said, her tone a little too bright. "I just thought you should know, in case you had to reach me, that I've checked into the Bluejay Inn for the night. I'll look for an apartment, but . . ."

Her voice trailed off, and Nick planted his elbow on his knee and leaned forward. "Why? I thought you were staying with your parents. Did—?" He took a deep breath and raked his hand through his hair. "Aw, no. Did you have a fight with them about working with me?"

He heard her sniff and knew she'd been crying.

"I just . . . felt it was better for all of us if I didn't stay at home."

Nick stood. "What room are you in?" he asked. "I'm coming over."

"No, you can't do that!"

"Why not?"

"Think about it," she said.

He could sense the pain in her ragged breath, and he braced a hand on his windowsill and gazed out at the moonlight glittering on the canal. Instead, he saw her face, twisted in pain and distress, her soft cheeks shining with tears.

"Remember that time you got a C on your English paper?" he asked. "Remember how upset you were when you came to my class . . . the overachiever who hadn't achieved? I was a good listener then, wasn't I?"

Brooke was quiet, but he knew that she remembered the way he had set her down in the art room that day he'd caught her crying, pushed her hair back from her damp cheek, and insisted that she tell him what was bothering her. "Yes, you were," she whispered. "And you fixed everything. You talked to Mrs. Deere and got me another chance to do the paper."

"Yeah," he said softly. "That's me. The fixer."

"I've always wondered what you said to her."

Nick dropped back to his bed. "Oh, not much," he said. "Just that you were an overachiever who saw anything less than an A as absolute failure and that I had really been working you hard in art because of your unique talent. I told her it was all my fault and that I'd let up a little."

She laughed softly then. "Let up? You never let up on me. You demanded perfection."

"And I got it," he said.

Her silence sent a warm feeling rushing up inside him, untangling the confusion in his heart. He could tell she had stopped crying. "I just need a good night's sleep," she said finally. "I'll see you tomorrow, okay?"

He hesitated. "Brooke, you're not going to skip town on me again, are you?"

"No," she said wearily. "I'll be there."

The line went dead, and Nick held the phone clutched in his hand and wondered why the thought of her created such loneliness in his soul. He went to his dresser and picked up his Bible, opened it, and sat back down on the bed. But even as he read, his heart ached for the pain he'd heard in her voice. Was this how it worked? Did God point people to that special person with an ache in their heart that wouldn't subside?

But God wouldn't point him to her. She wasn't a believer.

The memory of their words yesterday flashed like lightning through his mind. "You'll never find peace as long as you keep running away," he'd told her. But he had a feeling that Brooke didn't consider herself a candidate for peace at all.

He tried to concentrate on the book in his hand, but their conversation kept playing through his mind: "We can show them all what we're made of," he'd said.

"What is that, exactly?" she'd asked. "I'm not sure what I'm made of. That's part of the problem."

There was life right here, in this book, that could give her peace, confidence, and identity. Somehow, he had to find a way to show her.

*B*rooke leaned over the hotel's bathroom sink and washed her face, then looked in the mirror and saw a pale rendition of herself. Her eyes were red and swollen, and her hair fell around her face. She really should do something with it.

She heard a knock on the door and went to the window to peer out. Her mother stood at the door in the blue-white overhead light, and she saw her father waiting a few steps behind. Her heart tripped, and she felt the misery that Nick had so effectively calmed rising back to threaten her again. Swallowing, she opened the door.

Her mother looked almost as battle-fatigued as Brooke herself when she stepped inside. "We didn't want you to stay in a motel tonight," Alice Martin whispered, her lips trembling at the corners. "We love you, honey, and we want you to come home."

Brooke sighed and stepped back from the door, letting her parents into the room. They came in, looked around awkwardly and continued to stand as she lowered herself to the bed. "It's all right, Mom. I'm comfortable here."

"You can be comfortable at home," her father said, his gruff voice softened by his intention to make peace.

"No, not really," she said, shaking her head. "There's no comfort in hostility and accusations. I'm not used to it. I've lived alone for a long time. I just think it's best—"

"We won't accuse you anymore," her mother interrupted. "Will we, George?"

"No, we won't," her father agreed, setting his arm around his wife's narrow shoulders. "We just want you with us. If we promise to keep our opinions to ourselves, will you come home?"

Brooke looked critically at the floor, as if studying the worn-out carpet that clashed with the bedspread. She wondered if they could all really share a home together again, without judging or condemning each other. After all this time, she doubted it. "I don't know."

Her mother dropped into a chair and leaned toward her with her plea. "Do it for Roxy," her mother said, and Brooke looked up. "She needs you, Brooke. I'm worried about her. She's not happy, and I'm afraid we're losing her too. Maybe having you there will help her some."

Brooke stood up and went to the window, peered out over the dark parking lot lit only with two blaring lights. From her window she could see the neon sign of the After Hours Bar flashing its tacky glory. Tonight the parking lot was full of cars. "I don't see how I could help," she said, turning back to her parents. "She barely tolerates me."

"It isn't just you," her mother said. "She's quiet like that with everybody. She just needs to get to know you again. It would do her good."

Brooke tried to see them without reproach, without the pain that fogged her vision. Too much time had passed to really go home and pick up where she'd left off. But as Nick had reminded her tonight, it was never too late for a second chance. And if Roxy really needed her . . .

"All right," she whispered wearily. "I'll come home."

Her parents offered faint smiles, but there wasn't a great deal of victory in their expressions. Too much had been lost between them. "I'll have supper waiting," her mother said, and kissed her on the cheek. "I know you haven't eaten."

Brooke nodded. "I'll be there in about twenty minutes," she said. "I just have to get my things together and check out."

"Okay," her mother said awkwardly. She attempted a smile, and took a deep, uneven breath. "We'll see you at home, then."

"Yeah."

Brooke watched her parents walk toward the door, stiff with the emotion they both held trapped inside. "Mom? Dad?" she said just before they stepped outside.

They turned back to her, and she saw the naked love in both their faces. Suddenly she forgave them for all the mistrust, and all the pain. "I'll make you proud of me one of these days. I promise I will."

Her parents only smiled sadly and left her alone.

CHAPTER

10

*S*HADOWS SLID LIKE DANCING VISIONS along the moonlit wall of Nick's bedroom. It was almost midnight, but he felt about as sleepy as a hungry leopard. Wearily, he slung his feet to the ivory carpet and rubbed his eyes, then let his fingers slide down his face. His gaze drifted out the window, where a weeping willow blew and danced in the breeze with the same cadence as the shadows.

He got up and walked in darkness through the living room into the kitchen and opened the refrigerator, letting its light spill out to illuminate the room. He propped his elbow on the door and peered inside, at the leftover pasta and a lone apple.

He stared vacantly at the food and thought of the sound of despair in Brooke's voice tonight. He wondered if she was, indeed, all right. Of course she wasn't, he decided, shutting the refrigerator and letting the darkness swallow him again. Because of him, there was a rift again between Brooke and her parents. He must have been crazy asking her to come back here.

He went to the telephone on the kitchen wall, braced his elbows on the counter, and closed his hand around the cool receiver. If he called her just to see how she was and woke her, would it be such a crime?

There were worse things he could do—like getting dressed and showing up at her door. He looked up the number for the Bluejay Inn and dialed it.

It rang four times before the desk clerk answered.

"Would you please connect me to Brooke Martin's room?" he asked.

"Miss Martin checked out over two hours ago," the man said.

"She did? Why? Didn't she just check in?"

"All I know is what's on my books," the man said impatiently.

"Yes, thank you." Nick hung up the phone, running a hand through his hair. His heartbeat accelerated to a threatening speed as thoughts spun wildly in his mind, all leading to the same conclusion. *She's gone,* he thought. *She's left again.*

Before he'd consciously decided to do so, Nick snatched up the phone again and dialed information to get her number in Columbia.

"Hello." She answered on the first ring, and he caught his breath, though his heart fell miles to his feet. "Brooke, why did you—"

"This is Brooke Martin," her voice continued. "I'm not home right now, but if you'll leave your name and number I'll get back to you."

A recording! Nick realized with some relief. He heard the beep and hesitated a moment. "Uh ... it's Nick," he said. "I called the motel and you'd checked out. I hope you haven't gone home, Brooke. This is too important to give up on that easily. The windows, I mean. Don't give up, Brooke. It's worth whatever it takes to see it through. I really hope you haven't gone home."

Then, unable to think of anything else to say, he dropped the phone back into its cradle and rested his forehead on his palm.

He'd said too much. He hadn't said enough.

Well, there was no way to know for sure if she'd gone home until tomorrow.

The trick, he thought, would be getting through the rest of the night.

His question answered itself the next morning when Nick looked up to see Brooke standing in his office doorway, shining like a ray of sunlight on a stormy day.

"I don't believe it," he said, falling back against his chair with relief. "You're here."

Brooke smiled. "Well, that's some greeting."

He came to his feet and leaned haggardly over his desk. He imagined that the dark circles he'd seen beneath his eyes in the mirror that morning were still there and that his anxieties were written in every gesture he made. "Where were you?" he asked, schooling his voice to sound calm. "I called you last night. They said you'd checked out."

Brooke dropped her portfolio onto a chair. "My parents came by after I talked to you," she said. "We sort of made peace, so I decided to go back."

He stared at her for a moment longer, but as the simple truth registered, a slow grin spread across his face. "I thought you'd gone home to Columbia," he said. "I thought you'd given up again."

A poignant expression softened Brooke's features, and she shook her head. "I wouldn't abandon my partner without telling him."

"Good," he said finally. "We'd better get to work before the Hysterical Society gets here."

Brooke's smile died a little. "Too late. A few of them were driving up when I got here."

"Terrific," he said, coming around the desk.

He glanced out the door, shrugging. "Well, at least it can't go on forever. They're bound to run out of things to do soon."

A few of the women walked by and tried to look as if they weren't intentionally staring into the office as they passed.

"Morning, ladies," Nick called in a pseudo-cheerful voice.

The women mumbled various greetings that their tones negated and walked on, looking for work to be done.

For the next hour, both Nick and Brooke tried to concentrate, but even with the door closed they could hear the incessant humming of power saws and electric sanders, of banging and crashing, of cursing and yelling over the noise. The office was becoming cramped and hot as they tried to spread out, and with each new panel they sketched, it became more cluttered.

When they'd been at it for over two hours, Brooke threw down her charcoal. "This is never going to work," she said. "We need our workroom. That's what it's there for."

"They should be finished today," Nick said. "Things will be more normal tomorrow."

"In the meantime, we aren't really getting anything done. It's a mess in here. I don't know what I've done and what I haven't."

Nick leaned forward on his desk and propped his chin in his hand. "Look, why don't we just use the time to go to St. Louis to start getting bids for the glass and lead?"

Brooke looked at the stacks of papers that depicted some, but not all, of the panels. Even the ones they had roughed out didn't have details or exact colors—just the basic themes and ideas. "How can you order glass and lead when you don't know how much you need yet?"

"I can give them a ball-park figure and get some bids going, and when we're ready, we can give them exact amounts. Today's as good a day as any."

Nick's offer was sorely tempting, but something inside held Brooke back. Idly she fingered the chains at her throat. "We can't afford to waste time, you know," she said. "I could take some of this home and work on it there while you go to St. Louis."

"You're the expert. I need you with me."

A smile tugged at one side of her lips. "Don't give me that. *You* taught *me,* remember?"

"True, but you're the one who's been doing it for a living. You're way ahead of me."

Brooke shook her head. "Never. In my mind, you'll always be the teacher."

Nick's flip expression faded, and he looked down at his hands for a moment, then flicked a speck of dust off of his sketch. "I wish you could stop thinking of me that way. I haven't taught in years."

Brooke averted her eyes when he looked at her. "I wish I could too." She came to her feet, dusted off her pants as if she could shake away the growing sense of intimacy. "But maybe it's best that I do. It keeps the boundaries clear."

Nick's eyes were penetrating, waiting for her to look at him without defense. "Do you really need those boundaries, Brooke?"

Brooke tossed a wisp of hair back from her face. "We all need boundaries, Nick. They're like the lead work on the windows. They help support us. They keep us from buckling and cracking with the weight of whatever we carry around."

Nick nodded and looked down at his hands again, as if some script he needed to get through the day was hidden there, in the lines of his palms. Finally he got to his feet, too suddenly, too brightly, and clapped his hands together. "Well, all right, then. Let's just take those boundaries and go to St. Louis. What do you say we take the Duesenberg?"

Aware that those boundaries were blurring with each hour, Brooke followed a few steps behind him as he led her past the workers and out into the sunlight.

*A*bby Hemphill stepped over a dusty power tool that someone had neglectfully left lying at the entrance to the church and looked around for the culprit. *Who do these men think they are?* she wondered vaguely. From the way they slouched around, chomping on sandwiches and guzzling canned soda, you would think they owned the place.

It was a terrible day when one had to face the fact that the town's oldest church had been turned into a loafing place for every idiot with a saw, as well as a rendezvous point for Nick Marcello and that girl. It was a mockery to the solemnity of such a sacred institution.

Across the large room and through the corridor, Abby saw some of the ladies from the Historical Society. Straightening her hair and pristinely dodging cords and machinery, Abby made her way to the room where the ladies had congregated. "Well," she huffed when she reached them, "it certainly is refreshing to see that not *everyone* is wasting time."

The women looked up, all smiles and cordial greetings. They, at least, gave her the respect she deserved.

"It's lunch hour for the construction crews," Martha Inglish told her. "We were just thinking of going out to get a bite ourselves. But we couldn't decide whether we could spare the time. Our two *artistes*—" she pronounced the word with great sarcasm "—are getting a little annoyed that they have to share work space with us. We thought if we hurried we could finish this today."

"The Historical Society's duties should come first," Abby proclaimed. "Don't let them bully you."

"Oh, they aren't bullying us," Mrs. Inglish said. "In fact, we've hardly seen them in the last two days, since they've taken to locking themselves in his office. And we wouldn't *dream* of interrupting them."

The women snickered, but Abby didn't find it at all amusing. "Locked in his office? Are you serious?"

"Well, not now. They left about two hours ago."

"Have you actually *seen* them working? Cutting glass or whatever it is they do?"

The women all agreed that none of them had seen any work being done. "They just talked and whispered a lot—when we could hear them at all," Martha said. "Who knows what's been going on in that office?"

"That does it!" Abby spun around and started out the door. "I'm going to put a stop to this today!" She marched out like a woman with a divine mission.

CHAPTER

11

$\mathcal{T}$HE DUESENBERG'S ENGINE IDLED conspicuously at the red light in downtown St. Louis, drawing admiring stares from the drivers around them. Nick had pulled the top down before they'd left Hayden an hour ago, and the wind and sun had infused more energy and liveliness into his tired face.

The driver next to them, a businessman in a gold Mercedes, rolled down his window and leaned over to the passenger side. "Nice car!" he called.

Nick grinned. "Thanks."

The man dug into his pocket for a business card and stretched to hand it to Nick. "If you ever want to sell it, give me a call."

Nick took the card and noted that the light was still red. "Sorry. This baby's not for sale."

The light turned green, and the man shook his head regretfully. He gave the car a last look and drove off with a wave.

Brooke laughed and squinted over at Nick as the sun and wind hit her face. "You didn't even ask how much he was willing to pay," she said. "Aren't you even curious?"

Nick tossed the card to the floor. "Nope. Whatever it is, it's not enough. Some things just don't have a price.

Brooke glanced at Nick as he drove. The act of driving made him seem more relaxed, more at home than she'd ever seen him. It was as if the Duesenberg held his power, his worth, his confidence. "Was the grandfather who left you this car a rich man?" she asked.

Nick made a sharp turn, laughing. "No, not by any stretch of the imagination. My grandfather was a cobbler."

"Then how could he afford a Duesenberg?"

Nick pulled onto a street with bottlenecked traffic and idled for a moment. "He didn't buy it," he said. "One of his best customers for twenty years owned this car. Grandpa made everything that man put on his feet, and the man had a deep appreciation for the quality in his work. When he died, he left the car to my grandpa. He wrote in his will that my grandfather was the only man he knew who understood the true meaning of the word 'quality.' This car came to represent Grandpa's philosophy. It was his most prized possession."

A poignant smile touched Brooke's lips. "And he left it to you," she said.

"And he left it to me," Nick confirmed. "Before I was old enough to drive. He told me that he wanted me to depend on it like an old friend. So that's what I've done." He smiled as the memory played a sweet melody in his eyes. In an exaggerated Italian accent and with elaborate hand gestures, he said, "He told me, 'You put-a care and-a love into everything you do, Nicky, and that's-a quality. It don't matter about money. You do *everything* like you're doin' it for the Lord. He'll reward you. That's what this car stands for."

Brooke sat back and set her hand on the door, looking at the car from a new perspective. "What was your grandfather like?" she asked.

Nick's soft sigh was a whisper, and his eyes twinkled. "Grandpa was the only one in my family who saw my talent as a gift instead of a curse. He gave me my first box of paints when I was six years old. He was something."

Brooke's heart swelled at the look of love in his face. She suddenly realized that if anyone ever looked at *her* with such sweet, unconditional love, she would probably abandon all reason and devote herself to him completely. "You miss him, don't you?" she asked.

"Yeah," he whispered. "I miss him. But I have this car to remind me of him, and all my zany memories. He's not gone, really. And I'll see him again."

Brooke let her gaze drift out the window. She didn't know if she believed in heaven, but she didn't want to interrupt his musings by saying so.

"I was with him when he died," he said. "He took my hand and started quoting the Twenty-third Psalm. 'Yea, though I walk through the valley of the shadow of death, I will fear no evil.' And he didn't fear. Not at all. When he finished quoting that, he opened his eyes wide and touched my face. Then he said, 'Nicky, God's Word says that we do not-a grieve as those who have no hope. We will meet again, my boy.' And he squeezed my hand as hard as he could, and looked somewhere off behind me, and whispered, 'I'm gonna see Jesus!' And then he died."

Brooke watched him, aware that he'd just shared one of the most intimate moments of his life with her. She didn't know what to say.

"I want to die the same way," Nick said. "Without fear, looking forward to being with Jesus, and telling those behind me that there should be more joy than grief."

"Was there?" she asked. "More joy, I mean?"

"I cried," he said. "Cried my eyes out. But then I got to thinking of my grandpa in heaven, without the arthritis that made him limp and those brittle bones and the diabetes and high blood pressure and age . . . And Jesus there, teaching him unfathomable things, answering the questions he puzzled over, like why there had to be a Satan, and what he wrote in the sand that time . . ."

He spoke as if he believed in Jesus as more than just a myth-ical figure. She'd never known anyone who thought of Jesus in that way.

He smiled and glanced sideways at her as the traffic began moving again. "He would have liked you."

"I would have liked him," Brooke said, feeling as though she already knew the man who'd had such a profound impact on his grandson's life.

She looked around as the car pulled into the parking lot of an art gallery.

"What are we doing here?" she asked.

"I want to show you something." He cut off his engine, let-ting quiet surround them. "My grandfather always used to say that I could be whatever I aspired to be and that others would see me as I saw myself. Well, I think maybe it's time I showed you how I see myself, so that you'll stop seeing me as a teacher. You know, I haven't taught in seven years, and I've had to make a liv-ing somehow."

"I know you have," Brooke said.

He grinned with genuine amusement. "What exactly do you think I've been doing?"

"Well, you've . . . I guess you've been—" She caught her breath and felt the sting of embarrassment. "You're an artist, of course."

"Well, at least you do realize that," he said. "But you obvi-ously don't know if I'm a good one, or what that means in terms of who I am. To you, I'm still good ol' Mr. Marcello."

Brooke laughed. "Nick, you were never 'good ol' Mr. Marcello.'"

"Whatever," he said, opening the door and getting out. He came around the car and opened her door. "I brought you here to show you who I really am."

Tingling with anticipation, Brooke got out of the car—care-fully, lest he ban her from riding in it again—and followed him into the small gallery. It was a well-known place, with a shining reputation among art lovers in Missouri, a gallery Brooke had once secretly hoped would feature her own work someday, before she had decided to specialize in stained glass.

The gallery was quiet, though alive with the feel of exquisite art. Pieces hung from the slate-gray walls and graced lighted pedestals, which had been placed carefully throughout the rooms. Two patrons spoke in quiet tones to the gallery owner, a tall, wiry woman in billowy silk pants and an oversized silk blouse. Nick offered her a wave when they were inside.

"Nick!" she called, shattering the stillness. "It's been weeks! Darling, come over here right now and meet some of your admirers. We were just talking about you."

Brooke glanced up at Nick and noted his calm smile as he ushered her toward the people. Nick looked more alive and at home than she had ever seen him.

"My admirers?" he asked as he approached the couple. "Helena loves to exaggerate."

"No exaggeration this time," the man said, shaking Nick's hand. "We were just asking how to reach you for a specially commissioned project."

"Mr. and Mrs. Winston, this is Nick Marcello," Helena said.

Nick set his hand on Brooke's back. "I'd like you to meet Brooke Martin," he said. "She's my partner on my most recent project. I'm afraid I'm pretty tied up with it for a while."

The couple, from the "money is no object" strata of society, didn't settle for his polite rejection. Instead they went on to ply him with promises and offers, until Brooke decided to explore the gallery and allow them to talk privately.

Feeling emotionally stimulated by the caliber of art she saw, Brooke wandered among the walls of paintings and sculptures until she found a collection of paintings hanging like visual poetry on one side of the gallery. Without looking for the signature in the bottom corner, Brooke knew instinctively that the collection was Nick's. The colors reached out with a contemplation of life that was distinctly Italian in passion and fervor and conviction.

"He's wonderful, isn't he?" Helena said in a deep, smoky voice as she walked up behind her.

Brooke glanced at her over her shoulder. "Yes," she said, her voice laced with a reverence she hadn't intended. "I didn't know he had anything on exhibit."

"Nick?" Helena asked, surprised. "You've got to be kidding, darling. Without him, I might as well close this gallery down. He's been one of my staple artists for years now."

"Really?" Brooke turned back to the paintings, studying one that gave her an odd sense of joy deep in her soul, just in the way that he painted the source of light in the upper corner, as if it came from heaven itself.

"That's the one that couple likes most," Helena whispered, stepping closer to Brooke. "His work has such a rich, soulful feel. Sort of makes you want to step into it and live there." She grinned and cast a sidelong look at Brooke, her brow quirking up with her obvious appraisal. "So, tell me. Are you the lady in his life? He's so private it's hard to tell if there is one."

Brooke smiled. "No, not at all," she said quietly. "I'm a stained-glass artist. We're working together, that's all."

Helena sighed with dramatic disappointment and crossed her arms, her long, manicured fingernails tapping on her sleeve as she leaned back thoughtfully against the wall. Her tone was quiet when she spoke. "I've heard through the grapevine that there was some sort of scandal in his life a few years back."

Brooke chose to let that comment hang. She stepped down the wall, carefully absorbing the mood of each of the paintings, seeing . . . *feeling* vividly the romance Helena spoke of.

"How well do you know Nick?" Helena asked her, breaking into her reverie.

Brooke tore her eyes from the paintings and faced the tall woman. The gallery owner's expression was neither condemning nor competitive, only curious. "I knew him for a while a few years ago," she evaded. "But we were commissioned to do the windows . . ."

Helena's grin revealed that she wasn't buying the story. "No, darling. I asked how *well* you know him. Not how long."

Brooke tried to match the woman's smile, but knew that hers was strained and unnatural. "Not well at all."

"Oh, well," Helena said, stepping away from the wall to look at Nick's paintings again. "I was hoping there was a romance brewing here. Something smoldering he'd want to paint about. You have such style. I figured if Nick had a type, you'd probably be it."

Brooke dipped her face and wished she had something to do with her hands. She crossed her arms. "I . . . I don't know about that," she said.

"Don't get me wrong," Helena went on. "It isn't that I've never seen him with anyone. He's brought an occasional date to the parties I've thrown."

"You two aren't over here exchanging criticism about my work, are you?" Nick asked from behind them.

Brooke turned and saw him leaning against the wall, regarding her with a poignantly fragile look on his face. "Of course not."

"We were discussing the themes that inspire you, darling," Helena said, and Brooke's eyes darted back to the paintings as she struggled to look preoccupied. But she could feel Nick's eyes on her, gently appraising her.

"My themes, huh?" he asked.

"Brooke tells me you two hardly know each other."

Brooke met Nick's eyes and felt his gaze penetrating too deeply, searching her with an artist's eyes that filled in all the colorless places. "I was her art teacher a few years ago," he explained. "She was my best student."

Helena's eyebrows lifted in sudden understanding, and she turned back to Brooke, studying her with a new, more critical eye. "I see."

Brooke lifted her chin, trying not to look so self-conscious. "Nick, your work is wonderful. I had no idea."

"Thanks," he said, his modesty coming as naturally as his smile, though she sensed his pride in his eyes. "A guy's got to make a living."

"Give me a break," Brooke said. "This isn't just making a living."

He sighed and regarded the paintings with a subjective twinkle in his eyes. "No, this is more than that. It's just . . . what I do."

"It's making *me* a living," Helena threw in, her raspy laugh rattling the room. "And frankly, darling, I can't imagine what I'm going to do if you don't plan to produce anything until that dreadful church is finished."

"There are other artists, Helena," he said.

"Not like you, darling. Not like you."

CHAPTER

12

*T*HEY HAD BEEN ON THE ROAD for ten minutes before Nick said, "So, are you able to see past the teacher in me now?"

Brooke inclined her head pensively to one side and watched him as he drove. "Those paintings were fabulous, Nick. I mean it." She let her gaze travel to the other cars whizzing by. "I just wish you hadn't told Helena you were my teacher. She had just mentioned that there was some kind of scandal in your past. I think she knew I was the one the minute you told her that."

"So what?" Nick asked. "It isn't like it's some secret. Everybody in Hayden knows. Besides, Helena loves that sort of thing."

"I know." Brooke tried to smile, but found it difficult. "She also told me about the other women in your life. She's done quite a bit of speculating about your love life."

"Hasn't everybody?" Nick asked.

Brooke watched the wind flutter through his ha[i]
squelched the urge to ask about those other wo[

hadn't even considered until today. Instead, she asked the second most pressing question on her mind.

"How do you do it? Really, Nick," she said. "How have you been able to stand living in Hayden all these years, when you could have lived here, in a bigger city, and had respect and admiration—and where no one would have known or cared that you got fired for a bunch of lies when you were teaching?"

He laughed lightly, as though he'd asked himself the same question a thousand times. "There are more good people in Hayden than bad. I grew up there. I've never been one for running away from my problems."

Brooke recognized the indictment of her actions. "Like me?" she asked.

Nick kept his eyes on the road as he answered. "You did what you thought you had to do," he said in a flat voice. "I can't fault you for that."

She turned to face him in her seat, trying to make him understand. "Nick, those people are vicious. Maybe I'm not as strong as you. But the hostility . . . it's everywhere, in everybody in town. Like I killed each of their firstborn children, and they're determined to have their revenge."

"You're looking at the wrong people," Nick said. "Some of my closest friends, some of the people I love most in the world, are right there in Hayden. Good people."

"Good people who love gossip," she whispered. "Good people who don't care who they hurt."

"Good people are good people," Nick said. "I hope this time you'll stay around long enough to see that."

They visited three sources for the glass and lead they needed for the windows. By the time they were finished, they were both

little diner on their way out of town and studied the menus, the waitress came to n't Mr. Marcello and Brooke Martin."

at the woman, startled, as if she'd been he looked familiar, but Brooke couldn't

"Sharon Hemphill," Nick said after a pause, and he stood and gave her a one-armed hug.

Brooke stared at the woman who had changed so much since high school. She was bone thin, and had bleached her hair blonde, but her face looked older than her age, and she had dark circles under her eyes. "Sharon. I didn't recognize you," Brooke said.

"No one does. My mother finally got me skinny. It was her lifelong dream." She said it with such sarcasm that Brooke recognized the pain behind it. "So. . .are you guys ready to order?"

Nick and Brooke exchanged looks. "Sharon," Nick said, "I hope you don't mind my asking, but what are you doing working here? Your parents are the wealthiest people in Hayden."

"Didn't you hear?" she asked. "My parents cut me off. Threw me out when they found out I was pregnant."

"Pregnant?" Nick asked. "Sharon, I didn't know."

"Of course not. I left town so no one would. Couldn't take the chance of soiling my parents' lily-white reputations. My mother hasn't even seen my baby. She's two now. I've got to make a living, support my daughter somehow. Tips are good here. Lots of truckers stop in since it's so near the interstate."

Brooke's stomach tightened, and she found that she wasn't hungry anymore. The way Abby Hemphill had treated—was treating—Brooke suddenly seemed so minor compared to what she had done to her daughter . . . and her granddaughter.

"They had hopes of me marrying some upstanding rich jerk from one of the families they approve of. Instead I got tied up with the mechanic who serviced their Mercedes. The stuff nightmares are made of, as far as my mother is concerned."

"Did you marry him?" Nick asked.

"No. He wasn't interested, and neither was I. So it's just Carrie and me."

"Sharon," Brooke said, "why don't you take a break and join us?"

Sharon looked back over her shoulder, then slipped into the booth next to Brooke. "Guess I can spare a minute." She glanced over at Brooke with a grin. "So what are you two doing in St. Louis? I thought my mother ran you out of town, Brooke."

Brooke looked down at her hands. "She did, but I came back to work with Nick on the windows of St. Mary's."

"Oh, boy, I bet my mother's throwing fits over that."

"Actually, she is," Nick said. "I don't suppose you have any hints on how to appease her."

"Easy," Sharon said. "Just give her everything she wants. Do everything she says. Treat her like the queen dictator. Oh, and Brooke will probably need to leave town again. In fact, it would be best if both of you did."

Brooke smiled. "Other than that?"

Sharon's face grew hard, and her eyes went dull. "Tell you what. Watch my brother. He's a great model for getting along with her. He toes the line, bows down, does everything she tells him. He's the perfect son. Married well, ran for city council and won. Stands up straight, wears the right clothes. Keeps up appearances."

Quickly, Sharon got back up, and Brooke saw a glint of tears in her eyes. "You people must be hungry. We have great burgers."

They ordered, and Sharon scurried off to get their food.

Brooke looked across the table at Nick. "That's about the saddest thing I've ever heard," she said.

"Yeah," he said. "Abby Hemphill strikes again."

"She's ruthless. I'm not sure either of us is strong enough to take her on."

"Think again," Nick said. "I'm not going to let her win. Jesus said, 'In this world you will have trouble. But take heart! I have overcome the world.'"

"But did He mean even Abby Hemphill?"

"Even Abby. I have nothing to fear. Our work will glorify God in a mighty way, and I'm determined to do it. There are people praying for us, Brooke, and I'm praying. Prayer works. You'll see."

Sharon brought their burgers, then rushed off to serve some truckers at another table. They ate quietly, then said good-bye to Sharon and went back to the Duesenberg. It was mid-afternoon when they got back from St. Louis and parked the Duesenberg in Nick's garage, where Nick chose to leave the delicate old car most of the time. They got into Nick's old Buick and headed back to St. Mary's. Though the construction crews' trucks still filled the parking lot, the Lincolns and Oldsmobiles driven by the women of the Historical Society were gone.

"Alone at last," Nick said as he cut off his engine.

"The workroom is all ours," Brooke said, a smile finding its place on her face again. "Now we can get some real work done."

But as they climbed out of the car, Abby Hemphill pulled her shiny new Mercedes in beside them.

"Abby." Nick's greeting was strained as she got out of her car. "The ladies have gone home. I think you're finished here."

"Not quite," she said. "I just came by to inform you and your mistress that I intend to make a motion to stop the work on the windows tonight at the church business meeting. I'm going to have your commission for this job revoked. I have witnesses that you've been behaving inappropriately on the congregation's money . . . locking yourselves all day behind closed doors, disappearing for hours at a time . . . together. Checking into hotel rooms . . ."

"*What?*"

"Wait a minute!"

Brooke and Nick's outraged responses were simultaneous, but Mrs. Hemphill forged full speed ahead.

"The meetings are open, so if you care to fight for your jobs, I can't deny you the right to be there. It'll be held in the conference room at City Hall."

"You bet we'll be there," Nick shouted.

Brooke's heart rampaged in her chest, and something close to panic threatened to choke her. "Mrs. Hemphill, I hope you have proof to back up these lies," she cried. "Otherwise, you're setting yourself up for a whopping case of slander!"

"Oh, I have all the proof I need, young lady," Abby Hemphill said.

And then, leaving them both stunned, she got into her car, slammed the door, and screeched out of the parking lot.

CHAPTER

13

$\mathcal{T}$HE EVIDENCE THAT MRS. HEMPHILL presented at the meeting was flimsy at best, but in the minds of those present it seemed highly indicting.

Things began badly when Mrs. Inglish spoke to the church "on behalf of the Women's Historical Society," and related how Brooke and Nick had abandoned their workroom and locked themselves in Nick's tiny office "for hours on end," adding that she wouldn't venture to guess what they were doing in there since she was "too much of a lady to imagine such things." And referring to her notes as though it had been her task to log their goings and comings, Mrs. Inglish outlined the number of times they had left the church and disappeared "without a trace."

Brooke sat in her seat, her mouth clamped shut in anger as the accusations were fired at her. Nick bit his lip and continuously shook his head, but he remained silent as well.

Then Mrs. Hemphill pulled out her heavy artillery, and Brooke felt as if the bottom of the world had dropped out.

"Pastor Anderson," Abby Hemphill said in a tone as authoritative as a courtroom attorney's. "I would like to submit a copy of a hotel bill that shows that Brooke Martin checked into the Bluejay Inn last night, then checked out two hours later."

The members buzzed with disapproval, and Brooke's mouth fell open in mute fury. Her spine shot ramrod straight. She sensed Nick looking at her, and she feared he would try to touch her to calm her, an act that would make her snap completely. He didn't.

Before Brooke's rage erupted, Horace Anderson, the sixty-year-old pastor who'd seen this town through all of its peaks and valleys, stood up. "Abby, I'm sure this is going somewhere, but I can't imagine what all this has to do with Miss Martin and Mr. Marcello designing stained-glass windows."

"Exactly, Pastor," Abby Hemphill said. "It has nothing to do with stained-glass windows. But it has everything to do with wasting the church's money."

"Abby, I've known Nick a long time. I know his character. Before we go on with this gossip, I think we should give our victims a chance to defend themselves. Nick, Brooke, would either of you like to address these charges?"

"You bet I would." Nick came to his feet before Brooke could. He braced his hands on the chair in front of him, leaning in Mrs. Hemphill's direction. She lifted her nose and crossed her arms, regarding him with try-to-weasel-out-of-this smugness. His voice was as spuriously gentle as the wind in the eye of a hurricane. "You succeeded in smearing Brooke Martin's reputation and running her out of town once before, Abby. I'd like to think we're all a little older and a little wiser now, but I see some things never really change." He sighed and stood up straight, folded his arms and shook his head. "Pastor, Brooke and I were closed up in my office because the workroom that we would have preferred to work in was full of the ladies of the Historical Society. We simply moved to the office to work and closed the door to block out the noise of the construction work. It's deafening. Now, if you'd like evidence of the hours of work we've put in so far, you're welcome to come by the church tomorrow and get an update."

Nick left the chair and began pacing around the room, looking each of his accusers in the eye, daring them to look away. "As for our leaving today, we went to St. Louis to check out our suppliers and to get some bids on the supplies for the windows. Those are some of the things that go along with designing stained-glass windows of this magnitude. However, I don't plan to account to you people every time I get in my car or close my door."

"My point," Abby interrupted, "is that these two people have a scandalous history that I don't think anyone here needs to be reminded of. My fear is that they're using this project as a means of finishing what they started. He hasn't addressed the issue of the Bluejay Inn, yet, has he?"

"I can't address it, Abby!" Nick shouted. "I wasn't there! And as far as Brooke is concerned, I think she'll agree that it is none of your business!"

"No, wait a minute!" Brooke stood up, drawing all eyes to her. She felt like an eighteen-year-old girl again, even though she'd pulled her hair back in a chignon and worn a pair of black slacks with a white blouse. Her appearance was far from the artsy style she usually embraced. She'd left her jewelry at home, except for a pair of white studs in her earlobes. The effect was severe, she hoped. Not at all vulnerable. Her voice wavered with restrained wrath when she spoke. "I would like to address the motel issue."

Abby set her chin in her palm. "Go right ahead, dear," she said. "I can't wait."

Brooke offered the woman a sad, pitying smile. "I'm sure you can't. But I'm afraid I'm going to disappoint you, Mrs. Hemphill. The truth is that I had a disagreement with my family and decided that it would be best if I didn't stay at their house last night. I checked in, stayed awhile, and when they came and asked me to come home, I did. It's that simple."

"Then your parents were the only ones who visited you in the hotel room?" Abby asked as if she didn't believe a word.

"Absolutely," Brooke said. She turned to the other council members, her brows oppressively drawn together. "Why is it that I feel like I'm on trial here? Why am I having to defend everything I've done since I came into this town? Hayden is my home too. I came into this project against my better judgment, because I wanted a chance to work on something that meant something." She turned to Horace, who listened with a deep, ponderous frown. "You asked me to come here, Pastor. I didn't ask for the job. If we're wasting our time on this, tell us now. I'll just get right back to Columbia and pick up with my life."

"No, wait a minute," Horace blurted, halting her with an out-stretched hand. "That isn't what we want. I personally want you to do what you were hired to do." He rubbed his weary eyes and looked around at his congregation. "Look, if they provided sketches of the windows and made some kind of presentation to show us what they're planning, would that put your minds at ease?"

Some of the members agreed that it would, so the pastor turned back to Nick and Brooke, who now stood side by side, allies against the world. "All right then. This time next week, bring us eight or ten sketches, and I'm sure we won't have any more discussion about revoking the budget."

"Eight or ten?" Abby asked. "There are twenty windows. Let them bring sketches of all of them."

Nick and Brooke looked at each other, astounded, then turned back to the council. "All of our sketches?" Nick asked. "Each window has four parts. We're talking about eighty panels. We can't sketch all of those in enough detail to convince you people in one week!"

"We start with crude drawings called cartoons," Brooke tried to explain. "They look like puzzles. Unless you're used to looking at such things, you won't—"

"Do the best you can," Horace said. "We'll have to go by whatever you can show us."

Nick sighed and gazed at Brooke with troubled eyes, as if silently asking her if she was ready for the round-the-clock work it would take to prepare such a presentation. Her answering look told him she was.

"All right," he said. "We'll do the best we can."

*T*he hallway was dark when Nick and Brooke left the conference room, leaving the church members to conduct other business. Light spilled from the doorway of a room being cleaned a few doors down, filtering just enough light for Brooke to see Nick. She slowed her step and looked up at him, unable to stop the tears from filling her eyes. "They think we went to a motel together," she said. "As long as we live, Nick, whatever we do, whatever choices we make, right or wrong, they'll see us that way."

"I know it's hard for you, Brooke. But not everyone believes it. Horace didn't."

"Most of them do." Her tears began to flow and she covered her mouth with her hand and turned away from Nick. "It isn't fair."

"No, it isn't." Nick touched the back of her shoulder, and this time she didn't shrug him away. "We can't let it cripple us," he whispered. "That's what Abby Hemphill wants."

"Why?" Brooke turned back around, wiped at the tears in her eyes. "What have we *ever* done to that woman? Nick, we can't do all this in one week. It's physically impossible. Eighty panels?"

"We'll do what we can," he said. "I'm not willing to give up easily. We'll start working tonight. At my place."

"No!" she said again. "How many times do I have to tell you? We can't be caught alone at your house or anywhere except the church. And then we'll *still* be gossiped about."

He threw up his hands in frustrated surrender. "Sorry. I just thought since I had coffee there, and food. . . . We're going to be at this around the clock, you know. There's no avoiding it."

"Still," she said, putting him off with a trembling hand. "I just . . . I can't. Maybe tonight we should just work independently. I'll work at my parents', and you work at home."

Nick's discontent with the proposed arrangement was clear, but he didn't argue further. They began walking down the corridor, past the lighted room where the janitor was cleaning.

Brooke sensed the weariness in Nick's muscles, the heaviness in his stride. Idly, she recalled the ragged condition he'd been in that morning, as if he hadn't slept in days. She doubted tonight would provide him with much relaxation either.

They rounded the corner where Mrs. Hemphill's office was and came to the door marked "Records," where Roxy worked every afternoon. The lights were all off, creating an eerie, lonely atmosphere. The sound of their shoes against the floor was soft and rhythmic, but another sound, the sound of muffled voices inside the Records office, caught her attention.

Brooke's feet slowed. "Wait a minute," she whispered.

Nick stopped. "What?"

"I heard voices in my sister's office."

Nick wasn't concerned. "It was probably the cleaning woman."

Brooke listened for another moment, staring into the darkness, concentrating. The hall had fallen quiet. "I guess it was," she said, and started to walk.

Before they reached the glass doors that opened into the parking lot, Brooke could see the light from the street lamps surrounding it. Only a few cars were still there, most belonging to the church members. But one, set apart from the cluster of others, caught her eye.

Roxy's car.

"That's my sister's car." Brooke turned back toward Roxy's office, trying to decide whether to barge in. "What if she's in trouble in there? She wouldn't be in some dark office this late at night if something weren't wrong." She started back up the hall. "I'm going to check on her."

Nick followed her back to the Records room, and again they heard two distinct but muffled voices—a man's and a woman's.

Brooke knocked on the closed door, though there was no light shining beneath it. "Roxy?" she called.

The voices instantly stilled, but no one answered. "Roxy? It's Brooke," she said again. When there was still no answer, Brooke shoved open the door and snapped on the light.

The couple moved apart—Roxy and a man with blond hair. Roxy's hair was tousled and her expression panicked. She stumbled back.

"Roxy?" Brooke asked, astounded.

As if the confrontation were too much for her to deal with, Roxy snatched up her purse and started for the door.

"Roxy!" Brooke said again.

Brushing past, Roxy said, "Leave me alone, Brooke! Just leave me alone!"

Before Brooke could speak, Roxy was halfway down the hall, with the man fast on her heels.

Brooke stood numbly in the doorway, reeling from the hatred she had seen in her sister's eyes. Nick's face mirrored her pain. "I have to go talk to her," Brooke said.

"You can talk to her tomorrow," he whispered. "But not tonight, when she's in this mood. Tonight, we're going to my house. No arguments, okay?"

The emotional warfare of the day had drained all the energy from Brooke's spirit, making her too weak to fight. She released a deep breath and nodded. "No arguments," she said. "What have I got to lose, after all?"

The ride to Nick's house in his old Buick was too quiet.

Nick gave her a sidelong glance as he drove through town. "What are you thinking?" he asked softly.

She shook her head dolefully. "Nothing, really. Just wondering what's going on with Roxy. Worried she's messing up her life. She learned from watching me how complicated things can get."

"I'm not going to complicate things any more for you, Brooke," he said. "It's very simple. We're two artists working together for a few months. That's all."

"I know that, and you know that," she whispered.

He let out an aggravated sigh. "When are you going to stop letting them get to you?"

"When are you going to *start?*" she returned. "It all seems to roll off your back."

"Would you rather I let it *break* my back? I'm not going to cower in a corner just because some people have nothing better to do with their time than to throw stones at me."

"Are you saying that's what I've been doing? Cowering?"

Headlights from a passing car illuminated his face, then quickly disappeared. "I'm saying that there are a lot of excuses in life to keep from doing the hard things. I don't need excuses, Brooke. Maybe you do."

Nick pulled into his driveway, but Brooke didn't seem to notice. Instead she glowered at him in the darkness, silently denying his accusations. He let the car idle for a moment, but when she didn't say anything, he got out to open the garage.

Brooke stewed as she watched him walk to the garage door and pull it open with a jerk. His words still stung, but deep in the back of her mind, she realized that she couldn't find a comeback because she feared he might be right. Maybe she did need excuses. Maybe she was afraid.

She exhaled deeply as he got back into the car and pulled into the shelter of the garage, next to the Duesenberg. When he had killed the engine, they sat quietly for a moment, neither of them making an attempt to get out.

"Look, maybe I was out of line," he said, the lack of enthusiasm in his tone making the apology seem less sincere.

"It's okay," she whispered, not sure she meant her words either. "It's time I stopped hiding behind Mrs. Hemphill and all the others. It's time I really did grow up."

He looked at her in the dim garage light and offered a weak smile. "Let's go in."

They stepped into the kitchen from the garage. Brooke glanced around at the cluttered room that looked like a stop-off place for quick on-the-run meals. It was clean, though here and there lay a wadded napkin, an empty milk carton, a watered-down drink.

The faint, familiar smell of oil paints drew her deeper into the kitchen as Nick closed the door quietly and laid his things on the kitchen table. She peered through a door on the other side of the kitchen, where the strongest of the scents seemed to originate. "Is that your studio?" she asked.

"That's it," he said. "Go on in, if you want."

She turned on the light and tentatively stepped inside. The room was larger than the kitchen, and much more cluttered. Paintings in progress leaned against the wall. One back wall was made entirely of glass, overlooking a small canal lit with lanterns on either side. An easel dominated the middle of the floor, with a stool next to it, and a small table where dozens of colors of paints waited in tubes to be used. Paintbrushes soaked nearby in mineral spirits.

"I think this is exactly what I pictured," Brooke said with a self-conscious smile. "The room even smells creative."

She turned back to the kitchen and saw Nick making coffee. His expression was still sober. "Canvas seems to be your favorite medium," she said. "Why did you get interested in stained glass?"

He plugged the coffeepot in. "I had ideas for some things that I thought would turn out better in glass, and I like the freedom to be versatile." He got two coffee mugs out of the cupboard, and set them on the counter. "What made you specialize in glass?"

Brooke leaned against the doorway, suddenly feeling at home surrounded by an artist's tools, an artist's work, and an artist's understanding. It had been a long time since she had experienced such a sense of comfort in anyone else's home. "It's just such a beautiful art," she said. "The only one that sunlight plays a direct part in. I worked with it a lot in college, and I guess I got hooked. I was never that good at other media."

Nick stopped what he was doing and turned back to her, his eyes dark with disbelief. "Not good? You're kidding, right?"

"Well, maybe good enough to win a scholarship, but I don't think I could have ever produced anything good enough to sell."

Nick closed the cupboard door and turned to face her squarely. An astounded smile sparkled in his eyes, removing all traces of his earlier ire. "Brooke, has your memory really faded that much?"

"What do you mean?"

Nick abandoned the coffeepot. "Come here," he said.

Brooke followed him into his living room, a breathtaking showcase for some of the finest works of art she'd ever seen. The white carpet added contrast to the colors of the pieces hanging on the walls, and even the furniture served to accent the sculptures surrounding it.

Brooke's wandering eyes swept over each piece in turn, absorbing the richness of the beauty accumulated there. But Nick touched her shoulders and gently turned her around, where a piece of sculpture provided the centerpiece for the room.

It was *Infinity,* the sculpture of two hands, gently embraced, their touch so poignant that even now she could feel the emotions that had driven her as she'd worked on it. She inclined her head in a moment of awe. "You kept it," she whispered.

"Of course I kept it," he said. "What did you think I would do with it?"

Brooke laughed softly and brought her hands to her face. "I don't know. I guess I thought it was lying in your attic or something. Or that you'd thrown it away."

He led her to the sculpture, picked it up and set it in her hands. Immediately, she remembered the sweet familiarity of every line, the cool warmth of every vein chiseled there. She slid her hand over the male hand, then across the smaller hand it embraced.

"Does that look like something that could be thrown away?" he asked quietly. "Brooke, you have no idea how powerful this piece is."

She had some idea as she realized that *Infinity* held the key to her past, the lock on her future. It was both the beginning and the end. But it was *her* beginning, *her* ending, and as bittersweet as it was, she cherished it in a way that—she was certain—no one else ever could. "I don't know what you mean," she whispered.

"I've had offers for it," he said. "People see it, and they w it. It strikes so much emotion within them. That's what ar Brooke. That's why you were a born artist."

She frowned down at the hands, trying to see th objectively. "You had offers?" she repeated. "What

"Helena at the gallery saw it a few months ago and offered me $25,000 for it," he said, watching her face carefully for her reaction.

There was none. "Did you hear me?" he asked.

"I heard you." She locked her eyes on the sculpture again, then quickly set it back on the pedestal and backed away, staring at it as if it were a foreign, unfamiliar object. Assigning it that kind of price tag cast it into the realm of something alive and mysterious. Nothing an eighteen-year-old girl could have created.

"Why didn't you sell it?" she asked, still staring at the sculpture.

"Because it wasn't mine," he said.

She tore her eyes from the hands and looked up at him, stricken. "Yes, it was. I gave it to you."

"You gave it to me before everything fell apart," he said. "I always planned to give it back when I saw you."

He lifted the sculpture carefully and handed it back to her. Tentatively, she embraced it, not taking it from him, but holding it just as he did. "I want you to take it back," he said. "When you gave it to me, it was a poignant gesture of thanks. But after what happened, I don't think you really should have thanked me. Not for messing up your life, running you out of town...." He swallowed and looked down at the sculpture, unable to meet her eyes as he finished.

"But I don't want it," she said.

"Take it, Brooke," he whispered. "And when you start doubting your talent, you can remember just how powerful an artist you really are."

Brooke accepted the sculpture with mixed feelings, delighted ___ a place of honor all these years ... and ___ ven it back now.

CHAPTER

𝒯T WAS MIDNIGHT WHEN BROOKE slipped into her house and saw that Roxy was still up, sitting in the living room staring at some Japanese martial arts movie on television.

"Hi," Brooke said.

Roxy didn't look away from the screen. "Hi."

Brooke dropped her case on the couch, but she kept the wrapped sculpture in her hands. She was bone tired, and her spirit was full of holes, shot from every direction that day. She wanted nothing more than to collapse into bed and sleep unhindered, but Brooke knew that this talk with Roxy about the scene she'd interrupted earlier couldn't wait. She had to start laying some kind of foundation for a new relationship.

"Look, about tonight—" Brooke started.

But Roxy immediately cut in. "I don't want to talk about it."

Brooke sat down next to her, looked at the screen, and realized that her sister couldn't possibly have been interested in the badly dubbed film. Roxy had stayed up, Brooke surmised, exactly because she did want to talk about it.

"I want you to know that I only walked in on you because I heard your voice and the light was out, and I was afraid you were in trouble. I'm sorry, okay?"

Roxy kept her blank stare on the television, her eyes so devoid of feeling that Brooke began to wonder if her sister was, indeed, preoccupied by the movie.

"Who was he, anyway?" Brooke asked.

Roxy pulled her feet up on the couch and wrapped her arms around her knees. "No one you know."

"I might surprise you," Brooke said. "The town's pretty small. I got to know a lot of the kids your age going to school functions when you were little. What's his name?"

"He's not my age," Roxy said. "He's older." The tension on Roxy's face grew more pronounced, and her lips quivered. "It doesn't matter, anyway." She picked up the remote control and flipped the station.

"All right," Brooke said, crestfallen. "It's none of my business."

She sat motionless for a moment, struggling for some common subject she could broach. Her hands closed more tightly around the sculpture. Slowly, she began unwrapping it.

"Do you remember this, Roxy?" she asked.

Roxy looked down at the sculpture, and a grudging spark of interest ignited in her eyes. "That's the piece you did in high school. The one that won you the art scholarship."

Brooke nodded, turning the hands over, tracing the smooth lines with her fingertips. It fascinated her. Holding *Infinity* was like holding a part of herself she hadn't glimpsed in seven years. "Nick kept it all these years."

Roxy's gaze climbed to Brooke's face, amazement and wonder covering the jaded grays that had reigned there before. "You worked so hard on it. I always thought you had it or that you'd sold it or something."

Brooke shook her head. "I gave it to him. I couldn't have finished it without his help. Wouldn't have won the scholarship.

Wouldn't have even tried for it." She looked up and met Roxy's eyes. "Nick was a good teacher, Roxy."

The shutters over her sister's eyes drew shut again, and Roxy looked back at the television. "Why did he give it back?" she asked, her tone deliberately uninterested.

Brooke's eyes glazed over as she looked at the sculpture. "He said he always intended to. Just never had the chance until tonight." She laughed softly for a moment as the conversation played back over in her mind. "He told me that a gallery owner in St. Louis once offered him $25,000 for it. Can you believe that? And he turned it down."

Roxy's eyes left the screen and focused on her sister, her antagonism blatant. "Guess passion does crazy things to a person," she muttered.

"It had nothing to do with passion," she said tightly. "He just felt that it was mine, and that he didn't have the right to sell it."

"So are *you* going to sell it?" Roxy asked.

Brooke looked at the sculpture and realized just how much it meant to her, now that she held it again. She had put so much into it.

"No, I couldn't ever sell it. It means too much." Quickly she looked up at Roxy, as if she'd caught herself in her own trap. "Nothing happened between us, Roxy. And now our relationship is strictly business."

Roxy didn't seem content to let things go at that. Brooke saw the subtle challenge in her eyes. "If he doesn't mean anything to you, it seems like you could let it go. Especially since you haven't had it all this time, anyway."

"No," Brooke said, feeling as if the walls of free choice were closing in on her. She stood up and turned her back to her sister. "He could have sold it, but he didn't. I can't do it, either."

"Twenty-five thousand is a lot of money," Roxy said.

"They could offer me a hundred twenty-five and I wouldn't change my mind," she said. Then, looking down at the sculpture carefully cradled in her hands, she started out of the room. "Good night, Roxy. I'm going to bed."

*L*ater that night, as Roxy lay awake in her bed, she thought again of Brooke's attachment to the sculpture. *Twenty-five thousand dollars.* Just the thought of that amount of money made her heart beat faster. Twenty-five thousand dollars could take her so far away from this oppressive little town.

She turned over on her side, thinking of the sentiment Nick Marcello had shown in keeping the sculpture instead of selling it. She had to admit, it was a little out of character for the woman-izing cradle-robber she'd always imagined him to be. And the same old question that she supposed plagued everyone in Hayden cropped up again: Why would a handsome, gifted art teacher risk his career for an eighteen-year-old girl?

Brooke was different. The intuitive knowledge, the awe-struck memory, invaded her thoughts. Her sister had never been ordinary. So much style. So much substance. So much emotion. No one in Roxy's life had ever made her feel quite as special as her big sister had when she was little.

Maybe she was still angry at Brooke for driving away that day and leaving her on the doorstep, she admitted in the solitude of darkness. Maybe that was the big sin she couldn't forgive her for. That and all the others that had followed.

Time to grow up, Roxy told herself, staring at the ceiling. *Life won't let you stay innocent forever.* She understood that bet-ter than most people her age. She'd been fighting the inevitable for years. But the fight was coming to an end. If Brooke hadn't barged into her office tonight, her innocence would have been sur-rendered like the adoration she'd once had for her sister.

An angry tear rolled down her temple and over her ear, and she closed her hand over her mouth to muffle her sob.

When would her choices get less consequential? When was it supposed to get easier to make it through each day? And when could she stop caring about the hopeless, heartless whispers behind her back, the people waiting for her to mess up so that she could take her turn to wear Brooke's scarlet letter?

It was inescapable, really, she thought, burying her face in her pillow. It was just a matter of time until the bomb dropped. She would go on making choices based on the fickle, fathomless whims of other people, and stave off the chaos within until she could run away like Brooke had.

But unlike Brooke, Roxy knew she would never look back.

CHAPTER

15

$\mathcal{T}$HAT'S SO INTERESTING." IT WAS A thought Brooke had not meant to utter, but she couldn't help herself. Her fascination with Nick's concept for the windows had sent her to a bookstore for a Bible. Instead of answering her questions, her reading of it had raised many more.

Nick looked up from his sketch. "What's interesting?" he asked.

"The idea that God provided that ram." She swallowed and tried to steady her voice. "I know you're gonna think I'm incredibly stupid. I'd never read that before, about Abraham and Isaac, or how God provided that ram in place of his sacrifice of Isaac."

"Pretty powerful. Do you think we should show Isaac on the altar? The knife blade as Abraham prepared to sacrifice him?"

"Anguish and tears on his face."

"But his eyes focused on heaven," Nick added. "Because he knew God doesn't break covenant, and He had promised that a great nation would come through

Isaac. God would have to either stop Abraham from killing Isaac, or else raise Isaac from the dead."

She looked up at him. "Can we capture all that in stained glass? The very simplicity of the images might diminish the message."

"I think we can do it," he said. "We can give enough of it to make people hungry to read more in the Scriptures."

Brooke grew quiet as she looked down at her own sketch. "You're smart, Nick," she whispered. "This isn't just about art to you, is it? It's about getting people to read the Bible."

He smiled. "Shrewd as serpents, guileless as doves. That's what Jesus said to be."

She reached for the stack of sketches he had already finished and began to look through them. Her hand stilled as she came to the one of Mary holding her limp, bleeding son in her arms, weeping over him.

"This one," she whispered. "It just tugs at something . . . so deep."

He looked up at her. "Do you think it goes too far?"

She kept looking at the sketch. "It depends."

"On what?"

"On whether you want people to be able to glance away."

He smiled. "I don't."

"The pastor may have a hard time getting people to listen to him, when they can't keep their eyes off Jesus."

"That's the whole point of *having* a pastor," he said. "To keep people's eyes on Jesus. Horace will be thrilled."

She was quiet for a moment as not-so-quiet thoughts passed over her face like movie credits on a screen. Then she flipped through more of his sketches, stopping at a rough drawing of a man dressed in modern-day clothing—jeans, a T-shirt, tennis shoes—carrying a cross on his shoulder. "I don't understand this one," she said.

"Jesus is the New Covenant," he said. "And if we enter into that covenant with him, we're to take up our cross and follow him."

Take up her cross? How? What did that mean? But she didn't want to appear ignorant—not to Nick. So she vowed to find the answer herself when she had time to pore through the Bible more on her own.

"Is something wrong?" he asked quietly.

She shook her head. "No. I just wish I'd paid more attention in Sunday school when I was little." She didn't know why tears stung her eyes as she spoke, or why that yearning in her heart— for what, she wasn't sure—kept getting stronger.

He reached across the table and touched her chin. "I can tell something's wrong. Tell me, Brooke. What is it?"

She couldn't understand it herself, so she knew she couldn't articulate that emptiness, that hunger. . . .

"Hey, Picasso."

They both jumped. Sonny was leaning against the door casing, wearing worn-out jeans and a black leather jacket with a helmet tucked under one elbow. His eyes swept around the room, as round as those of a toddler at Disney World.

"Sonny!" Nick's voice was a degree less than enthusiastic at the sight of his nephew, but he forced a smile. "Come on in." Brooke quickly wiped the moisture from her eyes as Nick turned back around. "Brooke Martin, I'd like you to meet my nephew, Sonny Castori."

Sonny stepped forward, regarding her with a sly grin, and extended a hand to Brooke. "If you don't mind my saying so," he said bluntly, "now I can see what all the fuss was about."

Knowing intuitively that he referred to the scandal, though he meant the remark as some kind of compliment, Brooke tried not to bristle. "It's nice to meet you, Sonny," she said.

"What brings you by here?" Nick asked. "I thought you'd be in school about now."

Sonny glanced at his watch. "At five-thirty? Give me a break."

"Five thirty?" Brooke pulled her watch out of her drawer and gasped. "Nick, did we stop for lunch?"

Nick started to laugh. "No, I don't think so."

"Man," Sonny said. "You mean you two have been in here working all day and didn't even know how much time had passed?"

Brooke flung a sweeping hand toward the drawings and flopped back in her chair. "We've gotten a lot done. But we still have a long way to go."

Sonny studied the drawings, his expression one of awestruck admiration. Carefully, he began to flip through the sketches. A long, slow whistle eased out on his breath. "Man, these are great. I mean . . . these are *really* great."

Brooke's weary eyes brightened. "You think so?"

"Man." He turned back to Nick, not completely abandoning the drawings. "Listen, I just came by to see if I could take you up on your offer to use your studio tonight. But if I could help here, man, I'd love to be a part of this. I could trace the drawings for you or color them in or whatever you need."

Nick looked at Brooke. "What do you think?"

"I think he'd be a godsend. I didn't think we'd have time to do color presentations, but with help maybe we could."

Sonny took off his leather jacket, tossed it onto a chair, and rubbed his hands together anxiously. "Just mark each piece in the color you want and I'll take it from there," he said.

Brooke smiled and shook her head. Sonny was just like Nick.

"I'll order a pizza," Nick said, heading for the phone. "Brooke can get you started."

By the time he'd started to dial, Sonny and Brooke were head to head, working hard together.

It was after one in the morning when Nick realized that Brooke was fast approaching the zombie dimension, and he had to admit that seventeen hours of work was about his own limit as well.

After Nick had seen Brooke to her car, he and Sonny ambled toward the Harley parked near his Buick. "Your ma's gonna kill me for keeping you out so late."

"No problem," Sonny said. He threw a leg over the Harley, pulled his helmet over his head, and looked up at his uncle. "Hey, Picasso, I really appreciate your letting me help out on this. Can I come back tomorrow night?"

"You're welcome to come as often as you can," Nick assured him. "But don't thank us. Brooke and I needed help badly."

Sonny set his wrist on the handlebar, letting the keys dangle from his fingers. "She's a nice lady," he said. "Like I said earlier, I can see what all the fuss was about."

Nick issued a heavy sigh and looked in the direction she had driven. "Do me a favor and don't bring 'all the fuss' up in front of her anymore, huh? It's kind of a sore spot."

Sonny chuckled. "Yeah, sure. But really, man. She's not like most women. Something about her . . . she's different."

Nick smiled. "Yeah. She's definitely that."

Sonny kick-started his motor, revved it for a second before he pulled it off the stand. "Well, I'll see you tomorrow, then," he said.

Nick watched his nephew pull out of sight, one lone light disappearing with a grating shift of gears. For a moment he stood alone in the dark parking lot, feeling suddenly cold and alone. He had never spent so much time in one day with anyone in his life, and yet he had felt strangely deprived when she had to leave. *Give it up, Marcello,* he told himself. *You're just tired.*

Maybe so, he thought, but tired or not, there would be no getting Brooke Martin out of his mind tonight.

CHAPTER  16

$\mathcal{T}$HE ONLY LIGHT STILL GLOWING in the house when Brooke came in was the reading lamp in Roxy's room. She passed by the room quietly and saw that the door was ajar, casting a bright triangle of light on the comparative darkness in the hallway.

Brooke pushed the door open enough to see that Roxy lay asleep on top of her bedspread, still fully dressed right down to her shoes. A stack of travel brochures cluttered the bed beside her sister: Canada, Washington, Colorado, Jamaica, Idaho—places with nothing in common, except that they were all far away. Frowning, Brooke lowered herself to the bed, careful not to disturb the girl, and reached out to stroke the soft tangle of hair back from her face. Roxy looked so young tonight. So innocent. So unhampered by the bevy of secrets she hid behind her eyes. Tonight she looked almost happy.

But not quite.

Regret filled Brooke's weary heart. Why had she let herself miss these last few years with Roxy and lose touch with the crises that had altered her spirit? Was her pride really worth it?

At Brooke's touch, Roxy stirred, lifted her head, and squinted, disoriented.

Brooke withdrew her hand. "Sorry I woke you," she whispered. "I saw your light on."

Roxy sat up, looked around her. "Must have dozed off," she muttered. "What time is it?"

"One-thirty," Brooke said.

Roxy pushed her hair out of her face and settled her groggy eyes on her sister. "And you just got in?"

"With all the work I have to get done in the next few days, I don't have time to sleep at all," Brooke whispered. "Unfortunately, my body demands it."

Brooke knew that the wheels in Roxy's sleepy brain were turning, adding up the late hour and her work with Nick and coming up with the same old conclusion. Unwilling to argue about it now, Brooke gestured toward the travel brochures. "You going somewhere, Roxy?"

Roxy pulled her shoes off with her toes. They dropped to the floor with a thud. "As soon as I graduate and save up enough money."

Brooke tried to keep her expression neutral as she watched her sister slide off the bed and peel back the covers. "Where?"

Roxy slipped between the covers, still fully clothed. "As far from this town as I can get," she said.

The words hit Brooke like an icy tide, but she didn't speak. What was there to say, after all? That Roxy shouldn't run away from her problems? That the grass really wasn't greener on the other side? Her own credibility on that subject left something to be desired, so instead of digging deeper into Roxy's psyche, Brooke sat silently beside her for a few minutes as Roxy fell back to sleep, wondering if she had just imagined the misery in her sister's voice. Were the travel brochures just bits of a dream or crucial parts of an escape plan? And what, exactly, did Roxy feel she had to escape from?

The feeling that she had failed her sister by not being around enough assailed Brooke, exhausting her even more than she already was. Quietly she turned off Roxy's light and went to her own room, where *Infinity* sat on the bedside table, profoundly reminding her that she hadn't always failed. She just hadn't allowed herself to succeed, at least not at relationships. What would have been different if she had stayed in town seven years ago and faced the gossip? Would she and Roxy be friends? Would she and Nick have fallen in love?

She didn't know the answers. But Nick was different now. He had changed. Greater things than art occupied his mind. His goals were bigger, more important. His passions were more spiritual. She wished she could share them completely with him, but some of them were out of her grasp.

Covenants ... provisions ... covenants ... provisions. The image of first the rainbow and then the cross the jean-clad man had carried colored her dreams as she drifted off to sleep. Symbols of ... what? God's love? His sacrifice? His covenants and provisions?

Were they for her, or just a chosen few who had that gift of understanding? Would the peace she saw in Nick's eyes forever be foreign to her?

She didn't know. From the depths of her soul, she hoped she would find out before she left Hayden again.

CHAPTER

17

*B*ROOKE FELT WOEFULLY UNPREPARED for the meeting. It was ten o'clock on the night before the presentation when Sonny finally left them alone, sitting solemnly in Nick's house scrutinizing the work they had accomplished in the previous week. The drawings fell far short of what they had hoped for. Only half of them were finished, and none was done in any great detail. Thanks to Sonny, they did at least have color.

Nick slipped down to the carpet to sit across from Brooke on the floor, studying the panels she would love to have a second shot at. He poured more coffee into her cup, the sloshing sound punctuating the rhythm of a violin concerto on his stereo.

"We gave it our best shot," he said quietly. "And we can take care of some last-minute details tomorrow."

"Yeah," she whispered. She leaned her head back against the cushions of the chair and sipped her coffee. "They're going to hate it, you know. They won't have enough imagination to see what we see here. Not at this stage, before it's committed to glass."

Nick propped his wrists on his knees and stared down at his cup. "Oh, I don't know. Some of them had enough imagination once to drive you out of town."

She laughed softly.

"We'll do what we can to fire up their enthusiasm," Nick said, his voice little more than a whisper. "That's all we can do. God has to do the rest."

Brooke lifted her cup to her lips. "Do you think He will?" she asked. "I mean, does God even really care about the little town of Hayden and a bunch of stained-glass windows?"

"Of course He does," Nick said without a hint of doubt in his voice. "He cares about all of this."

Brooke wasn't convinced. "Does He really care about us? Two people who won't just be dragging these sketches in there tomorrow night—we'll be dragging in our history together and our alleged affair and everything that's ever been said about us."

"He knows they were lies," he whispered.

She stretched out her legs before her and stared down at one of the sketches. "It seems like I'm always on the losing side of lies," she whispered. "Why is that?"

Nick took a long sip from his cup, reached for the pot on a trivet on the coffee table, and poured himself some more. "Because you don't play dirty."

Brooke looked into her cup, considering it for a moment. "Where has that gotten me?" she asked. "Alone . . ."

"You're not alone, Brooke," Nick said quietly.

"Aren't I?"

"No. I'm here."

"But you're not," she whispered. "Not really. I used to think we were the same. Now I know that we're different."

"Different how?"

She sighed. "Our deepest-held beliefs. Our souls."

"We both have them."

"Yes," she whispered. "But yours seems full. Mine doesn't."

"It could be," he whispered. "That's always a choice."

She shook her head. "Not really. To have what you have, I have to believe something. I'm not sure I can." She blinked back the tears in her eyes, and laid her head back. "Maybe that disqualifies me for this job. Maybe because of my lack of belief, God is blocking what we're doing here."

"You're contradicting yourself," he pointed out. "You claim to lack belief in Him, and then you suggest that He's acting against you. How can both things be true?"

"I don't know," she whispered, closing her eyes. "All I know is that maybe the windows just weren't meant to be, and maybe that's my fault. I'm so sorry, Nick."

"No, it's never been your fault," he said. "I'm the one who's sorry."

"For what?" she asked.

"For asking you to put your work in Columbia on hold and come here for something that may not even materialize. For disrupting your life . . . again."

"It's okay, Nick. It was time for me to come home."

His face was only inches from hers, and she could see the warmth in his eyes and sense the apprehension in his heart. "Yes, it was," he whispered. "Time to come home, and time to forgive."

"It's myself I won't forgive," she said, "if I make you lose the second most significant job of your career."

His eyebrows drew together in troubled surprise. "You haven't been responsible for either one," he said.

His eyes were eloquent with his own emotion but cloaked with a sadness that went much deeper than the losses he had faced. It hinted at the losses still to come.

With all her spirit, Brooke wished she could hold that sadness at bay.

For a moment, as he gazed into her eyes, she thought he was going to kiss her.

And then he drew back, got up, and pulled her to her feet. "Guess you should go."

She swallowed, trying to steady her breath. "Okay," she whispered, puzzled. Had she done something wrong?

She drew in a deep, cleansing breath but found that it did nothing to banish the cluttered, clashing emotions within her. She started to stack some of the sketches, but he reached out and stopped her hand.

"But I was just—"

"I'll get them later," he said. "I'll bring them to St. Mary's tomorrow."

"Okay." She looked up at him with hurt, bewildered eyes. "I'll see you then."

She felt him watching her as she gathered her purse and her case, and started toward the door.

"Eight o'clock?" he asked.

"Sure," she said weakly.

He took a few steps to follow her to the door, but when Brooke glanced back, he stopped. "Try and get some sleep. Tomorrow's going to be rough."

She lifted her brows and offered a self-conscious smile that told him sleeping would be the last thing she'd do tonight. "I'll try."

He followed a few steps behind her to her car, watching her get in and dig nervously through her purse for her keys. When she found them, she gazed down at them for a moment, as if struggling with a question she couldn't make herself ask.

He spoke first.

"Hey, Brooke?"

She looked up at Nick, his hands jammed in his pockets and his eyes as vulnerable and gentle as she had ever seen them. "Uh-huh?"

"The things we're putting in the windows . . . I believe them with my whole heart. I almost kissed you in there. But alone in my house . . . I didn't trust myself." He stepped toward her, his eyes glistening in the moonlight. "God treasures you, Brooke. That's why He stopped me."

She felt her eyes filling with mist, and she smiled up at him as relief and gratitude played symphonies in her heart. He wasn't turning her away. He was just living his faith. "Thank you, Nick," she whispered.

As she pulled out of the driveway and started down the street, she saw him standing alone in his yard, watching her leave. Something warm burst in her heart, and she realized that she was important to someone. She was valuable to someone. Someone saw worth in her.

And so did Nick Marcello.

CHAPTER

18

$\mathcal{T}$HE CHURCH BUSINESS MEETING THE following night was once again held in the large conference room at City Hall. It was open to the public, and as Nick sat next to Brooke at the front of the room watching the people filing in, he wondered why the telephone lines in Hayden hadn't over-loaded during the past week. Some of those who came hadn't been to church in years. They couldn't be less inter-ested in stained-glass windows; that wasn't what they'd come to see. He watched their eyes sweep over the room and settle anxiously on himself and Brooke. What they really wanted was to be firsthand witnesses to any smutty little allegations he and Brooke faced, so that they could light up the telephone lines again.

He recognized some of the students he'd taught in school, Brooke's classmates, all gawking at her as if she were some legend they were finally getting a glimpse of after all these years. Others were his own ex-classmates or active grapevine contributors who wouldn't have missed tonight if they'd had two broken legs. Some, like Brooke's family and his own, were conspicuously absent. Nick leaned toward Brooke, who sat next to him, rigid and expressionless. "Do you believe this?"

"Of course," she said. "Best entertainment the town's seen all year."

"All decade," he muttered.

She shook her head and looked down at her hands, and he saw the threat of tears in her eyes. "Only this time they get to see exhibits one and two firsthand," she said quietly. "Last time they only enjoyed the dirt in print."

Nick wanted to reach for her hand and reassure her somehow, but he couldn't escape the feeling that if he did, cameras would begin flashing around the room and they'd be the headline story in tomorrow's news. The pastor, who looked as irritated as they, leaned over to Nick. "With all these inactive members here, I ought to preach a sermon. It's a shame to waste the opportunity."

Nick laughed. "Go ahead. I dare you."

The pastor only chuckled and got to his feet. "Could we have some order here?" he asked. "We have a lot of business to take care of tonight, and I'd like to get started."

It took a good ten minutes for the crowd to quiet, but when it did, he stood looking wearily across the crowd. "I dare say this is the biggest turnout I've ever had for a business meeting," he said. "And some of you haven't sat in my congregation in years. Maybe we need to have business meetings more often."

The regular church members chuckled, but the gawkers didn't find it particularly amusing.

"I'd like to remind you folks," he went on, "that our intention here tonight is to listen to the presentation Mr. Marcello and Miss Martin have prepared concerning the stained-glass windows in the church, and then to either continue with or withdraw their commission." He slipped his thumbs through the suspenders tucked under his coat and turned meaningfully to Abby Hemphill. "This is not about personal accusations or gossip. So I'd appreciate it if no one would waste our time with that stuff tonight."

A murmur of disappointment undulated through the crowd.

"If any of you would like to leave now that you've heard that, it won't hurt our feelings," Horace went on.

No one left.

"Well, I guess that means these folks are serious about stained glass. So Nick, Brooke, the floor is yours."

Nick and Brooke stood up, and Sonny, from across the room, stepped forward as well to assist them in setting up the first group of panel sketches they intended to explain. A round of whispers and mumbles were heard as they spread the drawings across the five easels they had set side by side in the room. When he finished, Nick ventured a glance at Brooke.

Her cheeks were flushed in sunburn pink, and he knew she struggled with all her courage to keep from letting the stares and whispers daunt her. He should have done this alone. He should have insisted that she stay home and let him make the presentation without her.

She finished arranging the panels on her end and looked up at him. Their eyes met. The apprehension on her face, the strain, made him want to comfort her. Instead he began the speech he had prepared for this night, hoping the church would defer its judgment and give them what they needed to go on.

*B*rooke's nerves calmed a bit as Nick read several passages from the Bible and explained the covenant theme to the members and spectators, and she found herself getting lost, yet again, in the passion in his voice as he explained the concept of each group of panels. He spent an inordinate amount of time explaining the cross, and finally it occurred to her that he was addressing those like her, who hadn't been raised in church. She glanced over the faces in the crowd. They were no longer gaping at her, for their interest had shifted completely to Nick's words.

It was as if he had planned his presentation to reach non-believers instead of just to persuade the church about the windows. And he *was* persuasive. With just the excitement in his voice and the zest in his eyes and the gestures of his hands he captured their imaginations and shown them the beauty that went beyond what she and Nick had done on paper. Brooke found herself listening with rapt attention as he moved from the Gospel to explain the process of creating the stained glass and the dimensions that couldn't be seen here. And with a few simple words, he made them imagine the colors as they might be, with the sun filtering through. He explained how the covenant themes all tied together, how they were designed to serve as visual parables that would reach into people's hearts and turn them to the Bible and ultimately to Christ.

When Nick's presentation ended, a hush fell over the room, undisturbed for a moment as the audience absorbed what he'd said. "We'd be happy to answer any questions anyone might have," he said finally, breaking the silence.

A thousand questions arose in Brooke's mind as her own hunger for understanding stirred to life. She would search for the answers later, she thought.

Hands went up throughout the audience, and Horace recognized one man by name. The man wiped tears from his face as he said, "This project must be anointed, Nick. I can just feel the Holy Spirit's part in this." Others agreed with a smattering of applause.

"How many people will you have to hire to help you with this?" a questioner asked.

"Quite a few if we're to stay on schedule and have the windows finished on time," he said. "We plan to subcontract experienced people to help cut and lead the glass, as well as some inexperienced help, part-time workers like teenagers, to help with some of the less intricate things. And then, of course, we'll have to have someone to install the panels, which should be included in the cost of the construction rather than our art budget."

Abby Hemphill slapped her hands theatrically on the table and bolted out of her seat. "I've sat here and listened to this nonsense long enough!" she blurted out. "We cannot spend our tithes and offerings to fill our church windows with gruesome, violent scenes that will frighten our children."

Nick spun around. "Frighten the children? Abby, if you see anything frightening here, would you please point it out to me?"

"Knives and fire and blood!" Abby said, coming around the table and waving a finger at one of the panels still displayed. "Take that one, for example!"

Brooke sprang up, ready to defend the panel. But Nick spoke first. "Abraham sacrificing Isaac?" he asked. "Abby, if it leads someone to the Bible to find out what it's about, they'll see that Abraham didn't have to go through with it. The next panel shows the ram God provided. You can't do the covenant theme without including Abraham and Isaac."

Abby Hemphill went to the series in question and jerked one of the pictures off the easel, waving it as if the audience hadn't seen it closely enough before. Fury constricted Brooke's throat, stopping her breath, as she saw that it was the one of Christ's nail-scarred hands. "Do you people really want *this* on windows where *children* can see them?" Abby asked. "Christianity already has enough of a PR problem without all of this blood imagery everywhere."

"Without blood there is no remission of sin," Nick threw back. "There's no point in pouring hundreds of thousands of dollars into restoring that building, and all the sweat and money that will go into those windows, if we plan to dilute the message until it won't offend anyone. Those who understand why Christ came understand that the blood is what cleanses us. We're supposed to have the truth at church, Abby, not some benign, politically correct gospel. And you know what? Christ had a PR problem. If it was okay with Him, it's okay with me." He turned away from Abby and faced the members of the audience. "This is a choice all of you have to make. You can listen to her and have a bunch of flowers and birds on the windows, or you can allow me to create something that will lead people to Christ and point them back to the Bible."

"We're supposed to *attract* people, not drive them away, Mr. Marcello."

"Is that right?" he asked. "Funny, but I thought your hobby was driving people away."

Brooke moaned inwardly as she saw the look of rabid loathing on Abby's face.

The woman's lips compressed in fury. "How dare you?" she hissed. She looked frantically around her. "You people can't really think that this man is the right one for the job. Horace, I move that we find someone else to oversee these windows and get Nick Marcello and Brooke Martin off this project! Our contract with him has a clause that says we can fire him if there is reason. Well, there is certainly reason."

Nick flopped back into his seat, his lips tight and nostrils flaring with each heavy breath. Brooke sat beside him, sensing the anger, the tension in every inch of his body. He leaned forward, propped his elbows on his thighs, and covered his face.

"For the record," Horace said, "I agree with Nick. We're all sinners, and the wages of our sin is death. If Christ hadn't taken our punishment for us, we'd all deserve to hang on that cross. I don't want to spend the Lord's money on anything that skirts around the truth of Christ. I want to use that money for a bold message that can change lives."

More applause sounded around the room, and Nick looked up, surprised.

"People don't convert to Christianity because of stained-glass windows," Abby Hemphill spouted.

"They can if the Holy Spirit is working," Horace said. "If the Holy Spirit has a mind to win souls, He can do it through the windows or in the parking lot or even in the bathrooms. And I believe He's working here. I sense the Holy Spirit in these plans, and I for one don't plan to squelch it. Any more discussion?" Horace asked. Then, without allowing much time for response, he clapped his hands together. "All right, then, let's vote."

As the church members voted, it became apparent that the decision was pretty evenly divided. Brooke's anxiety grew. But when the voting was done, there were a few more votes in favor of the windows than there were against them.

"Then let the record show that we voted—again—" Horace emphasized the word with vexation, "to allow Nick Marcello and

Brooke Martin to continue to design and create the stained-glass windows for the church."

With a final bang of his gavel, the meeting was adjourned. An eruption of voices suddenly filled the room, and Nick lowered his face into his hands.

Brooke set her hand on his shoulder and leaned toward him. "Nick, it's okay. We won."

"Just barely. Not exactly with overwhelming support." He looked up at her, self-deprecation evident in every line of his face.

Sonny zigzagged through the crowd and leaned over to slap his uncle on the back. "Hey, Picasso, you really did good."

Nick covered his face again.

Sonny's grin faded. "Hey, you're not upset, are you? I mean, you won. It's a go."

"Yeah, yeah," Nick said. He stood up and started to gather the drawings. "Let's just get our stuff and get out of here."

Across the room Brooke saw Abby Hemphill in a corner, surrounded by her cronies, babbling with nonstop fury. She was cooking something up already, he knew. She wasn't going to let this go easily.

"Congratulations," the pastor said from behind them.

Nick turned around and shook Horace's hand. "Thanks, Horace," he said quietly. "I appreciate your support."

"Don't thank me yet," Horace said, his gruff voice taking the edge off the victory. "Just between you and me, I'm concerned that Abby will try to reverse things on the budget end. Abby can be pretty vindictive when she wants to be."

"Tell me about it," Nick said, his eyes straying to the angry woman again.

"Horace," Brooke asked, keeping her voice too quiet for anyone to hear, "do you really think she can change the budget? I mean, can't she be outvoted?"

"Of course," Horace said, "and that's exactly what I hope will happen. But you never know about these things. It depends on which way the wind blows and how loud that woman yells. And when she starts threatening to withdraw her family's financial support of the church—well, some members of our finance committee depend more on that than on God."

He left them alone to speak to some of the other council members, and Brooke and Nick only stood staring at each other. "This is a nightmare," she whispered. "I thought it would be over tonight one way or another, but here we are, no better off."

Sonny shrugged, not entirely clear what the dismal mood was about. "Sure, you're better off. At least we can go ahead with our work . . . finish the cartoons. . . . At least some of the church members see that this gig is worthwhile."

Brooke scanned the faces in the crowd; some of the audience lingered with interest near the panels displayed on the easels. They *did* like them. But others were engaged in angry conversation, and still others snickered, throwing amused glances her way.

She turned back to Nick and saw that he still barely contained his rage as he stacked the drawings and dismantled the easels. She didn't know what to say to make him feel better. "Nick . . ."

"Miss Martin?"

She turned and saw a woman at the side door.

"Miss Martin, you have a telephone call. Your sister. She says it's important."

"All right." Reluctantly, Brooke started for the door. But before she left the room, she looked back and saw Nick staring down at the sketches, shoulders slumped.

CHAPTER

19

$\mathcal{T}$HE MAYOR'S OFFICE WAS ONLY partially lighted, and the secretary, who apparently was also a church member, said over her shoulder, "I just stopped in to drop off my notes after the meeting, and the phone was ringing. I almost didn't answer. Good thing I did. She said it was important." The woman pointed toward the telephone, and Brooke snatched it up. "Roxy?"

"Thank heaven they caught you!" Roxy was barely audible over the line, but Brooke could still hear the quaver in her voice. "I was afraid no one would answer the phone."

"Roxy, what's wrong?"

Roxy dragged in a shaky breath, and Brooke could tell that she was crying. "I need your help," she said. "I'm sort of ... stranded."

"Stranded? Where?"

Roxy cleared her throat. "You know that bar across the street from the Bluejay Inn? The After Hours?"

A sick feeling rose in Brooke's stomach. What was Roxy doing "stranded" alone at a rough place like that, a place where hoods and hookers hung out, where people got shot or stabbed on Saturday nights. She glanced at the mayor's secretary, who tried to pretend she wasn't listening. "Yes, I know the place," she said.

"Well, could you come pick me up?"

Brooke pushed her questions to the back of her mind. "I'll be there in five minutes," she said.

True to her word, Brooke made it to the After Hours Bar within five minutes. She pulled into the parking lot and saw a cluster of bearded men in denim and leather turn and ogle her as she put her car in park. Roxy was nowhere to be seen. She opened her car door and got halfway out, her lights still on and her motor still idling.

"Hey, darlin', you lookin' for me?" one of the men from the small crowd called out, and the others joined in with catcalls and vulgar remarks.

Trying to ignore them, Brooke looked around frantically for Roxy. Was she waiting inside? Did Roxy expect her to walk through those men to find her?

She was just about to turn off her ignition and take her chances when she saw Roxy slip from the shadows at the far corner of the building.

The men saw her. "Hey, there she is!"

"We thought you'd gone home, honey."

"You weren't hidin' from us, were you?"

As they moved toward Roxy, she ran toward the car. When she reached it, she yanked open the door and almost fell inside.

Brooke was pulling out of the parking lot before Roxy even had time to sit up and, more importantly, before any of the men had reached the car.

"They're like animals," Roxy cried. Her hands trembled as she groped for her seatbelt.

Brooke caught her breath and became aware that she was shaking, as well. "Did they hurt you?"

"No. I'm okay."

Brooke drove for several miles before she was certain her voice was steady enough to ask the questions that had to be asked. "Roxy, what in the world were you doing there?"

Roxy swallowed a sob, wiped her face, and lifted her chin. "Bill and I . . . we stopped in for a drink."

"A drink? Roxy, you're seventeen! You aren't old enough to buy liquor. Didn't they check your ID?"

"No!" Roxy flung back.

Brooke bit her lip, deciding to report the bar at the first opportunity. "Where is this *Bill?*"

Roxy didn't answer for a moment. Finally she spoke, slowly choosing her words. "He . . . he had an emergency, and had to leave—"

"He took you to a sleazy bar and *left* you there alone?" Brooke shouted. "Is he crazy? Are *you* crazy?"

Roxy glared out the window, tears streaming down her pale cheeks. "I don't need this from you, Brooke."

Brooke tried to contain her fury as she navigated the dark streets leading to their neighborhood. "I hope you don't intend to see him again," she said finally.

Roxy didn't say a word.

"Roxy? You don't, do you?"

Roxy remained silent, staring out the window.

"Roxy, you don't have to put up with this. You can do better than some insensitive jerk who—"

"You don't know anything about it!" Roxy screamed. "So just get off my back!"

Despair stabbed Brooke's heart. "All right, Roxy," she whispered, pulling into their driveway. "I'll get off your back. But promise me that if anything like this happens again, you'll call me."

"That's what I did, isn't it?" Roxy asked, her tone softer than before.

"Yes," Brooke said. "That's what you did."

Roxy got out of the car and started toward the house. The lights were off and Brooke knew that her parents were sleeping soundly, unaware that Roxy was going through some sort of crisis that Brooke didn't know how to handle. She locked the car and followed her sister to the porch.

Roxy stopped before she reached the front door. "Don't tell them, Brooke. Okay?"

Brooke regarded her sister for a moment, saw the desperation in her face. "That's asking a lot, Roxy."

"I've never asked you for anything before," Roxy said. "Not until tonight. I need you to promise me that you won't tell them."

Brooke saw the red, swollen evidence of misery and heartache in Roxy's eyes. She had no idea what her sister was going through, but going to her parents would only alienate Roxy further. Instead, Brooke vowed privately that she would find a way to take Roxy under her wing, win her trust, and guide her in the right direction again. Releasing a long, weary sigh, Brooke acquiesced. "All right," she whispered, though her better judgment warned her against it. "I promise."

CHAPTER  20

$\mathcal{N}$ICK BROUGHT THE SKETCHES INTO his kitchen. He set them down carefully, so as not to tear or bend them. Then, in direct contrast to that gentleness, he slammed his fist on the counter. Leaning over it, he clutched the edges of the counter top, his knuckles whitening with the force of his self-reproach.

What had come over him tonight?

Gritting his teeth, he kicked the cabinet at his knees, then headed into the living room, where he flung himself onto the couch.

He couldn't believe he had insulted Abby Hemphill in front of hundreds of people. Had he really said her hobby was driving people away? She was right. He didn't deserve to work on the windows. And what a terrible witness he'd been to all those nonbelievers who'd come just for the spectacle. He had given them something to talk about, all right.

Even Brooke had been disgusted. She had disappeared without a word.

The doorbell rang, and he sat up, looking at the door and wondering if it was a lynch mob come to finish him off.

Bracing himself, he crossed the room and pulled the door open—then started at the sight of his mother, his sister Anna, and her husband, Vinnie. Judging from the expressions on their faces, they might be the lynch mob he'd expected.

"Okay, what's going on?" he asked. "You guys never visit me. Something's wrong."

"Are you gonna invite us in or make us stand out here in the elements?" his mother asked.

Nick ushered them in and closed the door.

"We came to talk to you." Vinnie's words were edged with hostility.

"About what?"

"About what you're doing to Sonny," Anna said.

Nick frowned and shook his head, wondering if he'd missed something. "What do you mean, what I'm doing to Sonny?"

"Encouraging him in this art business," his mother threw in.

"How could you?" Anna asked, glaring at him with disgust. "How could you undermine our authority as his parents? Do you know what it's like to go through adolescence with a child?"

"Adolescence? The kid's nineteen!" Nick leaned wearily against the wall, telling himself that he was engaging in a losing argument, that he should stay calm. "Look, Anna, if I've upset you, I'm sorry. I didn't mean to—"

"Upset me!" she shouted. "I want to know how you could do this! When you know how bad Vinnie needs him in his business."

"Anna, you're overreacting," Nick said. "The kid has talent. I didn't do anything to cultivate that. He's done it himself."

"Yeah?" Vinnie asked, stepping across the room until his massive frame pressed threateningly close to Nick. "Then how come when we found that paint and stuff in his room tonight, and told him to get rid of it, he told us that if we wouldn't let him paint at home, he'd come over *here* and do it?"

"And then to find out that he was at the church meeting with you tonight," Anna said, "and that he's been helping you with those windows, when he should have been working with Vinnie."

"What are you people afraid of?" Nick shouted. "It's not like the kid's on drugs or something. He has a hobby, for Pete's sake."

"You should know better than anybody," his mother said, shaking her long finger at him. "Hobbies can turn into occupations. So maybe you've been able to make a living at it, but that doesn't mean Sonny will. He can make good money working with his father, and Vinnie needs him. They had it planned out. It was God's will. The direction He gave us for Sonny."

"If it was God's will, why didn't He tell Sonny?"

"He did! But the boy decided to listen to you instead."

Nick collapsed on the couch, wondering just how far his control was expected to stretch tonight. Anna sat down next to him, her face as intent as he'd ever seen it. He looked at her, wondering if she'd forgotten all the fights that had taken place between him and his father all those years ago, when he had been about Sonny's age. Hadn't she learned *anything* about human determination from the way he had conducted his own life?

"I want the best for my son, Nick," she told him, her tone quieter as she made an earnest attempt to reason with him. "I want him to have a good work ethic, and I want him to be able to earn a living."

Nick released a frustrated laugh and sprang off the couch, gesturing around him, at the home that proved—to him, at least—that he earned a living. "Don't I support myself?" he asked. "Don't I do okay? The bank that holds my mortgage doesn't have any complaints."

"You don't even have a family!" Anna shouted, as though that meant the ultimate failure. "How is Sonny ever gonna support a family drawing pictures? If it could be done, wouldn't you have done it by now?"

Nick strode across the room, rubbing the back of his neck, desperate not to explode in front of these people who meant so much to him. Trying to contain his rising wrath, he went to the window, propped a foot on the sill and looked out over the small canal behind his house. "My not marrying has nothing to do with my art."

"It has everything to do with your art!" his mother belted out. "It was because of your art that you made the biggest mistake of your life—having an affair with a student."

"What—?" The question whiplashed across the room as he spun around to confront that accusation on his mother's face.

"That Brooke Martin woman. She ruined your good name once already. And don't think we haven't heard about the latest episodes."

Nick opened his mouth to respond, but caught himself, bit his lip and told himself that he'd burned enough bridges tonight. It wouldn't pay to throw his family out of his house. Regardless of their lack of confidence in him, he needed them. "First of all," he said in a voice exceedingly calm despite the fire raging within him, "I told you seven years ago that nothing ever happened between us. I thought you, of all people, believed me."

"This whole project is just an excuse for being with her, and I know it!" his mother shouted.

Nick held his breath for a moment and coiled his hands into fists at his sides. He closed his eyes and reminded himself that he loved his mother. This was nothing new, after all. She'd been on him since the first day she'd discovered his intention to study art, rather than something more "practical."

"Ma, I'm going to say this one time, and I hope you'll hear it. Brooke Martin and I have never had an affair, and we're not having one now."

He reached out for his mother's arm, knowing she could feel that he was shaking. "Ma, I love you, but you have never understood the first thing about me. I learned to accept that a long time ago, and it doesn't even hurt me anymore. But don't you do that to Sonny. He's a great kid, and he deserves a chance to become what he wants. If that's an electrician, fine. But if it's not, don't force him to give up something so important to him."

"You're not going to help us, are you?" Vinnie asked.

Nick turned to his brother-in-law, who stood poised, like a tiger about to attack. "Vinnie, I'm not going to help Sonny defy you in any way. I won't condone rebellion or disrespect. But he's *not* an adolescent. He's nineteen years old, and if he wants to use my studio because he feels he has something in his soul that needs expressing, why can't he? Your trying to stop him is only going to make his passion for it that much stronger. Believe me, I've been there."

"I can't believe this," Anna shouted, tears coming to her eyes. "You're going to put us through this all over again, aren't you? All the fighting you and Pop did when we were kids, you're wishing it on us, now, aren't you?"

A fissure of pity cracked through his anger. His sister would never understand that embracing a gift from God did not amount to weakness or a betrayal of loved ones.

"I'm not wishing anything on you, Sis," Nick said. "You're bringing it on yourself. Just let him do it. I promise you it won't warp him."

Anna blotted her tears. "Let's go, Vinnie," she said. "Ma."

Nick's mother stood in the center of the floor, glaring at him with a confusion of emotions. "Give the kid some room, Ma," he entreated. "A little paint never killed anybody."

His mother said nothing as she turned and followed Anna and Vinnie out of the living room.

CHAPTER

21

*B*ROOKE'S ROOM SEEMED DARKER than usual, perhaps because the sky was overcast, or perhaps because her heart was turbulent with emotions she couldn't contain. Roxy, Abby Hemphill, Nick.... Worries and fears and more worries raged in her mind, making it impossible for her to sleep.

She heard the phone ring in another part of the house and wondered who could be calling so late. Roxy's boyfriend, perhaps, wondering if she'd made it home or gotten molested and left for dead? The thought made Brooke seethe, and she sat up and wadded her pillow.

A knock sounded lightly on her door, and then it opened. Roxy peered in. "Telephone," she said.

Brooke looked at the glowing numbers on the clock, then hurried out of bed. "Who is it?"

"Didn't say," Roxy told her, "but I have a strong hunch."

As she stepped barefoot out into the hall, Brooke clearly saw the look in her sister's eye. The look that said, *If there's nothing between you, why is he calling at nearly midnight?*

Brooke sat down on the stool next to the telephone and picked it up. "Hello?"

"It's me." Nick's voice was deep, gravelly, thick with pain. "Look, I know it's late . . ."

Brooke heard a click and knew that Roxy had hung up the extension. Nick paused for a moment.

"It's okay," she said. "I wasn't asleep."

She heard him sigh, sensed his struggle for the right words. "It's been a crummy day," he said. "I can't stop thinking that I owe you an apology. I owe everybody an apology. I was hateful to Abby Hemphill, and I put both of us in a terrible position. It's no wonder you left like you did."

She frowned, realizing that she hadn't told Nick good-bye. Her worries about Roxy had superceded everything else. "That's not why I left, Nick. I had a phone call. My sister was in trouble and needed me."

"Is everything all right with her?"

Brooke wilted against the counter, thankful there was someone she could confide in, if not her parents. "Oh, Nick. She was stranded at some sleazy bar. Her date left her there, and she had to call me to pick her up. I drove up there, and all these hoods were standing outside boozing it up. She had been hiding behind the building waiting for me.

"Who *is* this guy she's dating?" Nick asked.

"Some guy named Bill. That's all I can get out of her. I can't understand. One minute she's acting like I'm overreacting, the next she's hiding behind a building in absolute terror. I've got to keep an eye on her from now on. She's headed for trouble. I can see it."

Nick was quiet for a moment, and she sensed his concern. "Why don't you ask her to help us out at St. Mary's? Maybe you two could get to know each other again if you worked together."

Brooke was skeptical. "I don't know. It's a real sore spot with her that I have anything to do with you, Nick. Besides, she already works at City Hall and goes to school."

"School's out next week for spring break. And we need all the help we can get." He released a deep breath, and she could hear the self-deprecation in his tone. "Of course, after my diplomacy at the meeting tonight, we might not have jobs ourselves by the end of the week."

Brooke's voice softened. "Don't be so hard on yourself, Nick. You said what needed to be said. Abby Hemphill was going to jump on us, anyway. If the chuckles I heard were any indication, I'd say a few of the people there wanted to give you a trophy."

"That's just it," he said. "I shouldn't have said what I did about her driving people away. That was terrible. People shouldn't be laughing at her. That makes me no different than her."

"Everyone knows you're different."

"No, don't you see? If I can publicly insult her, then I'm *not* different. That bothers me a lot."

"Well, the fact that it bothers you shows how different you are. I guarantee you, Abby Hemphill isn't awake tonight worried that she insulted *us*."

He was quiet for a long moment. "And then my mother and sister and brother-in-law heard about the meeting and showed up to chew me out for getting Sonny involved . . . and for encouraging his art. They had his life all planned out, and I interfered."

She grew quiet, realizing they had more in common than she knew. "Well, I guess that's the job of family. To make sure you never feel too good about yourself."

Nick was silent for a few moments, then said, "That's why I called you. It was selfish, calling so late, but I couldn't help myself. You make me feel better."

She was quiet for a moment, weighing her words, wondering if she dared go on. The memory of the night before washed over her, when he'd almost kissed her. She closed her eyes, remembering what a gentleman he had been. He was so unlike all the other men she'd known. So different. And yet here he was, beating himself up for not being different enough.

"Nick, I think you're probably one of the most decent people I've ever known. And because of that, you make me feel better too."

He didn't answer for a moment, then he said, "I appreciate that. I really do." Silence reigned between them again. "I'll let you go now. Get some sleep," he whispered.

"Yeah, you too," she said. "And Nick? Don't think about what Abby Hemphill and your family said to you tonight. Just remember what *I* said."

"I will," he said. "Good night, Brooke."

"Good night, Nick." She hung up the phone and sat smiling down at it. Then, feeling better about everything in general—because he had called her when he needed her—she headed back to bed.

CHAPTER

22

$\mathcal{B}$ROOKE PASSED ROXY'S OPEN bedroom door on her way back to her room. Her sister sat at her desk in a long pink gown with her bare feet crossed on the floor, examining a paper under the dim light of her lamp.

"Studying?" Brooke asked quietly.

Roxy looked up. "No, I was just going over my savings account," she said. "I thought I'd have more money saved by now."

Brooke went into the room and sat down on the bed. "What are you saving for?"

"My escape," Roxy whispered. She closed her bank book and swiveled around on her chair to face her sister. There was no hostility in her voice or her expression, no belligerence in her manner. Only a gentle sadness that touched Brooke's heart.

"Escape from what, Roxy?" Brooke asked. "Me?"

"No," her sister said. She looked down at her gown, picked at a white dot on the fabric. "From this town. From the people here."

A faint note of alarm rang out in Brooke's head. "Are you planning to get married or something?" she asked.

Roxy laughed aloud, but there was no mirth in her eyes. "No, I don't plan to get married. I just want to leave town when I graduate, like you did. I want a chance to be somebody different."

Brooke pulled her feet up onto the bed and gazed at her sister, trying to view her as a grown woman rather than as the little sister she wanted so desperately to protect. "I like who you are already," she said.

Roxy's smile was wistful as she met her sister's eyes. "But you don't know me that well, do you?"

Brooke stood up and ambled to the desk. She leaned a hip against it and faced Roxy. Roxy's face looked so mature for her age. Brooke wondered what went on behind those beautiful, guarded amber eyes. "I'd like to fix that," she said.

Roxy looked away, as if embarrassed by Brooke's honesty.

"Listen, I don't know if you're interested, but Nick and I need to hire some people to help us at the church. If you really want to make some more money, you could work there whenever you could spare the time."

Roxy looked up at her, trepidation darkening her eyes. "With you and Nick?" she asked skeptically. "I do need the money. But I don't know, Brooke. I'm not real good at hiding the way I feel."

Brooke reached for a curl of Roxy's soft hair and tugged lightly on it. "That's okay," she whispered. "We couldn't have paid you for a while, anyway. At least not until Abby Hemphill is finished trying to pull our budget out from under us. It probably wasn't a good idea."

Roxy regarded the bank book on her desk, and an unreadable expression passed across her face. After a moment she glanced back up at Brooke. "What would I have to do?" she asked tentatively.

"Just simple things, like tracing the patterns, numbering them, coloring them. That way Nick and I can concentrate on the more technical work."

Roxy sat back in her chair and ran her hand through the roots of her hair. "You know, spring break is all next week. I have to work at City Hall for a few hours a day, but I could still put in some time at the church."

A smile began in Brooke's eyes and traveled to her lips. "Are you saying you want the job?"

"I guess," Roxy said. "When do I start?"

"We could use you tomorrow," Brooke said carefully, "if you don't mind working on Saturday."

Roxy nodded. "Just wake me up, and I'll go with you."

Brooke set her hand on Roxy's shoulder and wished she were close enough to her sister to lean over and kiss her cheek. But it was too soon for that. She would take things one step at a time. "I'll get you up at seven. Wear something you won't mind getting dirty."

She started toward the door, then turned back. "And Roxy," she said. "About Nick . . . you'll like him if you give him a chance. Really, you will."

Roxy's gaze fell to the floor, so Brooke left her alone, telling herself she could only expect one miracle at a time.

CHAPTER

23

"IF YOU CAN'T HAVE WHAT YOU WANT, Nicky, then want what you have." Nick's grandfather's old saw flew through his mind on the wings of a memory as he tried to sleep that night. He pictured the old, thin-haired man with his back curved from slumping over the shoes on his work bench. He vividly remembered the first time his grandfather had said those words to him, when Nick was ten or eleven, mourning the fact that his parents wouldn't send him to an art camp in southern Missouri.

"But it isn't fair," he'd mumbled, kicking at a rock in his grandpa's front yard. "I've saved the money myself, and it's just for two weeks. What do they care?"

"They care!" his grandfather had shouted, slapping his hands together. "And they won't let you go and that's that." Nick remembered how surprised he'd been when his grandfather had thrust his sketch pad and watercolor set at him, defying the boy to complain. "So stop-a moping and make the best of what you have! It won't get better 'less you make it so."

Nick had angrily lunged into a painting that had set the tone for those he had done for the rest of his career. Emotions had emerged in blacks, blues, and browns, for he'd discovered early that it was those dark shades that revealed the mysteries in his soul.

But now the color he saw foremost in his mind, the color he felt most inclined to mix on his palette, was the emerald-green color of Brooke Martin's eyes. She was becoming too important to him. He was thinking about her too much. They didn't have the same goals, the same needs, the same Spirit. She didn't know or understand the things most important to him, and until she did, he knew that a relationship between them would not work.

Of all the advice his grandfather had given him, that, perhaps, had been the most adamant. "You marry yourself a Christian girl, Nicky, and your life will be full. You do that for all of your kids and your grandkids. Won't mean they all follow down the right path, Nicky, but you give 'em the head start. Make sure they got that head start."

Would his grandfather have been so earnest in that advice, to hold out for a Christian woman, if he had even once seen Brooke's eyes?

Maybe he needed to spend more energy leading Brooke to Christ than he spent wishing he'd kissed her. Maybe then he would have been more careful about his behavior in the meeting tonight.

Wearily, Nick gave up on the idea of sleep, got out of bed, pulled on a pair of gym shorts, and went out to the garage, where he kept a can of the special car wax he had ordered for the Duesenberg. Mechanically, methodically, as if ministering to someone he loved, he began to apply the wax in small, gentle circles.

Nick's mind drifted back to last night. He had allowed himself to get too attached to her—again. Maybe it was too much to ask, that his emotions would stop where he told them to.

Maybe he had just made things more difficult for himself.

What would his grandfather tell him to do? he wondered as he gazed down at the car.

"Show her the light." The Italian-accented words breezed through his mind. "Show her, Nicky. She could still be the one. She's just not ready yet."

That's what his grandpa would say.

Hope welled in Nick's heart as he wiped the wax off his car with the firm but gentle hand of a lover. Hope that the time would come, if he could just show her the light.

CHAPTER

24

$\mathcal{N}$ICK WAS AT THE CHURCH AT eight o'clock the next morning, fatigued from lack of sleep. He had finished waxing his Duesenberg, changed the oil, and conditioned the leather upholstery before he'd finally gone inside and surrendered to sleep.

He heard the door open and close and the sound of rubber-soled sneakers across the church's dusty, cluttered floor. His heart leaped, and from his stool he looked up hopefully. But it wasn't Brooke who appeared at the workroom door.

"Hey, Picasso."

Nick tried not to look disappointed at the sight of his nephew leaning in his doorway, his tall frame slightly slumped in dejection. That smile that Nick had grown accustomed to seeing was conspicuously absent, and Sonny looked as if he'd gotten about as much sleep as Nick had last night.

"Hey, Sonny. You okay?"

"Yeah," Sonny said, stepping into the room and sliding his hands into the pockets of his black jeans. "Look man, I'm really sorry about last night. Ma told me about them ambushing you."

Nick leaned back against the work table, regarding his nephew with grim eyes. "They're worried about you." He uttered a gentle, self-deprecating laugh. "They're afraid you'll turn out like me or something."

"There are worse things I could do," Sonny said. He looked down at the floor, and Nick noted the deep frown beginning to chisel permanent lines in the boy's forehead, making him appear much older than his years. "What's so wrong with it, Nick? What do they care?"

"It's the work ethic," Nick tried to explain. "They honestly can't respect anyone who doesn't break his back all day to make a living."

"But you work harder than anybody I know," Sonny said. "I've never been to your house that you weren't deep in the middle of some project. And here, on these windows, you've been at it day and night. What do they want? Blood?

Nick grinned. "Maybe a little."

Sonny went to the worktable, picked up a mat knife, turned it over in his hands. "Well, I don't want them telling me what I'm gonna do with my life," he said. "I want to see if I can do anything with it."

Nick rubbed his forehead, wishing his encouragement of Sonny didn't mean direct defiance of his family. "Man, I wish you'd had a chance to know Grandpa. He's the one who helped me through it." He crossed his arms and shook his head. "Funny thing is, your ma got her work ethic from him. He was the hardest worker I'd ever seen. But you know what he told me when my family started giving me a hard time about my art?"

"What?" Sonny asked.

"He said, 'Nicky, the Lord don't dole out talents He don't expect-a you to use.' Then he held up the shoe he'd been working on, and said, 'If I had a talent like yours, I wouldn't be in here, pulling on the leather, I'll tell you that.'

"Man, I miss him," Nick said. He took a deep breath and pushed off from the table. "You know, if you go with your gut, there are going to be a lot of fights to come. Take it from me, the family may never understand. And that hurts, Sonny. Sometimes even I wonder if it's worth it."

"But that's just it," Sonny said, setting down the knife and balling one hand into a fist. "It's not like it's something I can just turn off. I want it bad."

Nick shrugged. "What can I say?" he asked. "I've been there. I'm still there. But I'm not sure that I ought to keep you working here, knowing how they feel. They think you're dishonoring them by working with me. Maybe I need to honor their wishes."

"But they don't understand! No one does, except you. I'm nineteen years old. When do I get to decide what I want to do with my life? What if it was ministry I wanted to go into? What if the folks didn't want that, but I knew God called me? Would you support that?"

"Probably. Yeah, I guess I would."

"Then what if God called me to be an artist? What if He gave me a gift. He wants me to use it, just the same as if He'd called me to be a minister? Isn't one calling from God just as important as another?"

Nick turned back to the table, saw all the work that still needed to be done. He needed Sonny's talent and passion, and Sonny could learn a lot about precision and detail from working with him and Brooke.

You're going to put us through this all over again, aren't you?

His sister's words echoed in his mind, and he weighed the pain they evoked against the plea he saw in his nephew's eyes. "Are you sure you're ready for this?" he asked.

"I've never been more sure of anything," Sonny said. "You won't regret it, Nick."

Nick laughed dryly and admitted that if he did end up with regrets about encouraging Sonny's art, at least they would feel very familiar. "All right, Sonny," he said with a sigh. "You can work here. But you're gonna have to make it okay with your folks. I'm gonna trust you to do that, okay?"

The echo of the door sounded throughout the church, and Nick knew that Brooke had arrived. His heart jolted again.

"Yeah, sure," Sonny said. "I'll do my best."

But Nick wasn't listening anymore. Instead, he was looking at the door, waiting for the sight of Brooke.

CHAPTER

25

$\mathcal{B}$ROOKE NOTED ROXY'S TENSION the moment she led her into the church, stepping over the electrical cords and around idle equipment used in the renovation. Because it was Saturday, the construction crews were off, and Brooke breathed a sigh of relief that she would be able to break Roxy in with relative peace and quiet.

"You've been working around all this?" Roxy asked.

Brooke looked over her shoulder. Her sister looked so young today, with her hair pulled back in a ponytail, wearing an old pair of jeans with a hole in one knee and a Hayden High School Tigers T-shirt. "Yeah. You should see it on weekdays. The noise level is so high you can hardly hear yourself think, and you can't walk through here without fearing for your life." She tossed a half smile over her shoulder. "I'm starting to get used to it, though. Our workroom is back through here."

Roxy hesitated. She crossed her arms, drawing her shoulders up defensively. Was she nervous about meeting Nick? Brooke wondered.

Slowly, with Roxy lagging behind, Brooke led her down the dark corridor to the workroom. Before she reached it, Brooke could see that the lights were on. She heard Nick's voice, then another's. Sonny? Maybe that was good. Maybe his being there would help Roxy to feel more at ease.

She stepped into the doorway, waiting for Roxy to catch up. Nick sat in his chair with his feet propped on the table. Sonny leaned back against the wall across the room.

"Hi," she said.

"Hi, yourself." Nick's face lit up at the sight of her. Then his eyes shifted to Roxy behind her, and he dropped his feet and got up. "Hi."

"Roxy has decided to work for us part-time," Brooke said. "She needed some extra money, and I told her how badly we needed help. She's willing to wait to get paid."

Nick offered Roxy a smile that would have charmed her right down to her toes if she hadn't already erected such strong barriers. "Hi, Roxy," he said. "I'm Nick Marcello."

"I know." The words were clipped and made it clear she wasn't interested in friendship.

Nick looked bemused when he shot a glance at Brooke. He turned back to Roxy and gestured toward Sonny. "This is my nephew, Sonny Castori. He's going to be helping out here some too. *If* his folks agree."

Roxy cleared her throat and tried to smile at the young man in the black T-shirt. "Hi."

The clouds passed out of Sonny's eyes, and he brightened at the sight of the small blond standing at the door. "Hey, I remember you," he said. "You went to Hayden High, didn't you?"

"Still do," Roxy said.

Sonny grinned, slid his hands into his back pockets, and took a cocky step toward her. "Yeah. I remember seeing you in Ole Lady Hannah's class a couple years back. I was in the class across the courtyard. You sat by the window."

The awkward smile tugging on Roxy's lips was hard to miss, but it was evident that she struggled to look unaffected. "I don't remember you," she said.

Sonny shrugged and ruffled his dark mop of hair. "Yeah, so what else is new? I have one of those faces that's real easy to forget."

Roxy grinned. As if to distract herself from her grudging interest in Sonny, she stepped over to the worktable, perusing the tools and patterns lying there. Behind her, Nick gave Brooke a wink that said he knew it would work out with Roxy, if Sonny had anything to do with it.

Even so, Brooke decided that Nick should be warned of Roxy's reluctance. She set the case she was carrying on the table. "Before we get started," she said, looking pointedly at Nick, "I need some help getting some things out of my trunk."

Sonny started for the door, but Nick stopped him. "I'll go," he said. "Sonny, why don't you just show Roxy where everything is, for now? We'll be right back."

Roxy looked at Nick, then at Brooke. She dropped her gaze to the floor, as if she knew without a doubt that Nick had more on his mind than getting anything out of Brooke's car.

As if oblivious to Roxy's disapproving glare, Nick escorted Brooke back out into the corridor. "So you talked her into it, huh?" he asked quietly as they walked.

"Yes," Brooke whispered. "But she's skeptical about it. She isn't exactly crazy about you, you know. She believes everything she's ever heard about us."

"Well, I'll just have to work hard to win her over."

"Yeah, me too," Brooke said. "But she's a tough one. Thanks for suggesting that she work with us, Nick. It means a lot to me. Maybe there's hope for Roxy and me yet."

CHAPTER

26

$\mathcal{N}$ICK STILL HAD HOPES THAT THEY would get the job done on time. The four of them worked diligently for hours, Nick and Brooke enlarging sketches and numbering them to keep the pattern pieces from getting lost, and Sonny and Roxy tracing pictures through sheets of carbon so that there would be three precise copies of each cartoon, the paper pattern and the working drawing.

Although Roxy occasionally exchanged a quip with Sonny, she was quiet for the most part, hardly speaking to Nick at all. Her silence added another level of tension to the already charged atmosphere, and Nick could clearly see that she was alienated not just from him but from Brooke as well. Near lunchtime, when Brooke had gone to retrieve something from Nick's office and Sonny was out running an errand, Nick found himself alone with Roxy.

"You're doing great," he said, looking over her shoulder at the drawing she'd just finished tracing. "I'm glad you decided to help us out."

"Thanks."

Undaunted by the monosyllable, Nick pulled up a stool and sat down next to her. "Are you interested in art too?" he asked.

Roxy's face turned pink, but she didn't look at him. "No. The art teachers at school now aren't nearly as interesting as they were when Brooke was there."

Nick accepted the verbal dart with a lift of his brows. "Ouch."

Still not looking at him and clearly not amused by his response, Roxy continued to work.

Nick heard footsteps approaching. He studied Roxy for a moment longer, searching for a clue to unlock her bitter resentment. But she was too tightly barricaded.

Brooke came back into the room, carrying a stack of fresh paper. "It's getting late," she said, putting the paper on the table and surveying both their faces for a hint as to what had transpired while she was gone. "I think I'll take Roxy to lunch. We don't want her to starve to death on her first day here."

Roxy pretended to be too engrossed in her work to eat. "That's okay," she mumbled.

"I want to," Brooke said, feigning brightness, despite the clouds hanging over the room. She turned back to Nick. "Can you do without us for an hour?"

"I'll manage," he said. "You go ahead."

Nick watched as Roxy reluctantly put up her tools and followed Brooke from the room.

"Jonny seems to like you," Brooke told Roxy as they sat in the popular little café, Back Street Deli, which drew people from miles around for its savory cheeseburgers. "What do you think?"

Roxy moved the uneaten potato chips around her plate with an idle finger. "I hope you don't plan to try to push us together," she said. "The last thing I need right now is another man in my life."

The weary way she spoke, as if she were a forty-five-year-old divorcee, disturbed Brooke. Roxy was too young to be so bitter. "I don't plan to do anything like that," she said. "But you've got to admit he's cute."

"If you like his type," Roxy said, indifferently. She pushed her half-eaten burger away and set down her wadded napkin.

Brooke cleared her throat and tried again to find a subject they could share. "So, do you like the work?"

Roxy nodded. "It beats filing at City Hall. All the hassles ..."

"You could quit and work more hours for us," Brooke said. "You said you were leaving town after you graduated, anyway. It isn't like you'd be giving up anything long term."

Roxy studied the wood grain on the table. "I can't really count on your budget, can I?" she asked. "What happens if I quit my job, and then Abby Hemphill pulls the rug out from under you?"

Brooke didn't have an argument for that. "Well, maybe you can think about it after the budget's secure."

Roxy nodded noncommittally.

Brooke broke a French fry in half and nibbled on it absently. "It hasn't been so hard today, has it?" she went on. "Working with Nick, I mean?"

Roxy scanned the room idly, as if bored by the conversation. "It's okay. There's no law that says I have to like him."

Brooke set her French fry down and knitted her brows together. "You don't like him?"

"No," Roxy said, bringing her jaded gold eyes back to her sister.

"Well," Brooke said. "I guess that's your right." She laced her hands together on the table, wondering what had happened when she left Nick and Roxy alone today. Had Roxy sniped at Nick when she'd left the room? Had Nick made Roxy angry? A heaviness settled over her at the idea that her two favorite people might have the capacity to hurt each other.

She watched her sister, desperate to find the words that could break the ice between them. Last night she had almost felt close to Roxy. They had met each other halfway, both of them trying to bridge the gap between them, and when Roxy had accepted the job Brooke offered, Brooke had embraced a hope that their relationship was healing. But now Roxy's exposure to Nick seemed to have made her shut down again.

"Are you—?"

"Do you—?"

Their words came out simultaneously, and they each stopped, yielding to the other.

Feeling the renewed awkwardness between them, Brooke tried again. "Are you ready to go back?" she asked quietly.

Roxy stood up. "I was going to ask the same."

Brooke left a tip on the table and followed her sister to the cash register near the door. She was busy digging through her bag for her credit card when she heard, "Hi, Rox. How's it going?"

Brooke looked up to see the man she had seen with her sister in the dark office at City Hall last week, standing with a woman who looked to be at least five months pregnant.

Roxy's face turned a startling shade of crimson as she shot a guilty look Brooke's way. "I'm . . . I'm fine . . ."

Knowing that her thoughts flashed across her face like the messages of a neon sign, Brooke kept her jaw from going slack.

She glanced too conspicuously at the woman's left hand and saw a wedding ring sparkling there. On his hand was a matching band, confirming that the two were married to each other.

"Bill, the hostess is waiting at our table," the woman said, tugging on his sleeve.

A wave of dizziness swept over Brooke, and she gaped at them as they moved past her and Roxy. Her eyes clashed with Roxy's in harsh reprobation. Incipient tears glistened in her sister's eyes, and Brooke wondered if they were tears of shame or heartbreak.

Mechanically, she paid the bill with her credit card. The cashier could have charged her three hundred dollars for a cheeseburger, and she would have signed for it without a thought. All that mattered was that her little sister was involved with a married man. Roxy was straddling the edge of a scandal, one that would ruin her life just as Brooke's had been ruined.

Neither said a word as they got into the car. Quietly, but on the verge of tears, Brooke pulled the car out of its parking space, waited for a break in traffic, then headed for the church a few miles away.

"It's not what you think." Roxy's voice was weak.

"Oh?" Brooke asked, her voice restrained. "What do I think?"

One tear spilled over Roxy's lashes and she lifted a shaky hand to wipe it away. "I don't know," she whispered.

"I'll tell you what I think," Brooke said, unable to stop herself. "I think you're having an affair with a married man. And despite how that infuriates and upsets me, it does explain a few things. Like why you have to meet in dark offices at night, and why he has sudden 'emergencies' come up that force him to leave you stranded in sleazy bars." She slammed to a stop at a red light, and sat seething until it changed color.

Roxy sat like a cold, rigid statue in the seat next to her, holding in whatever feelings she had.

"His wife is pregnant!" Brooke railed on, growing angrier the longer Roxy sat quiet. "Don't you even care about that? Doesn't that bother you at all?"

"Don't you dare judge me!" Roxy said through her teeth, the pitch of her voice rising with every word. "You had a fling with your art teacher at my age! Maybe it runs in the family, Brooke. Maybe those promiscuous genes are hereditary!"

Brooke screeched into the parking lot, killed the engine, and sat smoldering. "You can't blame this on me or your stupid genes," she said. "This is something that *you* are doing, Roxy. I want you to think about that."

"Think about it?" Roxy cried. "Do you think I've thought about anything else in the past few weeks?"

Brooke pressed her face into her hands. "You're going to get hurt, Roxy," she said. "It isn't worth it."

Roxy shook her head and opened her car door. "I can't talk to you about this," she said. "There is no way you would ever understand."

And before Brooke could stop her, Roxy had bolted out of Brooke's car and around the building, undoubtedly intending to walk home.

*N*ick was just leaving to get his own lunch when he found Brooke still sitting in her car, slumped over her steering wheel, weeping into the square of her arms. Opening her passenger door, he got in beside her. "What's wrong?" he asked. "Tell me."

Brooke shook her head. "I . . . can't."

"Yes, you can," he whispered.

"I met Roxy's boyfriend," she said. "Her married boyfriend . . . and his pregnant wife."

Nick moaned, sat back, and closed his eyes.

"What is she trying to do?" Brooke went on. "Follow in my footsteps?"

Nick looked up at her, struggling for the answers she so sorely needed. "Maybe it's not what you think," he ventured. "Maybe there's not really anything going on. I've been watching her today, and she doesn't seem like the home-wrecker type. She's withdrawn, and . . . almost shy. Sonny keeps trying to flirt with her, and she honestly doesn't seem to know how to respond to it. Not like someone who's had all that much experience with men."

"Oh, Nick," Brooke cried. "She practically admitted it. Said we both had promiscuity in our genes!"

"Ah, so that's it," Nick said. "So it's time to turn the tables and make you out to be the one who has to defend herself, huh? Sort of takes the focus off her, doesn't it?"

"That's not what she's doing!" Brooke said. "She really sees me that way!"

"Then she doesn't see you at all," he returned.

She dug for a tissue in her purse, blew her nose, and wiped at her tears. "We've got to go back in there," she whispered. "We have work to do." She got out of the car, and Nick followed.

"Brooke, when are you going to realize that I was the teacher? It was me they blamed most. I was the villain."

"Neither of us should have been the villain. We didn't *do* anything."

He let her get a few steps ahead of him, then finally said, "Maybe I did."

She turned around, stricken by the confession. "What, Nick? What did you do wrong?"

"I let myself fall for a student."

Brooke caught her breath, and turned to face him fully. It was then that she saw Roxy from the corner of her eye, standing motionless at the corner of the building.

And she knew that her sister had heard the confession, as well.

$\mathscr{B}$ROOKE TRIED TO KEEP HER FRAYED emotions in check for the rest of the day, but they were too sharp and jagged, too fresh, too extreme. Pain and anger swirled through her head like a drug as she worked in a solitary corner of the room, but in its wake came the sweet, burning sting of Nick's words. He had fallen for her when she was in high school. Somehow, in ways Brooke didn't begin to understand, that made everything look different.

Roxy had ended up walking home, after all. When Brooke got home, she went straight to Roxy's room. "Look, Roxy, I know you heard what Nick said today." The speech she'd mentally worked on all day rolled off her tongue, her tone quiet, hesitant. "I want you to know that it's the first I've heard of it too. But it doesn't change anything. No matter how I felt about him or he felt about me, we didn't do anything wrong back then."

"And I haven't done anything wrong, either," Roxy whispered, staring dully out the window.

Brooke wet her lips and tried to keep her voice even, despite the anger reviving inside her. "You've gotten involved with a married man."

She saw Roxy's bottom lip quivering and knew she was about to cry again. "You don't know anything about it."

Brooke dropped wearily into a chair, counting out her breaths until she could speak without reproach. "Then tell me," Brooke pleaded. "Don't make me guess. Do you love him? Is that it?"

Roxy uttered a harsh, cold laugh that only made her seem more distraught. "Love has nothing to do with it."

Brooke focused her astonished eyes on her sister, desperate to view the world as Roxy did, just long enough to understand. "Then what is it?"

"It's power," Roxy said, meeting Brooke's eyes directly, injecting all her energy into every word she uttered. "That's what it's all about. And if you can feel better about what happened to you in high school by believing that Nick Marcello was in love with you, fine. But the plain simple truth is that he had power over you, and he used it. That's what men do."

Brooke gaped at her sister, fresh, futile tears in her eyes. "How did you get so bitter?" she asked on an incredulous whisper. "Where did you get such a distorted view of things?"

"From watching my big sister," Roxy said simply. Then, leaving Brooke to deal with that pronouncement alone, Roxy went into the bathroom.

Paralyzed, Brooke sat in Roxy's room for a moment, staring at the air. Her parents were in the kitchen, no doubt, brimming with a million questions about Roxy's first day at St. Mary's, full of a million unspoken reservations about both of their daughters working with Nick. Brooke couldn't face that tonight, not when Roxy's words had scraped deeper into already bleeding wounds.

Brooke slipped out the back door and got into her car, not certain where she would go. After a while, she found herself cutting back through town, toward St. Mary's, the only place she was sure she could be alone.

Since the side door could only be unlocked with Nick's key, she parked on the street and went to the front door to use her own. The door opened and closed with an echoing thud, and she smelled the familiar scent of sawdust and paint, of dust and mortar.

Brooke made her way to the middle of the large, dark room and sat on a drop cloth crumpled there, crossing her legs and peering up at the boarded places where her windows would go when they were finished. Would she and Nick really be able to impart truth in colored windows?

But truth was such an abstract term, she thought miserably, rubbing her eyes. Roxy's truth was that there was no such thing as love—only power. But love was what *gave* one power. And that was Brooke's own truth.

She looked up at the front of the building, where the pulpit had once been. *Is there another truth, God? Is there truth in those windows we're doing? Does it make any difference?*

Her heart swelled within her, as if trying to give an answer. But still the questions came.

"I don't know if I believe in you," she said out loud as tears ran down her cheeks. "I don't know if you're really even there. But if you are, I could sure use some peace. You must be big enough to help me with some of these problems, God. If you're real, then surely you're powerful enough for that."

The front door opened, and she jumped. Swinging around, she saw Nick standing in the doorway, enshrouded in shadows. "Brooke?" His voice was tender.

"Nick. You scared me."

"I decided to come back and get some more work done. I saw your car." He let the door close behind him. "Are you okay?"

Brooke looked down at the drop cloth beneath her. "I had another round with Roxy," she said. "I just needed to think."

Nick went to the wall and turned on one dim light near Brooke. She found herself in a soft yellow circle, surrounded by darkness. Slowly, he stooped down in front of her. "So, you're *not* okay."

She shook her head. "No. I'm just a little ... depressed ... about my sister, and my parents, and your family, and Abby

Hemphill . . ." She looked up at him. "Roxy heard what you said today . . ."

"I know she did. I'm sorry. But it was true, Brooke."

Her heart swelled and shifted as it had when he'd said it earlier. "And I had a fierce crush on you," she whispered tragically. "When do we stop paying for that?"

Nick sat down on the floor next to her and draped his wrists over his knees. Slowly, he drew in a deep breath. "I was twenty-four years old. You were eighteen. I never made one inappropriate move toward you."

"If I had only known," she whispered. "I thought you would never forgive me for making you lose your job."

"Forgive you?" he repeated. "Brooke, there was nothing to forgive. Getting fired from that nice, safe teaching job was probably the best thing that could have happened to me, because it forced me to use my talents. If I were still teaching, I may have never taken that plunge."

She looked at him, marveling at his peace. "How do you do it, Nick? How do you find peace in terrible things? How do you make something good out of something bad?"

"Because I believe that everything that happens is for a reason. I believe that God is running this show. I believe that no matter what happens, He's going to make it work for good." His eyes locked with hers. "You could have that kind of peace, Brooke."

She shook her head. "If I have to get it from God, I don't think I can. I don't know God like you do."

"But He knows you."

She looked at him, struck by the idea that the Creator of the Universe knew or cared about her. She was so small. And if God was really there, He would have to be so big.

"How do you know that He even gives me a thought?" she asked.

"It's in the best-known Bible verse. 'For God so loved the world, that He gave His only begotten son.'"

"That didn't have anything to do with me," she said.

"Brooke, it had everything to do with you."

She looked down and remembered the prayer she had prayed just before Nick came in. She had asked for peace. Now Nick was trying to give it to her.

Was this an answer from God, or just a coincidence? After all, she had been the one to bring up the idea of peace to begin with.

Still, she had asked, and the next thing she knew, there the answer was. *For God so loved the world* . . . The thought of that, in itself, did promise peace. If she thought God loved her, what peace that would be.

But some part of her couldn't believe that.

"If you want to know Christ, all you have to do is ask Him."

She looked back up toward the area that would hold the pulpit, as if she could see God there. "Maybe someday I will."

When she glanced back at Nick, she saw the disappointment in his eyes as he gazed down at the floor. Somehow, what she'd said had been wrong. "What is it, Nick?" she asked.

"I just . . . want you to have peace now," he said. "I want you to have all the things that I have. I want you to know the fullness I feel."

"Fullness?" she asked.

"Yes. As opposed to emptiness. I want that for you, because I care about you, Brooke. Promise me," he said. "Promise me that you'll think about Christ. Promise me you'll consider what I've said. And that you won't wait."

She nodded. "I will."

He swallowed, then sighed, and got to his feet. "Let's go get some work done, unless you want to go home."

"No, we can work," she said.

But as she followed him into the workroom, she felt as dismal as she had before. Nothing had really changed.

CHAPTER  28

*T*HE TELEPHONE AT THE MARTINS' house rang at nine-thirty, but Roxy, who had been alone in her room for most of the evening, didn't answer it. She was busy turning the pages of the scrapbook she'd kept as a little girl, searching the joyful faces in the cracked and faded photographs for a sign of the happiness she had known before Brooke had left home.

Her one-time hero worship of her protective big sister had been a fantasy. Brooke could no more protect Roxy now than Roxy could have protected her seven years ago.

Her mother knocked on her door and stuck her head in, interrupting her reverie. "Telephone, Roxy. Someone named Sonny."

Roxy frowned and looked at the extension on her bed table. "Sonny? What does he want?"

Her mother smiled. "I guess he wants to talk to you."

Roxy cast a beseeching look at her mother. "No. Tell him I'm not here."

Her mother stepped into the room, still smiling, as if she had caught her shy, awkward daughter on the threshold of her first budding romance. "I've already told him you're home. You know, with that attitude it's no wonder that you're sitting at home on a Saturday night. Now, answer that phone."

Roxy watched her mother leave the room. Reluctantly she took a deep breath and picked up the phone. "Hello?"

"Yo, Roxy, it's me. Sonny."

Roxy sighed impatiently. "I know. What is it?"

"Well, I was just sitting here thinking about you leaving today, and I wondered how you were feeling."

"I'm fine," she said.

He hesitated a moment, and she realized that, just maybe, the conversation wasn't easy for him, either. Maybe he had sat looking at the telephone for a while, and only now had summoned the courage to call.

"Listen, I know it's late and everything, but would you like to go out for a Coke or pizza? I could have you home by eleven."

Roxy caught her reflection in her dresser mirror, saw the dark circles from too much crying today, her pallid complexion, the bedraggled state of her hair. What could Sonny possibly have seen in her, on a day when she was at her absolute worst? "Why?" she asked suspiciously.

"Why?" Sonny laughed, but it didn't disguise the tension in his voice. "Well, why not? I mean, I'm hungry, what can I say?" He laughed nervously again. "Tell you the truth, I didn't really expect to catch you at home tonight, but I figured I'd take a chance."

She sat quietly, unable to believe his invitation was that simple. There had to be more.

"I don't want you to think it's *normal* for me to be home on a Saturday night," Sonny qualified quickly. "Usually I have this long line of women lined up at my door, and they drag me out until all hours. But it's so exhausting, you know, my busy social schedule . . ."

A grin made its slow journey across Roxy's lips, but she didn't speak.

"So, what do you say?" he asked. "You feel like goin' somewhere? I could be there in ten minutes."

Her smile faded, and she felt her mouth go dry. "No. I couldn't get ready that fast. I look awful."

"Hey, Roxy," Sonny cut in. "If you look anything like you looked today, you'll knock my socks off."

She frowned, wondering if he could really be serious. She had rolled out of bed this morning and dressed in grubby clothes, without showering or anything. Talk about a bad hair day. "No, really. I can't . . ."

"Oh, I get it," Sonny said. "You've got one of those mud packs on your face, right? And all that greasy conditioning gunk in your hair? And sponges between your toes?"

She laughed in spite of herself. "No!"

"Then what could be so bad?" he asked, more seriously. "My standards are real low these days."

Roxy laughed again, becoming more uninhibited the more he carried on. "Thanks a lot."

"Hey, I'm trying to raise them some," he said. "What can I say? So will you wash the mud off of your face and come with me, or not?"

She smiled softly and brought her other hand up to the telephone. Something deep inside her urged her to say yes, but the part of her that had kept score over the past year warned her to stay at home. "I really can't," she said.

Sonny gave a great, exaggerated sigh. "All right," he huffed. "Then I guess I'll have to resort to that line of women outside my door."

"I guess."

"But I'm not fooled," he went on, undaunted. "I can hear in your voice that you really want to come. At least you aren't snapping at me anymore." He paused a moment, lowering his pitch. "Maybe I *won't* go out, after all. Maybe I'll just save myself for you."

A soul-deep smile welled up inside her chest and pushed out all the pain and misery she'd been dragging around with her. "I'll see you at St. Mary's Monday," Roxy said, and for the first time, realized she actually looked forward to it.

"I'll count the minutes," Sonny teased. "Don't leave the mud on too long, now, okay? I hear it wrinkles you up like a prune."

Laughing, Roxy hung up the phone and kept her hand over the receiver for a moment. Funny, she thought. Ten minutes earlier she wouldn't have believed that there was a person in the world who could make her smile today.

Sonny had proved her wrong. She only wished she were wrong about other things, as well.

It was just before ten when Brooke went home that night. She said goodnight to her parents, then passed by Roxy's room. The light was off.

She stepped into the doorway, watching Roxy sleeping soundly in her bed. Her sister's features were soft and youthful in repose, as innocent as they had been when she was a child. Quietly, Brooke reached down and pulled a blanket up around her.

Her heart twisted again at what she had discovered about her sister that day. Little Roxy, who used to crawl into bed with her to look at the clouds on her ceiling, involved with a married man.

She sighed, went back to the door, leaned against the casing. The tragedy of it all was that Roxy wouldn't find what she was looking for in sleazy bars and secret affairs. But for the life of her, Brooke didn't know how to show her where she could find it. In many ways, Brooke knew she was just as lost as her sister.

Quietly, she went to her room and got out of her clothes, then tried to empty her mind of its troubles as she climbed into bed.

CHAPTER

29

ONDAY AFTERNOON, ABBY HEMPHILL hung up the telephone and checked off one more name on the long list on her clipboard. "Gerald, I've already convinced over fifty church members to support my recommendation that the Finance Committee revoke the budget."

Gerald was busy reading the paper.

"Gerald, did you hear me?"

"Yes, dear," he said, lowering the paper. "The Finance Committee budget."

"No, the budget for the windows."

He looked at her and nodded, but his eyes didn't quite focus on her. His mind was a million miles away.

"Already I've convinced over fifty church members to support my recommendation not to grant the money necessary for the stained-glass windows. When the pastor tries to override our verdict, they'll all be there, backing me up."

Suddenly Gerald tuned in. "Tell the pastor that he wouldn't be able to renovate the *closet* at St. Mary's without our substantial donations."

"That's exactly what I plan to tell all of them," she said. "And when I made the phone calls, all I had to do was point out the more immediate needs of the church, and the proof I have that our artists in question are using the windows as a pretense to be together."

Gerald raised the newspaper again.

"Of course, I didn't bother to call the ones who won't agree with me."

"Good thinking," he said absently. He set the newspaper down and looked at his watch. "Time for me to go to the club. I'm meeting John Schaeffer there."

"Tonight?" she asked.

"Yes." He didn't wait for her approval. He never did.

"When will you be home?"

"I can't say. Don't wait up, though."

When he was gone, she glanced down at the gold watch shackling her wrist, noting that it was after noon. By now, Nick Marcello had probably been notified of the committee meeting. Already, he and Brooke Martin were probably desperately rallying whatever support they did have in the church. Wouldn't they be surprised when they saw how outnumbered they were?

She crossed the immaculately decorated living room—quite appropriate for a woman of her station—to the end table, and flicked off a piece of dust she had seen illuminated between the shadowed bars cast by the vertical blinds on the windows.

It was so quiet. Too quiet.

The quiet made her feel cold, lonely, detached . . . and she caged her arms with her hands and wandered into the study, to the small file cabinet where she kept her personal things. There was no need to lock it anymore, as she once had. The kids were grown and gone, and Gerald . . . well, Gerald would never in a million years have cared.

She pulled out an overstuffed scrapbook and opened it. A soft smile played across her face at the memories of her glory days. She had been in control then. No one had ever questioned that. And she had been a good role model for all those who looked up to her.

Maybe too good.

Her eyes fell on an old, fading snapshot of a young man, grinning at the camera as if he planned to pounce on the photographer as soon as the shutter snapped. He *had* too, she mused. He had chased her across the park, and when he'd caught her, he had tickled her until she'd collapsed with screams of glee.

She turned the page, seeing herself, young and pretty and full of spirit, brandishing the tiny engagement ring he had saved for a year to buy her.

"It's hardly more than a crumb," her father had pointed out distastefully. *"It'll probably turn your finger green."*

And then her mother had gotten all huffy and told her that she had to consider what people would think. It wasn't appropriate that a debutante would marry the son of a woman who cleaned houses for a living.

Little by little, her parents had chipped away until she had begun to blame him more and more for not being from the right side of the tracks, for not being someone her social circle respected, for not being the man her parents wanted her to marry.

Eventually, she had chosen propriety over love. Gerald Hemphill, a more *appropriate* choice from a wealthy family, had come along and proposed to her.

But not everyone would have understood her choice. Some would have followed their instincts—or their traitorous hearts. Some would have dived headfirst into the wrong kind of relationship. People like Brooke Martin, or Nick Marcello . . . or even her daughter, Sharon. People who *knew* that their actions were inappropriate and didn't care.

She flipped through the pages, finding other snapshots of the young man in a variety of candid poses that brought back unsettling memories. He had married, she'd heard through the grapevine. Had two children and a dog and a wife who had no more money than he had. She wondered if he were happy—if ever, in the dead of night when his family was sleeping and life stood quietly frozen, he thought of her. She wondered if his memories were pleasant or if he still blamed her for the choice she had made.

He had never understood her need to live her life properly, no matter what sacrifices had to be made.

There had to be a consequence for taking the easy way, as Brooke and Nick had done, and even as her own daughter had done, with that pregnancy that humiliated Abby so. And if she, Abby Hemphill, was called to be the one to administer those consequences, she was willing. Propriety, after all, was everything.

CHAPTER

30

W HAT WE'RE SAYING," PASTOR Anderson said in a round-about manner, trying to make the news sound less cruel than it was, "is that we realize the personal sacrifices both of you have made for the windows, and we appreciate it and intend to compensate you for your time. However—"

"However, we're fired, right?" Nick finished, making the job easier for him. He leaned forward, elbows on his knees, tapping his mouth with steepled fingers as he surveyed most of the members of the renovation committee on one side of the table, and Abby Hemphill and her Finance Committee on the other. He and Brooke had guessed what had transpired the moment the pastor called him that morning to ask them to attend the evening meeting. The somber tone of his voice had been an immediate clue.

"No, not fired," Horace said, his face pinched with distaste at the hateful task he'd been assigned. "Technically, the job has been approved—twice—and the Renovation Committee has approved you to do it. We just . . ."

He lowered his eyes in defeat, and slumped over the table. "We just can't pay you."

Brooke looked at Nick and saw that he was as confused as she. Nick stood up and regarded Abby Hemphill, who sat perched on the edge of her seat with her nose high and a satisfied smile on her lips. "Let me get this straight," he said quietly. "The Finance Committee revoked the budget for just our salaries or for the expenses of the windows as well?"

"The budget," Abby Hemphill said, "is nonexistent."

"But as I've said, we're not firing you," Horace repeated, as if that softened the blow.

Nick fixed his astonished eyes on the pastor, impatient with his inability to be direct. "Is that supposed to be some consolation?"

The pastor rubbed his face, and Brooke could see that the ordeal was costing him a great deal. She reached up and touched Nick's arm to calm him. He peered down at her, saw the censure in her expression. He turned back to Horace.

Horace cleared his throat and tried to explain. "I know it's not much," he said. "But I want people to know that you were capable of doing the job and that this decision had nothing to do with you." He looked down the table at Abby. "But the Finance Committee does control the budget."

"So, what you're saying," Brooke began, struggling to get the ruling clearer in her mind, "is that it's over? All the work we've done? All our plans . . . they're worth nothing? The windows we designed will never be built?"

Horace sat back wearily in his chair and rubbed his temples. "I guess that's about it," he said. "The renovation will continue, but there won't be any stained-glass windows."

The harsh reality of the decree assailed Brooke. No stained-glass windows . . . no notice for her work . . . no redemption from Hayden . . . no excuse to stay.

Her heart plummeted and her eyes flitted to Nick's. Was history destined to repeat itself? Another job lost, another relationship broken, another defeat to overcome? Would she follow the script Abby Hemphill had written for her and leave town again?

Would seven more barren years go by with nothing but regrets and recriminations?

The emotions evident on Nick's face told Brooke that the same questions plagued his mind. He got up, and she followed. Without saying another word that could be rebutted or repeated, the two left the meeting together.

By the time they reached the parking lot, Brooke's veins pumped with fury. "She's done it again," she rasped. "How could she do this to us *again?*"

"I don't know," he whispered. "I don't know. But don't blame the church. There are good people there. Those like Abby are just louder and angrier. It seems like they're getting their way, but—"

"They *are* getting their way," she said.

Behind them, the door to the building opened, and the somber Renovation Committee members spilled out one by one, along with Abby Hemphill's team of supporters who bubbled and buzzed with the elation of their "moral victory."

But what had they been victorious over? Brooke asked herself miserably. Over the distaste of a misunderstood relationship? Nick opened Brooke's car door for her, then slipped in next to her. Together they watched those who had condemned them going to their cars and driving away without even a look back. Abby Hemphill, in all her glory, was one of the last to leave. They watched her march to her gold Mercedes, get in, and start the engine. When she pulled out of her space, she made a U-turn and drove up beside Brooke's car. Her automatic window drifted down, and within the solitary shadows of the car, they could see Abby's cold, smug smile.

"I trust you'll have your things out of the church as soon as possible," she said. "And leave your forwarding address, darling, so Horace can send you a check for the little bit you've done."

"What makes you think she's leaving town?" Nick asked.

"Well, maybe I was a little premature," she said chuckling. "I assumed she had to make a living. One of you really should, you know." Then, rolling up her window and disappearing behind the tinted glass, Abby Hemphill drove away.

Nick didn't speak for a long time. When he did, his voice was shaky . . . his tone tentative. "Well, I guess I'll go to the church tonight and gather up our things."

"I can't believe this," Brooke whispered, looking dismally up at Hayden City Hall and the buildings beyond. Despite its hatred of her, there was something innocent about the town that Brooke still loved. "Those windows could have been so special."

"Yeah," Nick whispered. "A sermon in themselves. But maybe you can't really do that in windows. Maybe we were just kidding ourselves."

Brooke gazed off into the distance after Abby Hemphill. Her anger shot bursts of adrenaline through her, giving her an energy that demanded a confrontation. Maybe some people never could be convinced, but they could be confronted. They could be made to think. And they could be forced to see the truth in themselves, no matter how ugly it was.

"So, you want to come back to St. Mary's with me?" Nick asked.

Slowly Brooke shook her head. "Not yet. There's something I need to take care of first."

His eyes were a misty black beneath the light in her car, and she saw him swallow. "Brooke, you aren't going to leave now, are you?" he asked. "Not yet?"

"No, Nick," she said. "I'll see you later tonight. I promise."

Slowly, he got out of her car. As she drove away, she looked in her rearview mirror. He stood watching her with sad apprehension and dread in his eyes. The tragedy was that she didn't know how to banish that pain from his heart. All she did know was that, whether it helped matters or not, there were a few things she had to settle with Mrs. Hemphill tonight.

CHAPTER  31

ABBY HEMPHILL'S HOUSE WAS ON the upper-class side of town, nestled in a neighborhood of bankers, lawyers, and doctors. Brooke pulled into the woman's driveway and peered through the darkness at the huge Tudor-style house. Much too extravagant for a superintendent's salary—but everyone in town knew that both Abby and Gerald Hemphill came from old money and that they had brought equal portions of wealth into the marriage.

Abby Hemphill probably hadn't had to worry about money a day in her life, Brooke thought as she sat in her car, yet she was so concerned about the money Brooke and Nick would have made. Idly, Brooke wondered if the hateful woman had ever known the feeling of accomplishment, of creating something out of your own heart and with your own hands, of seeing a project through, of sharing it with another human being. Abby had probably never in her life known the satisfaction that came from intense involvement and struggle.

In a way, Brooke almost felt sorry for her.

She got out of the car, not knowing what she planned to say to the woman, but trusting that the words would come when she called for them. Hands trembling with the emotions wreaking havoc in her soul, Brooke went up the wide steps to the door and rang the bell. A chorus of chimes rang out with regal authority. She stood still, one hand in the pocket of her jacket, the other clutched around the strap of her purse as she waited for her self-appointed archenemy to answer.

In just a moment the door opened, and Abby Hemphill stood looking at her. Abby's expression became instantly guarded, as if she braced herself for a physical attack.

"I'd like to talk to you, Mrs. Hemphill," Brooke said, her tone dangerously calm. "You don't have to worry. No screaming, no yelling, nothing distasteful. Just one adult to another."

Abby Hemphill crossed her arms and stroked the column of her throat with her index finger. "I don't really believe you and I have anything to discuss. My mind certainly won't be changed."

"I'm not here to change your mind," Brooke said, stepping inside despite the fact that she hadn't been invited. "I just want to try to understand." She turned around inside the foyer, making it clear that Abby would have to contend with her. Stiffly, Abby closed the door, bolted it, and turned back to Brooke. "I wanted to ask you to explain it to me," Brooke went on, "this vendetta you have against Nick and me."

Abby smiled condescendingly and shook her head. "Don't flatter yourself. It's no vendetta. It's business."

"Was it business seven years ago," Brooke asked, "when I was eighteen and you lied about what you saw Nick and me doing in the art room? Was it business when Hayden High School lost the best art teacher they've ever had? Was it business when you spread smut around town about what we were doing when, the truth is, we were working day and night on those windows, knowing that you would do everything in your power to pull the rug out from under us?"

Abby's pale, pampered skin flushed to a rose color. "Whether you can understand this or not, the church trusts the Finance

Committee to oversee how their money is spent. We can't allow church funds to be misspent as a cover for your little affair."

Brooke tightened her lips to keep them from trembling. "Why are you so threatened by the idea of Nick and me?"

"Because you brought scandal upon my husband's school system seven years ago!" Abby shouted. "It took us *months* to recover from that, and I won't have it tainting our church!"

"*You* brought scandal on *me!*" Brooke returned, the fraying thread of her control snapping. "I *still* haven't recovered from it, and it was all lies! All I did was thank him for all he did for me to help me get the scholarship, and then I gave him an innocent hug. I've had to pay everyday since." She paced across the room, groping for the reins of her control. Then she spun around, knowing that she was exposing all her wounds to Abby Hemphill. "Is your life so empty that you have to do cruel, bitter things like this to find reason to get up in the morning?"

Myriad emotions passed like a color wheel over the woman's face. "Get out!" she said, reaching for the door. "You are not welcome in my house."

"Of course I'm not," Brooke said. "Why would you welcome me when you won't even welcome your own daughter and the grandchild you've never seen?"

The woman drew in a deep breath. For the first time since Brooke had known her, Abby Hemphill was speechless.

"That's right," Brooke said, her lips trembling. "I saw Sharon, working in a diner to support her child."

"I told you to get out!" Abby shrieked.

Knowing that she'd said even more than she had come to say, Brooke started through the door. But behind her another door swung open.

"Mother? Is everything all right?"

Brooke turned and saw her sister's boyfriend—the infamous, mysterious, cheating Bill—standing in an inner doorway with his pregnant wife peering out from behind him.

"Yes," Mrs. Hemphill said, trying to steady her breath. "Miss Martin was just leaving." She looked pointedly at Brooke, who stood staring at the man. He met her eyes with incredulous recognition, but rather than the guilt she would have expected, he offered her a cold, amused smile that dared her to expose him.

For a moment it occurred to Brooke that doing just that to his wife and his mother would provide justice for them all.

Run this through that value system of yours, Mrs. Hemphill. Your married, soon-to-be-a-father son is involved with my sister!

For a moment Brooke glared at him, until his grin faltered the slightest degree . . . until she could see the briefest flash of fear in his eyes. He had miscalculated her silence.

The revelation on the tip of her tongue faded, as clear thinking prevailed. She couldn't use this ammunition on the Hemphills without destroying Roxy in the process. The last thing she wanted was Mrs. Hemphill blaming her sister. Besides, some gentler voice in her throbbing heart cried out, his wife probably didn't deserve this family she'd married into, much less the misery the news would inflict upon her. Despite her wish to put Mrs. Hemphill in her place, to repay her vindictiveness with a little of her own, Brooke couldn't be that cruel.

Slowly she tore her eyes from Bill and turned back to the woman waiting for her to walk through the door. "You know, Mrs. Hemphill, if I were you I'd make sure my own house was clean before I started trying to clean up the town."

The second she was through the door, it slammed behind her. Hurrying to her car, Brooke realized she felt no better than before she'd come.

Her car flew with a vengeance—not to St. Mary's where Nick would be waiting for her—but to her parents' home, where Roxy probably sat waiting at the smutty beck and call of that man.

The car screeched to a halt in the driveway, and Brooke saw that her parents' car wasn't there. Roxy's light was on, so Brooke went into the house and stormed back to Roxy's room.

"How could you?" she yelled, before Roxy even knew she was there.

Her sister looked up, confusion distorting her face. "What?"

Brooke's teeth came together, and she bit out each word. "How could you have an affair with Abby Hemphill's son?"

Roxy came to her feet. "Brooke, don't—"

"Mrs. Hemphill's son! The *married* son of the town dictator!" Brooke repeated. "Do you know what will happen if it ever gets out? Do you know what that woman will do to you?"

"You don't—" Roxy started to answer, but Brooke stormed across the room.

"Roxy, are you trying to self-destruct? Is your life so terrible that you're just trying to ruin it once and for all? Or are you just determined to follow in my own miserable footsteps?"

"Maybe I don't have a choice, okay?" Roxy cried. "Maybe I've never had a choice! Maybe because of you, I've had my life mapped out for me!"

"Don't you *dare* blame this on me!" Brooke said. "Don't you dare!"

Roxy threw herself onto the bed and thrust a fist into her pillow as she glared at Brooke. "You don't know anything about me," she cried. "So don't come in here judging me when you don't have a clue what you're talking about!"

Brooke looked at her, her green eyes frosty as ice, feeling as if every miserable moment since she and Nick had been caught hugging in the art room seven years before had been compressed and packed into this one. "Why not?" she asked her sister. "You've judged me for the last seven years."

Turning her back on her sister, Brooke ran out of the house.

CHAPTER

32

*T*IME IS RUNNING OUT, LORD, Nick prayed as he sat alone in the darkness of his Buick. *It's just a matter of time until Brooke leaves again. I don't want her to go.*

He opened his eyes and looked at the church, dark and dormant under the cover of night. Aloud, he said, "I don't understand, Lord. I thought these windows were Your doing. I thought all the talent You had given me was about the windows in St. Mary's."

He had misread God. That was all there was to it. He had wanted it himself, so he made himself think he was following God's will.

But now it had all tumbled down. His ma's artist son had lost another job.

You be what God made you to be, his grandpa had advised him so long ago, sitting at his favorite fishing hole and teaching him how to look busy while taking time to think. *And when they chide you about it, you just-a smile and nod and go on about your business. Soon they'll get tired of you and find somebody else to bother.*

176

He saw headlights pull into the parking lot, and Brooke's car pulled into the space next to his. She saw his shadow in the car, got out of her own and came to the passenger side. Without a word, she got in next to him.

"What are you doing?" she whispered.

"Thinking. Praying. Stay here with me for a minute," he said quietly. "Then we'll go in."

Brooke laid her head back against the seat and closed her eyes. He could see that the thoughts raging through her mind were no more tranquil than his.

CHAPTER

33

*T*EARS BURNED DOWN ROXY'S FACE as she paced furiously across her room. She heard a car outside and knew that her parents had come home from the grocery store. Peering through her mini-blinds, she surveyed their faces as they got out of the car. Had they heard yet about the latest scandal developing in their family? And if not, how much longer would it be? It would come out eventually. She hadn't doubted that when the whole thing had started, and Bill had been very careful to remind her how humiliating the consequences could be.

She went to her mirror and tore a tissue out of its box, wiped her eyes carefully. Dabbing a little makeup on her finger, she tried to touch up the red circles under her eyes.

Maybe she should just come right out and tell them. Maybe she should just get the whole thing out in the open and accept whatever came of it. She was so tired of hiding. So tired of all the lies and the sneaking around. So tired of the limits it imposed on her life.

But what would they say? What would they do? Vividly, she remembered the night seven years ago when Mrs. Hemphill had called her father to tell him about his fallen daughter. Roxy hadn't known, then, what was going on, but she would never forget her father's storming across the house threatening to kill Nick Marcello. Would her dad want to kill Bill too? Or Roxy herself?

His reaction might serve to make the scandal bigger, she thought, starting to cry again. It would just be that much more to deal with.

"Hi, honey." Her mother's voice came from her doorway, and Roxy kept her face turned away. "I thought you'd be out somewhere tonight since you don't have school tomorrow."

"No, Mom," Roxy said. "I had some studying to do."

"Studying?" Her mother stepped into the room. "I've never yet met a senior who studied during spring break."

Roxy shrugged and grabbed one of her books. "Yeah, well. I'm having a little trouble in history."

Alice Martin sat down on her daughter's bed. Roxy knew that she wasn't fooling anyone. Her mother would have to be blind not to see the remnants of tears on her red-rimmed eyes or deaf not to hear the rasp of hoarseness in her voice. "Honey, I'm worried about you."

"Don't worry," Roxy said too brightly. "I'll pull my grades up. I'm just a borderline B."

"I'm not worried about your grades," her mother said. "I'm worried about the way you've withdrawn lately. You've been crying, haven't you?"

"No," Roxy denied, as if the thought was absurd. "Why would I be crying?"

"I don't know," her mother said, frowning. She cupped Roxy's chin and tipped her face up. "But you have. And here you are, holed up in your room again, like you're afraid to come out . . ."

Thankfully, the phone rang just as new tears emerged in Roxy's eyes. Turning from her mother, she snatched it up. "Hello?"

"Hey, Rox. It's me, Sonny."

"Hi." She glanced back at her mother, who waited for her to finish the call so that they could continue their talk. But the prospect terrified her.

"Listen," Sonny was saying. "I was wondering if you might want to go out for a pizza or something. Now, before you say no, let me remind you—"

"Yes," Roxy said quickly. "Yes, I'd like that."

"What?" Sonny asked. "Did you say yes?"

"Yes," Roxy said again. "When can you be here?"

"Fifteen minutes," Sonny said. "No, ten."

"I'll be ready," Roxy said.

She hung up the phone and turned back to her mother. "Well, looks like I have a date."

"Really?" Her mother's smile inched back over her face. "Who with?"

"Sonny Castori," she said, rushing to the dresser to finish applying her makeup. "He graduated from Hayden last year." Deliberately, she neglected to tell her mother that he was Nick's nephew. All that concerned Roxy now was getting out of the house and away from her mother's probing questions, at least until the rumors that had reached Brooke somehow reached her parents too.

If the truth didn't come out of its own accord, Roxy wasn't sure how much longer she could hold the sordid secrets tightly within herself. And she wasn't sure how much longer she wanted to try.

Her energy was almost gone, and the humiliation of having to face Brooke with the truth had already been too much. How much worse could it be for her parents to know, after all?

CHAPTER 34

𝒯HE CHURCH WAS DARK WHEN Brooke and Nick went inside for what was to be their final time. Nick flipped the switch on the wall, casting the place in a dim half-light. Tonight the shadows around them seemed too big to conquer, providing a mystery that couldn't be unraveled. Together they walked to the center of the large room and looked up at the boarded windows they could have transformed into such enchanting works of art.

"Funny," Nick said, his soft voice echoing in the room's emptiness. "Art is supposed to be expression. It's supposed to be pure and untainted. But what it really comes down to, what really is the bottom line, is the almighty buck."

Brooke walked across the floor and lightly kicked the drop cloths. "When I accepted this job, money wasn't an issue," she said. "I just wanted a chance to prove myself as a stained-glass artist. Make a name for myself."

Nick brought his hand up and clenched it into a fist. "It could have been so good, Brooke. It could have been so . . . beautiful." His eyes misted over as his voice broke. He turned from her, inhaling a deep breath that made his shoulders rise and fall in weary defeat.

Brooke offered no answers, and he sensed that her own pain kept her reflectively quiet.

Finally they walked back to the workroom to view the progress they had made, the seeds of masterpieces they had planted together. Their work, spread out on the tables and around the room, greeted them like still-hopeful children about to be abandoned.

Nick went to one pattern pinned to the table with the cartoon and working drawing beneath it. He slipped his fingertips under the edge, poised to rip it off the tacks, but Brooke reached out and stopped him. "Let's . . . let's just keep them together," she whispered. "We worked so hard . . ."

"Why?" Nick's face reddened as he brought his eyes to hers, and she could hear the anger in his voice. "Why should we hold onto them?"

His hand whipped across the pages, ripping the heart out of the drawing. "We might as well just rip them *all* up!"

"No!" Brooke grabbed both his hands and held them. "Don't, Nick," she cried. "They're ours. The church can stop us from designing them for this building, but they can't keep us from creating them somewhere else. Don't tear them up, Nick. Please."

He looked at her then, his eyes softening. Nick regarded the torn drawing in his hands helplessly and dropped down onto a stool. "We can't do this anyplace else," he said in a metallic voice. "It wouldn't be the same. This building is perfect for them."

Brooke wouldn't give up. "It would work if we tried hard enough to make it work," she whispered. "If God was with us."

If God was with us.

The significance of her words struck him full force. Was this the first seed of her faith? Had it been planted? Was it taking root? Was she beginning to believe?

If God was with us.

He swallowed and tried to find the words to voice his thoughts. "You know, a few years ago when I became a Christian, it all came together for me. My art ... my gift ... I knew God planned for me to use it to His glory. It never occurred to me that any part of it could be about money. I knew the Bible said the workman is worthy of his wages, so I didn't have any guilt about taking payment for my work, but that wasn't the force behind it, you know?" He raked a rough hand through his hair and shook his head. "Now, I've made so much money on my work that I *expect* to make money on it. It's almost like I can't conceive of doing it just for the love of it. And when it starts to be about money, somebody who knows nothing about my calling can always come along and take it away."

"I know," she said, leaning her back wearily against the table and gazing off into the distance as memories gave an extra clarity to her life. "Looking back, I see that my deepest expression, my most intense work, was on the sculpture of the hands. I haven't been that absorbed in my work since then, but I've made a lot of money. And I never dreamed, while I was working on it, that that sculpture would ever be worth a cent."

Nick set his palms down on the tabletop. "My family was so down on my being an artist that I always felt I could prove my worth by putting a big dollar sign on it. But these windows meant so much to me." He looked at her with sad eyes. "I would have done them for free, Brooke."

Brooke inclined her head and inhaled a breath that seemed weighted with the tragedy in Nick's eyes. "So would I," she admitted. "But our salaries were only half of it. It costs thousands to construct windows like these."

Nick's eyes lit up like lanterns that had suddenly been turned on to flood the night. "Do you mean it, Brooke?" he asked. "Or are you just saying it because you know it's moot now?"

"Saying what?" she asked. "That I would have done it for free? Of course, but ..."

Nick's heart leapt as an idea came to him. He grabbed her shoulders and sat her down on the couch, then stooped in front of her. "I have no right to ask this," he whispered, breathless with brimming excitement, "but I'm going to. Would you consider—even consider—staying here and finishing this project without pay ... if we could come up with the money somehow to finance the windows?"

"*How?*" Brooke asked. "We can't get our hands on that kind of money."

"*If* we could, would you stay?" he asked again. "If somehow the money just appeared for the supplies, would you help me finish the job?"

Something in the intensity of his voice told her that the money *would* appear from somewhere. Her eyes slowly widened with excitement. "Yes, I'll stay," she whispered. "I'll help you finish the windows."

"We'll get the money," he promised. "Horace said that we weren't fired. Our budget just wasn't approved. If we got the money, we could stay. Would you do it?"

"Yes," Brooke said, almost inaudibly. "Count me in."

CHAPTER 35

$\mathcal{B}$ROOKE'S MOTHER WAS WAITING up when she came home that night. Brooke stepped into the dimly lit living room and set her things on the telephone table. "Mom, you didn't have to wait up for me," she said quietly.

"I heard about the decision of the church Finance Committee tonight," her mother said apprehensively. Along with that apprehension was an unmistakable, if subtle, note of relief. "I wanted to see how you took it."

Brooke sat down next to her mother. "Well, we've decided not to roll over and play dead. As a matter of fact, Nick and I are going to try to get the money on our own and do the project without pay. So I won't be leaving just yet."

"Oh?" Her mother brought her hand to the collar of her robe, idly stroking the velour. "Brooke, won't that be a lot of money? You aren't going to borrow it, I hope."

Brooke almost laughed, but the subject was far from funny. "Borrow it? Not a bank in this country would loan money for something like this, especially when the Finance

Committee isn't behind it. It isn't like there's any kind of return on our investment. No, whatever we put into it, we have no hope of getting back. At least, not monetarily."

Brooke could see her mother bristling as she stood up and paced across the room, struggling to keep her mouth shut despite her reservations. "Then how?" she finally asked. "You don't have that kind of money, do you?"

"No," Brooke said. "But we'll get it from somewhere. I know we will."

Her mother turned around slowly, regarding Brooke as if she'd lost all good sense. But for the first time in her life, Brooke realized that it didn't matter whether her mother understood or not. "I know I said that I wouldn't nag," her mother said, trying to keep her tone even. "But I don't want to see you do something stupid in the name of . . . of . . ."

"In the name of God, I think," Brooke provided quietly.

The word seemed to bring her mother's spirits down further. "Oh, Brooke," she said. "I didn't know you even believed in God."

Brooke looked up at her. "You never taught me to believe in much of anything, Mom. Least of all, myself." She sighed, got up, and met her mother face to face. "I'm not real sure I believe now. But what if He does exist? What if we're all wrong? And what if He's been in control of my life all along, watching over me and taking care of me even when I don't give Him a thought? What if He's the one who brought me back here, so I could put my past behind me? So I could finally move on?"

"Brooke, I think your coming back here had more to do with Nick Marcello than God."

The comment didn't even make Brooke angry. "You know, Mom, the thing about not believing in God is that, when things go wrong, they're hopeless. There's no place to turn. I wouldn't think you and Dad would want that for me . . . or for Roxy."

"Believing in something that doesn't exist doesn't change your life, Brooke. And it won't regenerate your bank account after you've poured everything into those windows."

"It's not coming out of my bank account. I don't have nearly enough. My car isn't worth much, and I rent my apartment, so there's nothing to mortgage. Even if I sold everything I owned, it wouldn't begin to get us started."

"But Brooke, if you don't have the money, how can you—?"

"The money will come from somewhere," she cut in before her mother's negative words could weaken her fledgling faith. "And if it does . . . I think I have no choice but to believe."

With a sigh, her mother dropped into a chair across the room. Her face was as strained as if she carried the weight of the galaxy on her shoulders.

"Has Roxy heard about the church's decision?" Brooke asked quietly to change the subject.

Her mother shook her head. "No. Roxy had gone out before I got the call. She had a date."

"A date?" Brooke asked, her face burning in sudden anger. Had Roxy actually gone out with Bill tonight, after Brooke had confronted her? Had he actually had the nerve to see her, knowing that Brooke knew?

"Yes," her mother said absently. "With a boy named Sonny. I met him when he picked her up. I was a little worried about the motorcycle, but he brought her a helmet. He seemed like a nice boy."

Relief stole the fury from Brooke's eyes. "I know Sonny," she said. "He is a nice boy. Very nice."

Brooke's mother just looked at her, and she knew that she yearned to ask more questions about her work with Nick. Finally, knowing that more conversation would only wind up in argument, Brooke kissed her distraught mother goodnight and went to her room.

Her room was already aglow with the little lamp in the corner, lighting *Infinity* like a halo. Brooke stepped in and closed the door behind her. She picked up the hands, held them against her heart and lay down on her bed. She had sculpted it selflessly, out of love and not for recognition, and Nick had helped her, with no thought of payment or reward. The competition for the scholarship had seemed secondary. The hands had been a labor of love, and had given her a reason to go on day after day . . .

And they could do it again, she suddenly realized.

Helena at the gallery offered me twenty-five thousand for it.
Nick's words came back to her, reminding her that there *was*
something she could sell. Something worth far more to her than
mere dollars.

Why didn't you sell it?

Because it wasn't mine . . .

Now, holding the sculpture in her hands, Brooke wondered
if *Infinity* was really hers to sell. Wasn't it really *theirs?* Hadn't
she created it, if only unconsciously, as a symbol for that nameless
bond between them seven years ago that had changed the course
of their lives and, now, had led them right back to where they'd
started?

No, she couldn't sell it. There must be another way.

But if there wasn't, what would happen? Would she be able
to put the windows off long enough, perhaps, to do some expen-
sive panels for her best clients in Columbia, long enough to save
that impossible sum of money?

Brooke set the sculpture down and heaved a great sigh, realizing that since she'd been here, she hadn't even called her machine
at home once to see if anything pressing had come up. Since she
might have to get her job back sooner than she'd thought, she
strolled barefoot into Roxy's dark room, picked up her extension,
and dialed her home phone number in Columbia.

Her own voice greeted her, the voice of someone she hardly
remembered, someone empty, someone lonely, running as fast as
her memories could chase her. She pressed out her code on the
push-button dial, and heard the beep that followed.

A shiver coursed through her as she recognized the gravelly
voice. "Uh . . . it's Nick. I called the motel and you'd checked
out." She sat up straighter, listening to the message that must
have been recorded the night she'd checked into the Bluejay Inn.
"I hope you haven't gone home, Brooke. It's too important to
give up on that easily . . . the windows, I mean. Don't give up,
Brooke. It's worth whatever it takes to see it through." There was
an eloquent pause, and finally he said again. "I really hope you
haven't gone home."

She hung up the phone without even listening for the rest of her messages and sat in the dark, letting the warmth of Nick's voice envelope her, making her decision more clear.

Slowly she went back into her room and looked down at the sculpture, knowing finally that Nick had given her the strength to do what was necessary.

It's worth whatever it takes to see it through, he had said. And he was right. It *was* worth it. She and Nick had had two beginnings. Tomorrow she would sell the sculpture to buy her chance at an ending . . . an ending that both of them could live with.

CHAPTER 36

$\mathcal{S}$ONNY AND ROXY WALKED ALONG the courtyard outside the little strip of restaurants where they'd eaten. A fountain played in the center, spraying up, then cascading down, frivolous and frothy. "I tried to hide it from them," he was saying, "but when they found what I'd been working on, I realized that it was stupid, pretending that I don't care about it."

"Why don't they want you to paint?" Roxy asked. She had been disinterestedly quiet when Sonny first picked her up, but over the course of the evening she had found him so comfortable to be with that he had coaxed her out of her shell. Now she found herself able to talk to him freely. And even more surprisingly, she found herself actually interested in what he was saying.

"They think it'll keep me from working with my pop. It's what I'm supposed to do, see? Be an electrician and work in Pop's business." He paused and looked toward the fountain. "My great-grandfather was the only one in the family who ever thought art was worthwhile. I never knew him—he died right after I was born—but he's the one who left Nick that car. The way Nick treats it, you'd think Grandpa's spirit was sewn into the upholstery or something." He shrugged, picked up a pebble from the side of the fountain and tossed it in. "I guess, in a way, Nick is doing for me what Grandpa did for him."

"Nick?" Roxy asked. "What's he doing?"

Sonny shrugged. "He believes in me," he said. "He's the only one who thinks I've got something."

Roxy sat on the fountain's edge, looking down at her feet with listless eyes. "Sometimes maybe it's best not to encourage talent, if it's only going to wind up defeating you."

"Hey." Sonny leaned over her, touching her nose with a fingertip. "It can't defeat you if you don't let it."

"Sometimes people don't have a choice," Roxy said. "Sometimes life has a way of just dragging you along by the throat."

Sonny chuckled, making her despair seem thinner and less significant. "I don't know who you've been hanging out with, Rox, but it doesn't have to be that way." He took her hand and pulled her to her feet. She couldn't help looking at him.

"Have you ever had a dream?" he asked. "Or a talent that you just had to go after, no matter what anybody else said?"

Roxy's smile was almost too subtle to see. "I'm no artist, if that's what you mean."

"Something else, then," he said. "Hey, I'll bet you can sing. Go ahead, hum a few bars."

Roxy laughed for the second time in months. "No, I can't sing. And I can't play an instrument. And I can't act." She smiled up at him, saw that he wasn't relenting and, almost embarrassed, lowered her gaze to study her feet. "But ... I used to like to dance. Once, I wanted to be a ballerina."

"A ballerina?" he said, inclining his head in awe. "Have you studied ballet?"

"Until about a year ago," Roxy said. "But my teacher kept making me dance solo in the recitals ..." Her smile faded as the memory came back to her of one particular man sitting in the audience. "I was always really self-conscious about all those people looking at me . . . so I quit."

"You *quit?*" Sonny asked, astounded. "Just because of that?"

She shrugged. "It was a big thing to me."

Sonny leaned against the brick wall, a poignant smile on his lips. "Do you ever dance anymore? When you're by yourself, I mean?"

Roxy grinned at him self-consciously, wondering how he'd managed to make the awkwardness pass. "You'll laugh."

"No, I won't. Scout's honor," Sonny said. "'Course, I'm not a scout, but . . . if you do, we have more in common than I thought. I paint alone in my room. Because, you know, you don't have to have someone's approval to be good. All you need is your own judgment." He pushed away from the wall, and took her hands out of her pockets, held one over her head in a crude ballerina pose. "Dance for me, Roxy," he entreated softly, not making fun of her, and not diminishing the art she loved. "I'll bet you're a beautiful dancer."

Roxy laughed nervously and shook her head. "I can't . . . really. It's been a long time."

"Come on, just a few steps," he coaxed. "I'll show you my painting if you do."

Roxy wet her lips, looked up at him, and realized that the balls and chains she had felt weighing her down before she'd come out with Sonny tonight didn't seem to be dragging her down just then. She felt light with him, and for a moment she was able to forget her fear and shame and guilt and heartache. For the moment, she just wanted to dance.

Roxy stepped back, stood on her toes, and did a soft pirouette, lowered into a *plié*, then ended in a delicate curtsy.

Sonny threw both hands over his heart and stepped back, grinning with delight. "Oh, Rox, you've got to start dancing again. That's too nice to waste."

Roxy bit her lip, wondering why she wasn't embarrassed. "Thank you," she whispered. "Now you have to keep your part of the bargain and show me your painting."

"Okay," Sonny said. "But my moves aren't nearly as graceful as yours."

They rode his motorcycle back to Sonny's garage apartment, and Roxy knew he could feel her hand shaking as he held it and led her in. Something in her head warned her that she could be walking into trouble . . . that men could not be trusted . . . that they were all ruled by rampant hormones instead of the heart. But somewhere deep inside, instinct told her that Sonny was indeed different and that he could be trusted.

He turned on the light, robbing the room of its mystery, and closed the door behind him. "Ain't much," he said, "but it's mine. At least, until my folks kick me out."

Roxy smiled. "So, where's the painting?"

Sonny lifted the spread on his bed, slid out the canvas lying face up on the floor beneath it. He held it up, its back to her, and assessed it himself one last time. Finally, reluctantly, he turned it around to show her.

Roxy stepped closer, surveying the detail of the house depicted there. There was a Norman Rockwell poignancy to the faces of the people around it, emotion in every stroke. "It's got so much," she whispered. "So many stories in this one little canvas. So many feelings." She looked up at him, surprise in her eyes as she regarded him in a new light. "Sonny, have your parents seen this? I mean, really looked at it?"

"No, not really," he said. "I mean, they saw it long enough to get mad, like I'd been growing pot in my bathroom or something. But I don't think they took the time to *see* it."

"They *have* to," Roxy said. "Sonny, you have to make them. It's wonderful. It reminds me of . . . family. When the family is young and colorful and bright. Before everything turns gray."

"You think?"

"Yes. That painting shouldn't be hidden."

"Well, it's not finished. But thanks, Rox. I appreciate it."

He took a deep, shaky breath. "I'd better take you home," he whispered with an affected grin.

Roxy looked at him, wide-eyed, surprised that he wouldn't at least try to take advantage of the situation. The respect in his choice filled her with relief. "Yeah," she whispered. "I'd better get home."

Sonny took her hand and led her back to his motorcycle.

CHAPTER

37

$\mathcal{M}$ORNING LIGHT SHONE THROUGH the windows in Brooke's room the next day, offering new hope and an exhilarated feeling that something good was about to happen. Dressed and ready to pursue the finances needed to finish the windows, Brooke took the sculpture and sat down on her bed, holding it in her lap and stroking the smooth lines, quietly absorbing the feel of it for the last time.

She heard a knock and looked up to see Roxy standing in her doorway. "Hi," she said.

"Hi." They were both stiff, awkward. The fight they'd had the night before weighed on Brooke's heart, making her regret that she had ever confronted her sister. Maybe she should have kept it to herself and tried to find covert ways of helping Roxy out of this hole she had dug for herself.

"Mom just told me about the committee's decision," Roxy said. "I'm really sorry. I know how hard you worked on those windows."

Brooke's eyes dropped to the sculpture. "We'll pay you for the work you've done," she said. "They did agree to compensate us for what we've already done."

Roxy crossed her arms and looked at the floor. "That's okay," she said. "Just keep it."

A moment of silence passed, but Roxy still lingered on the threshold of Brooke's room.

"Did Mom also tell you that we're going ahead with the project?" Brooke asked. "Without pay?"

"Yeah," Roxy said. "But I don't understand how you plan to raise the money."

Brooke touched the fingertips of the man's hand in the sculpture, placed her own hand over the woman's. The thought of letting the piece go made her heart ache. "Nick said someone had offered him twenty-five thousand dollars for this," she whispered. "That'll get us started on the windows."

"What?" Roxy stepped into the room. "Why would you sell that for the stupid people at that church? You'll never get the money back, and the sculpture will go into strange hands, and the church members won't even care."

Tears emerged in Brooke's eyes, and she looked up. "What else can I do?" she asked. "I've caught Nick's vision for those windows. I feel right on the verge of so many things. I just have this feeling that working on the windows can change my life somehow. And I want to change it. I don't think I can stand to go back to the way it was before, living day to day, never daring to look ahead. I feel like abandoning the windows now will leave us right back where we were seven years ago—with everything taken away from us because of one woman and her lies."

"You're in love with him, aren't you?" Roxy asked.

Brooke set the sculpture down carefully and ambled to the window. The morning sunlight was shining on her parents' back lawn. It warmed her face. "All I know is that I have a connection with Nick that I've never had with anyone else. Even in high school, I felt it so strong that it almost overwhelmed me. But I never acted on it, not once, and neither did he. He treated me just the way a teacher should treat a student. If we don't have these windows to do, I don't know what will happen to us. I can't stay here, and he probably won't leave." She turned around, faced her sister, bracing herself for her reproach, her disgust, her judgment. But this time there was none.

Roxy simply stood looking at her, a frown forming between her thin brows—a frown of deep concern—not of angry disapproval. "But, Brooke," she whispered, "isn't the sculpture just as important? He kept it all these years. He could have sold it himself."

Brooke went back to the sculpture, picked it up, and held it as if it were alive. "These hands represent the beginning," she said. "But I want more than just a beginning. I want a future." She looked up at her sister, her mouth twitching in pain as she lifted her brows decisively. "I'm going to sell it today."

Roxy swallowed, and her face softened, her expression as unguarded and sympathetic as Brooke had seen since she'd come home. "Can I come with you?" she asked.

Brooke tried to laugh, but her effort failed. "I'd really appreciate that," she said, "because this is going to be one of the hardest things I've ever had to do."

In that moment it seemed as if Roxy was her little sister again, anxious to join Brooke in whatever adventure she embarked on. Brooke crossed the distance between them and hugged Roxy in a way that she hadn't done in seven years. Miraculously, Roxy hugged her back. In that hug, all the regrets and injustices and condemnations between them fell away, leaving just two sisters who desperately needed each other's love.

CHAPTER  38

$\mathscr{H}$ELENA, THE GALLERY OWNER, was busy with a client when Brooke and Roxy first arrived, so while they waited, Brooke led her sister to the wall where Nick's work hung.

"He's good, isn't he?" Brooke whispered, holding the wrapped sculpture against her like a newborn baby.

Roxy hadn't yet surrendered her grudge against Nick completely, so she nodded without saying a word.

Brooke leaned back against a corner of the wall and gazed at her sister's sad eyes. "Roxy, I know you don't like him," she whispered, "because you think that directly or indirectly he's responsible for a lot of the hurt in both our lives. But what you have to understand is that Nick was as much a victim as I was."

Roxy settled her eyes on one painting, and Brooke could see that she made an honest effort to see, to feel the bright poignancy Nick had captured there. "I know about being a victim, Brooke," she whispered.

"I know you do," Brooke said quietly. "You've been a victim of my scandal, and now, you're also a victim of a married man who probably promised you the moon and the stars. But he's married, Roxy, and no matter how you add that up, you come out shortchanged."

"I don't want to talk about it."

Brooke watched Roxy step away, arms crossed defensively as she glanced at other pieces displayed in that portion of the gallery. "Just remember something," Brooke said. "There's someone out there for you, who has the same dreams, the same imagination, the same kind of soul. When you find that person, Roxy, you'll understand how destructive this relationship is now."

"I know it's destructive," Roxy said. "You're not telling me anything new. I'm hoping not to see him anymore," she said. "Really hoping." She looked toward the gallery owner, who was walking her clients to the door, then moved her focus back to Brooke. A shred of a smile glimmered in her eyes. "Sonny's nice, though."

Brooke's surprise at Roxy's declaration not to see Abby Hemphill's son anymore, as weak as it was, was usurped by this new development. "Yeah, Sonny's real nice."

Brooke smiled at her sister, praying that the enchantment she saw on her face meant that Roxy was allowing herself another chance to find the happiness she deserved.

But before Roxy said more, Helena was free and heading toward them.

"Sorry, darling," she said, her voice loud now that they were alone in the gallery. "You're Nick's friend, aren't you?" She took her hand and kissed her cheek, as if Brooke was a long lost friend. "That was one of my best clients. Didn't find anything she wanted this trip, though. I could use some new pieces from him. Is he working on anything?"

"A few things," Brooke said, not wanting to disappoint the anxious woman. "The stained-glass windows are his main priority right now, though." She felt her heart pounding painfully, like that of a mother offering a child for adoption, at the moment of surrender. "I came to see if you'd be interested in buying something from me."

"What, darling?"

Slowly, she uncovered *Infinity*, and the woman gasped.

"He—" Brooke's voice faltered, and she swallowed. "He told me you like this. That you had made an offer on it."

Helena's face lit up as she drew in a deep, reverent breath. Carefully, she took the sculpture from Brooke and turned it over in her hands as if she knew its value vividly. "The sculpture he wouldn't sell me!" she said. "I *begged* him for it." She looked at Brooke, her eyes filled with a new respect. "He said it wasn't his. You wouldn't be the sculptor, would you?"

Brooke nodded and wondered if her face looked as pale and lifeless as it felt. "Yes, I am."

"I see." Helena inclined her head and offered her a knowing smile. "The last time you two were in, darling, I figured out that you were the woman in Nick's past. Now I understand why he wouldn't part with the sculpture. I thought his attachment to it was a little unusual. Especially when it wasn't his own work. And honey, I offered him a *lot* of money."

Brooke tried to ignore the comments regarding their relationship and seized the opportunity. "Does the offer still stand?" she asked, her voice suddenly hoarse.

"Does it ever!" Helena said. "I can write you a check right now."

Brooke looked down at the sculpture and realized that it could fall into a stranger's hands, someone who didn't know the history, the pain, the heartache associated with those hands, who'd set it on their mantle somewhere and forget to dust it.

"Do . . . do you plan to keep it . . . for yourself? Or do you plan to sell it?" The question came out as broken and wavering as her heartbeat.

Helena set a gentle hand on Brooke's shoulder. "I'm keeping it for myself, of course. I've been wanting it for years. But if an offer comes along that I can't refuse . . ." She took the sculpture and let out a low, long breath. "Oh, but it would have to be *some* offer." She looked into Brooke's eyes. "Are you sure you're ready to part with it, darling?"

Brooke's mouth went dry, but still she managed to speak. "I'm sure," she said. "It's all yours."

I can't believe you did it," Roxy said two hours later, after Brooke had opened a Hayden bank account for the stained-glass window expenses and deposited the twenty-five thousand.

"I can't believe it, either," Brooke whispered as she drove, aware that the color had still not returned completely to her face. She had gone through the transactions that morning in a zombie-like daze, doing what she had to do, but refusing to dwell on the pain it caused. "But I have to concentrate on what it will mean in the long run. We'll have the chance to do the windows. This won't cover all of it by a long shot, but it'll get us started until we can think of something else."

Roxy just looked at her. "And you'll be around Nick a little longer."

"Well . . . honestly . . . yeah, there may be something to that. But I'm not sure how he feels."

"The same," Roxy said. "He feels exactly the same."

"How do you know?"

"I can see it in his eyes when he looks at you." The words were uttered without pleasure.

"Well . . . anyway . . . it looks like we will be working together for a while." She breathed a deep sigh and tried to smile. "I'll drop you off at home before I go to the church."

Roxy looked out the window, her expression pensive as she chose her words. Finally she looked at her sister. "You know, Brooke, I think this is really unselfish, what you're doing. And if you still need me, I'd like to keep working at the church. You don't have to pay me."

"Really?" Brooke asked, taking her eyes off the road long enough to gape at Roxy. "You'd do that?"

"Yeah. I'm out of school the rest of this week, and then I can help weekends and after school sometimes. I think I'm going to quit my job at City Hall."

The sweet, forgiving offer was like an injection of positive energy that made Brooke's smile more genuine. "All right, Roxy. You can work today, if you want."

For the first time since she could remember, Roxy answered her smile. They drove to the church in silence as a sense of well-being washed over Brooke. She had the money to get a substantial start on the stained-glass windows. Already, in her mind's eye, she could see the surprise and delight in Nick's eyes when she told him.

And that, she realized, was worth ten *Infinities*.

CHAPTER

39

*Y*OU SAID YOU WEREN'T FIRING US," Nick reminded the pastor as they sat in the office at St. Mary's, figures and projected cost estimates spread out on the table. "If we come up with the money ourselves, we can go ahead with it, right?"

Horace rubbed his loose jaw and straightened his heavy glasses. "I don't like it," he said gruffly. "It doesn't seem fair. You and Brooke don't have that kind of money."

Nick leaned forward, anxious to get his point across. His eyes were alive with conviction. "Horace, I'm going to get the money. Now, are you with us, or not?"

A grin stole across Horace's face. "Yes, I'm with you. If you're willing to put yourself on the line like that, not even Abby Hemphill can stop you."

Nick took Horace's hand and shook it heartily. "You're a good man, Pastor."

"And you, my friend, are a devoted artist. I really believe God is going to bless your sacrificial spirit."

A knock sounded on the office door, and Nick leaned over and opened it, laughter still in his voice as he greeted Brooke and Roxy. "Great news," he sang out before either of them could speak. "Horace gave us the go-ahead."

"Then we're in business!" she said. "I just opened an account and made a deposit this morning."

Nick got up. "What? A deposit?" His smile began to waver as she brandished the bank book she clutched in her hand.

He took it, opened it, and read the amount. "Twenty-five thousand? Brooke!"

Brooke stemmed his questions with an outstretched hand. "Don't worry," she said, laughing and winking at Horace. "I didn't do anything illegal."

"But Brooke—"

Brooke cut him off and turned back to the pastor. "So, I guess we have enough to get a good start on the windows, anyway."

Horace let out a boisterous laugh and shook his head. "That ought to quiet Abby."

Brooke laughed, then looked back at Nick.

"Brooke, I have to know where you got this money," he said quietly.

Brooke's smile vanished. "We'll talk in a minute," she said, restoring her smile and taking Horace's arm. "I'll walk you out, Pastor."

Nick watched her disappear with Horace, then turned his suspicious eyes on Roxy, who stood mutely just inside the door.

"What did she do, Roxy?" he whispered. "Where did she get it?"

She shook her head and said, "It should come from her. It's really none of my business."

The significance of the girl's evasion hit him boldly in the heart. "She sold it." His voice was weak, as though the truth had knocked the breath out of him. "She sold *Infinity*, didn't she?" Roxy stood motionless, but Nick came toward her, forcing her to answer. "*Didn't she?*"

"She had to."

"I knew it!" he shouted. "How could she do that? How *could* she when I told her that I would get the money?"

He threw down the bank book and pushed past Roxy, out into the hall and past the construction crews working inside the church. He paced back and forth in front of the door, watching through the window until the pastor drove away. The moment Brooke was alone, he rushed into the parking lot.

"You sold it!" he shouted, bolting toward her. "How could you do that?"

Her face filled with confusion. "Nick, wait a minute," she said, stepping toward him. "I did what I had to do! We needed the money, and now we've got some!"

"I told you that I could come up with the money. You didn't have to do something so drastic." Angrily, he strode toward his old Buick and opened his car door.

Brooke yelled, "Nick, where are you going?"

He closed the door and started the car. Before she could stop him, he was out of the parking lot.

CHAPTER

40

$\mathcal{B}$ROOKE WAITED AT ST. MARY'S for the rest of the day, hoping Nick would come back, but when darkness finally swallowed the old church, intruding in the workroom and making her feel more isolated, she realized that he didn't plan to return.

Where had he gone?

She thought of going home, but couldn't bear the thought of facing her parents and opening herself up to their scrutiny and probing questions. She had called Nick's house so many times today, but he wasn't home. He was somewhere nursing his anger, his pain ... but why selling the sculpture had caused him such anger, she wasn't sure ...

Everything always came back to that sculpture. Like a magnet, it drew the two of them together but also had the power to repel them. How could something so sweet create such bitterness?

Quietly she walked through the church, wishing, praying, that Nick would appear before she left and tell her that he understood what she had done, that he appreciated the sacrifice.

"Why don't you just go buy it back?"

She turned and saw Roxy standing in the doorway, watching her pace. "I can't," she said. "We do need the money for the windows."

"There must be another way to get it," she said. "Nick must know of one."

"Another way," she whispered, shaking her head. "I wish I knew what it could be." She thought of last night, when they had agreed to finish the windows without pay and he had told her that he could get the money. Today, her failure to wait seemed to have hurt him worse than her selling the sculpture. Was that what this was about?

"Buy it back," she muttered again, a smile slowly curving her lips as she brought her weary eyes back to Roxy. "That's what I'll do."

CHAPTER

41

*N*ICK LEANED BACK AGAINST HIS Duesenberg and let the river wind whip through his hair.

As if he sat beside him, Nick heard his grandfather's laughter. *"That's the thing about women,"* he had told him once. *"Just-a when you think you got 'em figured, they change all the rules."*

Nick shook the voice out of his head and looked at the car that had been his main source of pride for as long as he'd been able to drive. He could see his grandfather in every detail, from the gold-plated wheel covers to the leather seats. His grandpa, who had believed in him and shown him what was real, despite the pain it cost. His grandpa, who had planted the seeds of faith.

Nick's eyes misted over, and he realized he'd give every day he'd had as an artist for one more day with his grandfather. He could use a little advice right now. He could use some help.

The night grew more opaque as clouds billowed overhead, and a chill wind crept around him, reminding him that he was a couple of hours from home. But he had no intention of going back there tonight. Not until he had sorted some things out. Not until he had set some things right.

It was clear in his mind what he had to do. He only wished it had been as clear in Brooke's.

*B*rooke was up at dawn the next morning, pacing in front of the telephone until a decent hour when she could call the gallery and plead with Helena to let her buy back the sculpture. Her parents came in for breakfast, looked at her with concern, and asked what was wrong. She explained as briefly as possible, giving no details.

Before long, Roxy came in as well, and all of them sat quietly as Brooke dialed the gallery. She let the phone ring ten or twelve times and finally gave up until she could try again.

"What is it with that statue?" her father asked, irritated by her persistence.

"It's important, Daddy," Brooke said, not in the mood to go into her relationship with Nick. "It was a mistake to sell it."

"If you ask me, you made a mistake holding onto it all this time," he said, picking up the paper and flipping to the sports section. "How much did they give you for it, anyway? Fifty, sixty?"

"Twenty-five," Brooke said absently, flipping through the phone book for Helena's last name as it had appeared on her check, desperately hoping to catch her at home.

"Then what's the big deal?" her father asked. "I could have loaned you twenty-five bucks."

Roxy's sudden burst of laughter surprised both parents. "Thousand, Daddy. Twenty-five thousand."

George dropped the newspaper with a sharp intake of breath. *"Twenty-five thousand dollars!"* he bellowed. "They paid you twenty-five thousand for that, and you think you made a mistake?"

Oblivious to her parents' shock, Brooke eyed the clock on the wall, and saw that it wasn't yet eight. "Maybe they open at eight," she muttered. "Maybe I ought to just go there." She turned back to Roxy, ignoring her father's and mother's shock. "Roxy, do you think I should just go there?"

"It wouldn't hurt," Roxy said. "You'll have to go to pick it up, anyway."

Her mother bolted out of her seat. "You're going to give that money back? Are you crazy?"

"Yes, Mom," Brooke said, grabbing her purse and heading for the door without a second look back. "I guess I am."

CHAPTER

*W*HAT DO YOU MEAN, YOU'VE SOLD IT?" Brooke's voice wobbled with panic as she stood in the gallery, gaping at Helena.

"Last night, darling. I don't run a pawn shop, you know. I didn't expect you to want it back."

A wave of dizzy disbelief washed over Brooke, and she lowered herself onto a white leather chair. "But you . . . you said you'd bought it for yourself . . . that you would keep it!"

Obviously alarmed at Brooke's near-wild state, Helena sat down next to her, lowering her voice to a calming pitch. "Darling, I said I'd keep it unless someone made me an offer I couldn't refuse. I meant that, but that offer came last night."

Ignoring the tears inhibiting her speech, Brooke dug into her purse for a pen and a piece of paper. "All right. Who did you sell it to?" she asked. "I'll go directly to them and buy it back.

Helena shook her head slowly, and set a kind hand on Brooke's shoulder. "Love, I couldn't in good conscience disclose that client's name to you and let you show up with that wild look in your eyes. It's just not . . . professional."

Brooke pressed her face into her hands and tried to catch her breath. After a moment she looked up, her pallid complexion contrasting with the redness in her eyes. "Helena, look," she tried again. "I know you hardly know me at all. But if you've ever cared about Nick, please help me. It means so much to him. I want it back for him."

Helena shook her head resolutely, but her face was not without sympathy. "I'm sorry, love. It's out of the question."

Brooke's shoulders drooped as if this final refusal punctured her determination once and for all. "I can't believe this," she whispered. "I thought I was doing the right thing. And now I can't even afford my own work, and I have no idea where Nick is." She came to her feet, almost dazed, and started for the door.

Helena followed her. "He's a complex man. It shows in his work." She stopped as Brooke opened the door. "If he's that upset about the sculpture, darling, it isn't really about the sculpture. It's about something else."

"I know," Brooke whispered. "I know."

She bade Helena good-bye, then got in her car and sat for a moment. It was gone. The sculpture she had made for him, *sold* for him, was gone. And so was he.

She started her car and vacantly drove back to Hayden. Tears rolled down her face—tears of regret, tears of guilt, tears of waste. *Infinity* was gone, handed over to a perfect stranger who hadn't a clue that it meant so much to two such vulnerable souls. She would never see it again. *Where are you, Nick?* Her heart cried as she drove. *Help me cope with what I've done. Don't you condemn me too . . .*

But he did condemn her, she knew. That was a fact, just as vivid as the loneliness of her past seven years. Nick condemned her, just as everyone else did.

But if there was an up side to the constant sense of failure she had experienced for seven years, it was that she had become conditioned to living with it, accepting it, and even forgiving it. So she drove to Nick's house, praying that, despite how things looked at the moment, the two of them would have one more chance to forgive each other.

When she arrived, the garage was open and his Duesenberg was gone. Still, she went to the door and knocked. There was no answer. She left a note, pleading for him to call her, and headed back for St. Mary's, praying that she would find him there, hard at work.

His car wasn't there, but Brooke went into the church, stalked past the workers, and checked his office and the workroom.

He wasn't there. Brooke sat for a moment, racking her brain for some clue, some memory, to lead her in the right direction.

Nick's family lived in town. Maybe they would know where he could be reached. Maybe he was with them.

Quickly, she drove to a pay phone and looked up the name Marcello. There was no listing. But Sonny's last name was Castori— she flipped over to the Cs. Still no listing.

Maybe Roxy will know where they live, she thought suddenly.

Brooke headed across town to City Hall, praying that she would find Roxy there.

The parking lot was cluttered with everything from buses to pickup trucks, but Brooke found Roxy's car and pulled into a space nearby. A fleeting doubt passed through her mind about disturbing her sister at work, but she told herself this visit couldn't wait. She had to find Nick.

She went up the stairs to the building and stepped aside as a small wedding party came out of the justice of the peace's office. The young bride, adorned in a short white dress with a spray of baby's breath tucked into her French twist, laughed melodically as she tossed the bouquet toward the half-dozen well-wishers surrounding her.

Such was the stuff of other people's lives, Brooke thought, fighting sadness. But were things really ever that simple, that uncomplicated?

What was it about the Martin girls that such happiness could never belong to them?

She went to the office marked "Records," where Roxy worked. Distracted by her urgency, she pushed open the door without knocking. Hushed voices came from the corner of the room behind a row of file cabinets.

"No, Bill!" Roxy was saying, her voice somberly low. "Leave me alone."

Realizing that she had walked into something embarrassingly private, Brooke had started to back out of the office when she heard something slam against the file cabinet. "Oh, no, you don't," the man said viciously. "I'm warning you. I call the shots here, not you. And you're not finished with me until I say you are."

Alarmed, Brooke leaned around a cabinet far enough to see that Bill Hemphill had braced an arm on each side of Roxy, trapping her. "Please, Bill," Roxy said, her voice raspy with emotion. "I can't take this anymore."

"Well, you'll have to," he told her in a syrupy sweet voice. "If you want to keep this job—"

"I don't!" Roxy pushed him away and twisted out of his reach. "I'm sick of this job, and I'm tired of dealing with you!"

Bill's laugh was calculatingly intimidating. "Do you think that's all there is to it, babe? That your job is all that's at stake? I have more than that to hold over you."

Brooke stepped back out of sight, covered her mouth and held her breath in horror at this revelation of the truth—which sounded even worse than she had feared.

"I hope your wife finds out about this! I hope she throws you out!"

Though she couldn't see him, Brooke could hear Bill chuckle. "Do you really think that anyone would blame me if word did get out? I'd just say that you chased me. Since that sort of behavior runs in your family, anyway, it wouldn't be that hard to sell."

"You're sick!" Roxy shouted.

Brooke jumped at a sudden loud crash and looked around the cabinet to see that Bill was holding Roxy with brute force against the wall.

The final filament of Brooke's control snapped, and she barreled toward him, aflame with outrage. "Let go of her!" she demanded. "Get your slimy hands off my sister!"

Bill spun around, letting Roxy go, and Brooke realized that at that moment, had she been holding a weapon, she could have killed him without one second's hesitation.

"If you want a scandal, you'll get one," Brooke said through her teeth. "Because if there's anything we Martins have learned from your family, it's how to play dirty."

As Roxy slipped behind her, Brooke took a few intimidating steps toward the tall young man, who stepped back uncertainly, as if he saw the capability for violence in her eyes. "Does the term 'statutory rape' mean anything to you?" she asked, her eyes glowering with intense hatred. "Have you ever heard of sexual harassment?" She uttered a deep, humorless laugh. "Oh, we're talking about a lot more than family embarrassment, here. We're talking about prison!"

"Hey, wait a minute!" Bill said. "I didn't do anything. It was just a game."

"A game?" Brooke bit out. "A *game?* Is that some sick hobby you and your family have? Destroy the Martins if you can? Hit them while they're young? Win a Kewpie doll?"

Footsteps sounded in the doorway, and Brooke glanced back to see Abby Hemphill standing there, head cocked and nose indignantly thrown in the air. "What is going on here?" she demanded, addressing Brooke. "This is a government office, and you have no business here."

Brooke turned from the son and faced the mother. "I'll tell you what's going on here," she said, pointing a scathing finger at the woman. "Your son has been sexually harassing my sister. You and your family have made your last attempt to ruin my family. And I suggest you watch the headlines very carefully tomorrow. There's going to be a story that'll curl your hair. See how it feels,

Mrs. Hemphill. You love scandals so much. Enjoy one of your own for a change." She reached for Roxy, then turned back to Bill as they started to leave the room. "I wouldn't wait too long to get yourself a lawyer," she warned. "You're going to need one."

Then, leaving Mrs. Hemphill and her son gaping after them in horror, she and Roxy stormed out of the office and down the steps of City Hall.

When they were safe in the sanctuary of Brooke's car, Roxy leaned her head back on the seat and threw her hands over her face, as if absorbing the final release from her personal prison. "Thank you, Brooke," she whispered.

Brooke tried to catch her breath, but rage still spiraled up in her throat. "Did he hurt you?"

"Not physically," Roxy whispered, her voice coming out in a strained vibrato. "But the intimidation . . . it's been going on for months now. I was so scared . . ." She wiped her tears, mascara smearing on her hands, and looked at her sister.

"When I first started working there he hardly knew I existed, so he didn't bother me. But then one night he saw me dance in a recital." Her voice broke and she hid her face from her sister. "Ever since, he's been after me. At first I thought he was harmless, but for the past few weeks he's been making ultimatums . . . demands . . ." She drew in a sustaining breath to help her go on. "Brooke, that night when you picked me up at that bar? At first he drove me to a motel, but when I refused to go into the room, he dumped me out at that bar. He said that if I was so anxious to hold onto . . . my virtue . . . I could try holding onto it there."

"I could kill him," Brooke whispered. "I could honestly—"

"He had me so scared that I really believed if I didn't give in to him soon, he was going to spread a bunch of lies about me, and there would be another scandal all over again." She shoved her hand through her hair, leaving it tangled. "I've run all my life from a scandal, Brooke. That's the thing I'm most afraid of, and he knew it. I just couldn't stand the idea of being involved in one."

Brooke closed her eyes and let the truth cast some light on the darkness she had stumbled through. She had been wrong about Roxy, and the fact that she had assumed the worst shamed her. When she could finally speak again, she pulled her sister against her. Roxy hugged her just as she had when she was no more than a toddler. "I love you, Roxy," Brooke said, "and I hope you can forgive me for thinking the worst about you."

"Only if you can forgive me for thinking the worst about you," Roxy whispered.

They held each other for a long while until a new thought occurred to Brooke, and she leaned back against her car door, facing her sister. "Do you want to press charges against him?" she asked. "I'd love to see him in jail."

"No." Roxy's answer was firm, as if she'd already given the question some thought. "I wouldn't have much to stand on, since he never really got what he was after. And I sure don't want my name in the paper." She looked toward the front doors of City Hall, contemplating her plight. "But let's not let him off the hook just yet. Let him watch the headlines everyday, wondering when the story will hit. Let him lose a few nights of sleep. I think he deserves at least that, don't you?"

"Are you sure?" Brooke asked with a disappointed sigh. "Not even *one* night in jail?"

Roxy shook her head sadly. "No. He'd have the town believing that I was some kind of temptress. I'd rather let him build his own prison."

Brooke squeezed her sister's hand, knowing that this decision was one only Roxy could make. "All right," she said. "I guess I can live with that if you can."

"I don't know what would have happened to me if you hadn't been there," Roxy said quietly. "What were you doing there, anyway?"

Brooke remembered her mission. "I came to ask you if you know where Sonny lives. I don't think Nick's been home all night, and I don't even know where to look for him. I thought his family might know."

"He took me there the other night to show me his painting," Roxy said. "I think I can find the place again. You want me to go with you and show you?"

"Would you?" she asked. "I'm a little shaky today. I'm not in the best shape to meet his family, but I don't know where else to turn."

"Sure," Roxy said. "I owe you one." Roxy wiped the tears from her face. "I've learned a lot of lessons in the past few weeks. But the most important one is that things aren't always the way they look."

Brooke relaxed a little as a warm stirring of hope rose inside her. "We've all learned a lesson or two," she said.

Roxy directed her to Sonny's street, but she wasn't certain which house was his, for it had been too dark the night she'd been there. They drove slowly past each house, and had turned around to try again, when Sonny's motorcycle grumbled up the street toward them and pulled into a driveway.

"Bingo," Brooke said, pulling into the driveway behind him. Sonny took off his helmet, leaving his hair badly tousled, and looked back at them. A genuine smile tore across his face at the sight of Roxy.

He got off his bike and ambled back to the passenger window. "Hey, Rox. You remembered where I live," he said, bracing his arms on her rolled-down window. "I like that."

Brooke didn't have time to let Roxy react to the mild flirtation. "Sonny, have you seen Nick? I've been looking for him all day."

"He didn't come home last night," Sonny said. "I was over there using his studio till three A.M., and he never came home."

"Where could he be?"

"Beats me," Sonny said. "Did you two have a fight or something?"

"Yeah ... something ..." Brooke felt suddenly self-conscious, realizing that her eyes were tired and raw from weeping and that she had long ago cried all her makeup off. She was an emotional mess—in no shape for meeting Nick's family. But ... "Look, is your mother home? Or your grandmother? I'd like to talk to them."

"Sure," Sonny said, surprised. "I'll take you inside."

"No." Brooke got out of the car and looked at him over the roof. "You just stay out here and keep Roxy company. I have to do this alone."

Brooke went to the door and rang the bell, holding her breath as she waited. After a moment, a pretty Italian woman in her late thirties answered.

"Yes?" Nick's sister stood in the doorway, bouncing a fat baby on her hip. "Can I help you?"

"Yes." She cleared her throat, then swallowed. "I'm Brooke Martin . . . a friend of Nick's."

Anna stared at her for a moment, then stepped back. "Ma!" she yelled over her shoulder, then turned back to Brooke, held out a tentative hand, and murmured, "I'm Anna, his sister."

In less than a minute Nick's wiry little mother stood at the door, and Brooke saw a hint of resemblance to Nick in the old woman's dark features.

"Ma, this is Brooke Martin," Anna said.

Nick's mother regarded her without saying a word, then peered out into the driveway. "Where's Nicky?" she asked.

"I . . . I don't know," Brooke said, aware of the chill in the woman's voice. "That's sort of what I wanted to talk to you about. I don't think he went home at all last night. I thought you might know of some place he might be."

"Come in." Without ceremony, Mrs. Marcello took her arm and pulled her into the living room. She gestured toward an old, worn-out chair. "Sit," she ordered.

"No, thank you," Brooke said. She took a deep breath and decided to be as honest with the two women as she could. At this point she had nothing to lose. "Look, I know that you two probably feel the same way about me as my parents feel about Nick. The gossip that follows us is . . . well, it's pretty overpowering. But at the moment that isn't my concern. I'm worried about Nick, Mrs. Marcello. Do you have any idea where he could be?"

The baby started to fuss, and Mrs. Marcello took her from her daughter. "He wouldn't have told us. We had words."

"About me?" Brooke asked.

"Nothing against you!" Nick's mother blurted, shaking a finger at her so hard that the baby began to cry. "You were a child! He has no right influencing children. You, Sonny . . ." She tried to lower her voice, bounced the baby a moment, then handed her back to Anna. Two other children ran past, one in hot pursuit of the other, and Anna dashed out to intervene, leaving the two women to face each other alone. "He has no right influencing children," Nick's mother repeated.

Brooke stepped across the living room to view a collection of family photographs assembled on a shelf. Her eyes scanned them until she found a young man she was sure was Nick, standing beside an old man and his Duesenberg.

He would have liked you, Nick had said. If that was true, then maybe Nick's mother wasn't a lost cause, either. She turned back to the brittle old woman. "Mrs. Marcello, Nick always acted in the most appropriate manner when I was in high school," she said. "He isn't big on self-defense, so maybe he's never told you. Nothing happened between us."

"That's not what the newspaper said!"

"They were lies," Brooke said. "How could you know Nick, really know him, and not realize that?" In spite of her efforts to curb her tears, Brooke's eyes filled again, and she willed her lips to stop shaking. Anna came back into the room, her steps slower as she witnessed Brooke's impending breakdown. "Nick is the most honorable, gentle man I have ever known," Brooke went on. "He would never hurt anyone, but things hurt him so deeply. He's out there somewhere hurting right now, because of something I did. I want so much to tell him I'm sorry."

Mrs. Marcello's forehead wrinkled in grudging concern, but she didn't speak.

"Ma?" Anna asked. "Should we go look for him?"

Nick's mother turned to his sister, her eyes dark with mixed emotions. "After what he did? Filling Sonny's head full of dreams so that he didn't even want to work for Vinnie?"

Brooke had heard all she could stand, and of their own accord, her words tumbled out. "Mrs. Marcello, do you know what it's like to work twenty hours a day on a job that you may or may not get paid for? Do you know what it's like to believe in your work so much that you'd be willing to live on *nothing* for months at a time while you finished it, for a town that would never be grateful? Nick Marcello doesn't have empty dreams, Mrs. Marcello. He works as hard as his grandfather did, or his brother-in-law, or either of you. No wonder he misses his grandfather so much," she said. "He was the only one who could see how special your son really is."

Mrs. Marcello glared at her, stunned silence holding her in its grip, and Anna only looked at the floor. Brooke brought her shaky hand higher and covered her eyes, thinking how much she was going to regret having said these things to his family.

"Excuse me," she said finally, going toward the door. "I have to go find him." She was about to leave when Nick's mother touched her arm to stop her.

"Do you think he's all right?" she asked in a feeble voice.

Brooke turned and saw that the anger had drained from the old woman's face, and she felt her face growing hot. "I don't know. . . . If I could just . . . find him. . ." She felt herself breaking, wilting, and suddenly the old woman's arms were around her, pulling her back inside the house, leading her to the couch, making her sit down.

"Now, you sit," she said more gently. "When Nicky comes home, we'll make things right." She pulled a handkerchief out of her pocket and began dabbing the tears from Brooke's face. "And we'll tell him there are worse things he could do than to marry the girl who cries over him."

"Marriage?" Brooke laughed in spite of herself. "We've never discussed marriage."

"Then you should!" Mrs. Marcello said.

Brooke laughed again, but the pain in her heart chased that laughter away, making her sobs more racking . . . more intense.

And she knew that nothing would really make things right until she knew Nick was back.

Sonny finally summoned the courage to say what he'd been thinking since he'd seen Brooke and Roxy pull into his driveway. "You've been cryin'. Why?"

Roxy managed a weak smile for him. "I've had a bad day," she said. "I sort of lost my job."

"Really?" Sonny couldn't help grinning. "Does that mean I'll be seeing you at St. Mary's more?"

"I'll be there," she said, "but I didn't think you would. They can't pay us, you know."

Sonny took her hand. "The company there is a lot better than minimum wage, anyway," he said. "I'd pay them to let me hang around you."

Roxy grinned and bit her lip. "You're crazy."

Sonny smiled. "Out of my head. Ever since I saw you dance the other night."

Something about the way he said it didn't seem offensive. It didn't cast her as a seductress. Instead, his soft-spoken words made her feel beautiful. "That wasn't dancing," she said. "That was just a couple of steps."

"It was magic," Sonny whispered, cupping her chin. "And if you don't use some of your unemployed time to study dancing again, then I'm going to swear off art for the rest of my life. Think about it. You want that on your conscience?"

Roxy laughed aloud. "Of course not."

"Then you'll dance again? On stage and everything?"

Her smile faded into an expression of peaceful contemplation, and she looked down at her skirt, following the texture of one pleat with her index finger. "How can I turn down an ultimatum like that?"

"Hey," he said, "I must be getting harder to say no to. While I'm on a roll, I know this great little Italian restaurant that's not very busy this time of the week. They have tables outside and music playing and—" He offered a self-deprecating laugh. "And I can afford it."

Roxy's smile found a warm place in his eyes. "Like you said," she whispered, "you're on a roll. How can I say no?"

"You can't." His flirtation didn't frighten Roxy at all, for there was no sly insistence, no threat in his voice.

There was no hurry for either of them, she told herself. They would have plenty more time together.

CHAPTER  43

$\mathcal{N}$OT KNOWING WHERE ELSE TO look for Nick, Brooke talked Sonny into following her to Nick's house and letting her in to wait for him. Just the thought that he couldn't come home without her knowing about it made her feel a little better.

Roxy and Sonny left her there, and she found herself in awe of his home once again. She walked around the studio, looking at each of his works in progress, studying the line, the light . . . wondering just what he was trying to say. As always, his work had layers of expression, reaching out to her, engaging her heart.

What was it about his work?

The light, she thought again. That light, coming from above, in every one of the paintings. A bright, clean light that cut through darkness and desert and dense forest. A bright light that illuminated something in her.

She went back into the living room and sat down on the couch. Nick's Bible lay on the coffee table, its leather cover ragged from handling, its pages marked and worn. She opened it.

Except for her research on the windows, it had been a long time since she had read a Bible. Once, when she was eight or nine, she'd gone with a friend several times to one of the local churches. She had read one there, but since then, it had seemed so irrelevant to her life.

Yet Nick didn't think so.

She remembered the words she'd prayed to God the other night in the church. She had asked Him if He was really there, and told Him how much she needed peace if He was. So far, she hadn't felt that peace with any permanence. But maybe there was something she had to do first.

She opened to the book of John, from which those teachers had read when she was a child. Somewhere along the way she had memorized John 3:16. But long ago she had put it out of her mind, believing that enlightened people didn't read the Bible, that intelligent people didn't believe God became man.

Still, she began to read, and as she did, the light jumped out at her, just like it had in Nick's paintings.

"In Him was life, and the life was the Light of men. The Light shines in the darkness, and the darkness did not comprehend it . . ."

Was that why light was such a powerful element in Nick's paintings? Was that light his life? Could she have really loved him and not perceived that, when she thought she knew him so well?

She read down to verse nine and caught her breath. *"There was the true Light which, coming into the world, enlightens every man."*

Enlightened? Could it be that *she* was the one who needed to be enlightened?

Tears came to her eyes and she didn't know why. She read about the Word becoming flesh and dwelling among us. Through her tears, she read about Jesus being the Lamb of God. She remembered what she'd read in her covenant research, about lambs being sacrificed to cover the sins of the people. It all began to have relevance as she read page after page, hungrily devouring the Word of God, as if it truly did have life and light. As if it could change her life.

She began to weep as the truth dawned on her. "Lord, forgive me for thinking I was enlightened," she whispered. "I didn't know. Show me what to do."

And as that peace she had longed for fell over her, she gave her life to Christ. She asked the Lord to change her and to help her get rid of her bitterness about the Hemphills and the town, and to help her to forgive.

As she prayed, the bitterness left her, replaced by forgiveness. All at once, everything looked different, bathed in this stark new light. "Lord, take care of Nick. Send him home so I can tell him what I've done."

Warm in the peace that washed over her, she fell asleep on his couch, with his Bible open next to her.

CHAPTER  44

$\mathcal{T}$HE RENTAL CAR WAS A FAR CRY from the Duesenberg Nick had left town in. From now on, his Buick would be his only car, and that space in the garage would be empty. He looked down on the seat next to him, and even in the darkness, he could see the check with all those zeroes staring up at him. Would his grandpa have approved of what he had done? Nick missed him now more than he ever had. The memory of the tearful boy standing over his grandfather's deathbed came back to him with heart-wrenching force.

"How do you just stop loving someone, Grandpa?"

His own words played in his mind, as if it were yesterday, begging the haggard old man not to die.

"You don't stop loving them, Nicky. That's not what the Lord intended. You remember them, because you gonna see 'em again."

"But I don't want to remember you, Grandpa. I want you to be right here. With me."

"I wish that could be so, my boy. But I'm tired . . . I'm ready to go home."

He had wept that night when his mother drew him from his grandfather's bedside. And later, when the man he loved most in the world had passed into another world, he had felt it as a cold jolt in his soul.

Later he discovered that his grandfather had left him more than a memory. He had left him his car, the most treasured possession he had, even though Nick was years from driving age.

Tears filled Nick's eyes as he took the Hayden exit, and he blinked them back, determined not to weep over his grandpa again. He had done what he had to do to finish the windows.

The car was gone now, but his grandpa was not. He was still here, in Nick's memory and his heart. His grandpa's voice would never die.

"Joy is free, Nicky, but-a happiness has a price. It takes a big man to recognize its value."

He wondered if he had what it took to be happy. He'd been going to great lengths to get the money for the windows, but the Lord had shown him today that he was doing it more to be with Brooke than for any offering to God.

It had taken Nick days of wrestling with the Lord to understand that the windows had to just be about His Father. And if he wanted it to be a pure offering, then he had to give up any idea of a relationship that wouldn't work. Brooke wouldn't understand that offering to His Father, and she wouldn't be able to share that passion for his work with Him. Only a Christian could understand. That created too big a breach between them. He hadn't wanted to see it.

Exhausted from lack of sleep, he navigated the dark streets of Hayden and pulled into his neighborhood. The lights and lines and shadows looked different from the perspective of this different car . . . more dismal . . . more opaque. He reached his house, saw that he had accidentally left the garage open, so that he could pull the Duesenberg right in to shelter it from harm. But the Duesenberg was now a part of a grand collection of classic cars.

He pulled the rental into the garage, cut off the engine, and sat in the dark for a moment. How long had he been gone? Two days? Three? Had Brooke been looking for him, or had she given up and gone back to Columbia to forget about him and the windows? Was that the way the Lord wanted it?

He picked up the check and the box on the seat next to him, got out of the car, and went to the door. It was unlocked. Had he forgotten to lock up when he'd left?

He went into the kitchen, set the box and the check on the counter, flipped on the light, and looked around to see if everything was still in place. The studio was intact, though it looked as if someone had been there. He stepped into the room, flipped on the lamp, and noted that all of his works-in-progress were still in place. He turned to the living room, and his eye caught something on his couch.

A blanket . . . a woman . . .

Brooke's eyes opened, and she sat up in the half darkness, groggy as she looked up at him. She wore not a drop of makeup, and her eyes were red. Her hair framed her face in neglectful tangles. "Nick," she said, her voice hoarse. "You came back. Are you . . . are you all right?"

He wanted to reach out and hold her, but his fatigue and confusion and his determination to follow God's will were too strong. Instead, he stood stiffly back. "I'm fine," he said. "I didn't see your car. How did you get in?"

"Sonny let me in," she said. "And he and Roxy took my car. I didn't know where to look for you. I was so . . . worried."

"You shouldn't have been," he said. "I just needed some time."

"To do what?"

"To think." His eyes were hard beneath the shadows cast by the lamp. "About you and us and the windows." He slid his fingertips into his pockets and took a few somber steps closer. "About God's plan for my life . . . and your life. Trying to raise the money for the windows kind of made some things clear to me."

He saw the tears forming in her eyes, penetrating the shield in which he'd cloaked himself. "Nick, I tried to get the sculpture back," she said. "I went back to the gallery and begged Helena, but she had sold it. She wouldn't give me the name of the other person who had bought it, and there was nothing I could do . . ."

He couldn't look at her. "You shouldn't have worried about it."

"Nick, why are you so mad about this?"

"I'm not mad, Brooke. I'm tired. I haven't slept since I left. And to be perfectly honest, I'm not in the best mood."

"Because of the sculpture?" she whispered. "Nick, I only sold it so that we could go on with our work. So that I could stay in Hayden with you."

"See, that's what the Lord showed me. That raising the money, doing it for free, wasn't about Him, but about us."

"Nick, it was a sacrifice. An offering. Isn't that good?"

"Not if we have the wrong motives. The Lord showed me that it has to *just* be about Him."

"So . . . you don't want to work with me? You want to get someone else?"

"No," he said too quickly. "No, that's not it. I want to work with you. But it needs to just be about work. About God."

She stood there, stunned for a long moment, not knowing what to say. Finally, as if the silence was too stifling to endure, he grabbed the box he had brought in with him and opened it. Gently, he pulled out the sculpture, held it up to her.

She caught her breath in staggering relief. "You bought it back! *You* were the one who bought it! How?" she asked. "Where did the money come from?"

When he brought his eyes back to hers, all the anger was gone. "It came out of the offering I was going to give to the Lord. That's when I started to realize how upside-down this whole thing is. Brooke, I sold my car to get the money for the windows, and then I used part of that to buy back the sculpture. What's wrong with this picture?"

"You sold your car?" Her words wobbled on a faint wisp of breath, and she dropped her hands to her sides. "Oh, Nick. *Why?*"

"For all the reasons we talked about when we agreed we'd do the windows for free," he said wearily. "For the calling that I feel to do those windows. For the sacrifice I want to offer the Lord. But I ruined it."

She took a step toward him, but he backed away. "Nick, you didn't have to sell the car. We could have gotten the money some other way. We could have—"

"I wanted to do it," he told her. "It was my choice. My offering."

"And I wanted to sell the sculpture for the same reason. For the calling . . . and the sacrifice."

His face twisted in pain as he tried to find the words. "Brooke, what I did was wrong. I shouldn't have used what I had earmarked for God's house to buy something that—in my eyes—symbolized our relationship. I got my eyes off God. I've repented of that, and He's forgiven me. But He showed me the reality of our different values."

"I value the sculpture!" she said, confused. "You think I don't because I sold it, but I do as much as you valued your car."

"I'm not talking about the sculpture, Brooke," he said, turning his back to her. "I'm talking about our deepest beliefs. You said it yourself once. We don't see things the same."

She stared at him. "Nick, you should know that something happened tonight, when I was sitting here waiting for you. I prayed and told the Lord . . ."

He swung around at the words, meeting her eyes, but the heavy stone sculpture slipped out of his hands. He gasped as it fell to the ceramic tile floor with a bone-chilling crash.

Brooke cried out and fell to her knees, but it was too late. The fingers of the woman's hand had broken off. "Oh, no," she said, picking up the pieces. "Oh, no."

He stood motionless, so stunned by his own careless failure that he couldn't find his voice.

Brooke got to her feet, holding the broken sculpture in her hands like a wounded bird. There was no pleading left in her eyes, only a dull, exhausted glimmer of tears.

"Our relationship is your call, Nick," she said. "But I'm still committed to the windows."

Nick watched as Brooke cradled the broken sculpture in her hands and left Nick's house to walk home.

CHAPTER

45

$\mathcal{A}$BBY HEMPHILL STOOD IN HER Victorian gown at the front window of her living room, staring out through the vertical blinds and the wrought-iron webbing, to the houses up and down the street. Had they heard yet? Did they know that her son had sexually harassed a minor?

She turned from the window, hands shaking, and went to the sofa to fluff the pillows. Things could never be too neat. Never too ordered. If they were to come here— the police, the photographers—at least they would see that her house was immaculate, that her own life was without reproach, that she had tried to keep things sterile and secure.

Her mind drifted, and she sat down and stared at the portrait of her son on the wall amid those of her daughter before she had ruined her life. That morning, when his name hadn't appeared in the newspaper, he'd considered himself off the hook. It hadn't seemed to faze him that Brooke Martin and her sister had reason to press charges, spreading the news all over the front page. Hadn't she hurt the girl and her family in that exact way more than once? Wasn't this their perfect opportunity for revenge?

Abby stood up and drifted into the dining room and, with the hem of her gown, polished a smudge off the table. It left a dull spot. Maybe it was time to have it refinished.

Would the news come out in the paper tomorrow? She felt panic rising in her throat. Would that be the day the police snapped cuffs on her son and dragged him to jail in front of the entire town of Hayden? Would that be the day her life was ruined?

She went into the study, to the little drawer where she kept her private things, and sifted through the articles there that she had been particularly proud of. Her son's valedictory speech. Her husband's educator's award. The newspaper article condemning Nick Marcello and Brooke Martin.

She unfolded the yellowed article and re-read the headlines as they had appeared seven years ago: "Teacher Fired for Rumored Affair with Student."

Pretty cut and dried, Abby mused. Didn't leave much room for doubt. But she knew now, as she had known then, that it wasn't *exactly* the truth. And she had done nothing to correct it.

She found herself back at the window in the living room. Would the papers have a field day with her son? Would they too take the story a little further for drama's sake and allege that her son was guilty of statutory rape?

The back of her neck prickled with a thin sheen of perspiration, and she released the top button of her gown and tried to take a deep breath. This must be how Brooke Martin felt the night before her story broke. The feeling of being trapped in a steel box with no air and no escape. It was a miserable feeling. Worse than torture.

Vaguely, Abby wondered if she could stop it all by forcing her son to apologize to Roxy . . . she could even go so far as apologizing to Brooke herself. Maybe she could even reconsider the budget for the church. Maybe she could find a way to bring the matter to a vote again.

Feeling a tiny bit better now that she stood at the brink of decision, Abby went to the phone and dialed her son's house. His wife answered, her kind, gentle voice oblivious to the turmoil in her marriage, oblivious to the humiliation she might soon suffer. But Bill had been adamant about not warning her . . . for the sake of the baby, he'd said. Instead, "for the sake of the baby," he was going to wait and let his wife discover the truth in the paper. The thought sent a jolt of anger through Abby. Bill still didn't see that there were wages for his sins, consequences for his mistakes that he could be made to pay. He still didn't believe the Martin girls would expose him.

"Carol, can I speak to Bill, please?" Abby said.

"He's not here," her daughter-in-law said. "He had to go back to the office to take care of some things."

"The office?" Abby repeated. Instantly she knew that Bill had lied, for city employees rarely had to work at night. Where could he have gone? What could he be up to now?

"Yes," Carol said. "I'll get him to call you when he gets back. Is everything all right?"

"Yes, fine," she said. "Do get him to call me."

Tears came to Abby's eyes as she turned back to the window and stared out between the flat bars of the vertical blinds into the night again. The waste! Was it too late to change, or had it all been futile? All the years of doing the right thing, the appropriate thing. All the sacrifices of heart and soul to make things neat, to keep them organized. All the loneliness and hollow memories, in the name of propriety.

And now it had come down to a thoughtless son who in one fell swoop could wipe out all the years of work and care, and make her heart ache for that one mistake in her past, the one wrong choice, the other man she should have married. Maybe Bill would leave town before the gossip could get started. Sharon had already fled because of impending scandal, and it had worked—they had been able to keep her pregnancy a secret. Now Abby had no idea where Sharon lived or how she earned a living—other than what Brooke had blurted out to her. But sacrifices had to be made.

She closed her eyes and cupped her hand over her mouth, trying to muffle the sobs of despair.

Gerald came in, wearing a smoking jacket and holding his pipe. "Did I hear you crying?" he asked.

She looked up at him and dabbed at her eyes. "I was just thinking about Bill. Worrying about it coming out in the paper. Do you think it will happen tomorrow?"

"I don't know," he said. "But if that paper prints a scandalous story about my son, so help me, I'll use every resource I have to close them down. They must know that."

"Do you think? Is it possible that it won't come out?"

"It's possible," he said. "But then there's word-of-mouth. And the possibility of arrest. Everybody has a price, even the sheriff. We'll just have to pay it."

He ambled to the window and looked out just as she had moments before, then turned his concerned face back to her. She started to cry harder, but he only shook his head. "Pull yourself together, Abby. For heaven's sake, those tears won't solve a thing. You should see yourself."

Puffing on his pipe, he went back to his study.

CHAPTER 46

NICK STOOD FROZEN IN DISBELIEF. How could he have been so careless as to drop the thing he had loved so much? He replayed the scene in his mind, trying to understand: Brooke's words had surprised him, he had swung around to face her, the statue had slipped . . .

And now it was destroyed. He leaned back against the counter, suddenly weak. He realized that he had never heard what she was going to say. Something about praying, asking the Lord something . . .

The phone rang, and he ignored it. It couldn't be Brooke; she hadn't had time to get home yet, and when she did, he'd be the last one she'd want to speak to. Before he could talk to anyone else, he had things to sort out.

But the phone continued to ring, and finally, out of frustration and mounting anger, he answered. "Yeah."

"Nicky? Is that you?" His mother's voice came across the line on a sigh of relief.

"Yes, Ma. It's me."

"We were worried!" she cried. "What's the matter with you, disappearing like that without telling nobody? How were we to know that you weren't lying in a ditch somewhere? Where were you?"

Nick rolled his eyes and wished he hadn't answered the phone. "I was out of town," he said. "I took the Duesenberg to a collector and sold it." There. That ought to give her something to bash him with.

"You did *what?*" his mother shouted. "You sold the Duesy? Papa's Duesy?"

Nick gripped the phone tightly and considered throwing it against the wall. "Ma, I really don't want to talk about this right now. I've got a lot on my mind."

"Well, I should say so," his mother lectured. "First running out on that sweet girl and now selling the car. Have you gone crazy in the head?"

Nick squinted and shook his head hard, struggling to make some sense of his mother's words. "What sweet girl? Ma, what are you talking about?"

"I'm talking about Brooke Martin, that's who. She came over looking for you, and we had a nice little visit. She was crying for you. Now, I'd like for you to tell me what is taking you so long? Why haven't you snapped her up by now? Why isn't there a ring on her finger?"

Nick backed against the wall. This was one argument he'd never expected to come out of his mother's mouth. He closed his eyes and tried to picture Brooke breaking down enough to go to his mother in tears. Hard to reconcile that image with the young girl who had run away without looking back. "I thought you didn't approve of her, Ma," he said in a weary, husky voice. "You told me, just the other day, that it was wrong, my relationship with her."

"Well, maybe I was the one who was wrong," his mother muttered in a quieter voice, as if she couldn't let any other family member hear her admit that. "When a girl stands before me with tears in her eyes and defends my boy as the most honorable, gentle man she's ever known, what else can I do but believe her? That girl is God's pick for you, Nicky, you mark my word."

Nick pinched the bridge of his nose and closed his eyes. "You may be wrong about that, Ma."

"Don't you say that, Nicky," his mother shouted, and he could almost see her wagging her finger at him. "You marry that girl and finish those windows. And I'll tell everybody that my boy, the artist, and the sweet girl God chose for him, was the one who made them. Your grandpa woulda been proud. And he woulda liked that girl too."

Nick smiled softly. "Thanks, Ma," he whispered.

He hung up the phone and looked down again at the spot on the floor where he had broken the sculpture, and wondered what Brooke had been about to tell him.

Nick, something happened tonight, when I was sitting here waiting for you. I prayed and told the Lord . . .

She prayed and told the Lord what? He closed his eyes. Had she given Christ her life? If she had, maybe there was a chance for them. Maybe God wasn't going to make him give her up after all.

It was all Brooke could do to make it through her parents' house without breaking down completely, but the moment she reached her bedroom, she fell to her knees and began crying out to God. She had given her life to Him, and He had given her peace. Why had He taken it away so soon? Why had He convinced Nick that they were wrong for each other?

Was it a punishment for the sins she had confessed or a test of her new faith?

She didn't know, but as she prayed and wept, she felt as if the Lord was lifting her and gathering her onto His lap. She wept into His chest and cried out the desires of her heart. And as she wept, she realized that the peace was still there, even in the company of sadness. She had given her life to the Lord of the universe, after all.

He didn't condemn her for her grief. After all, He had become a man too, flesh and blood. He understood.

"I'm still yours," she whispered as she wept. "Whatever you want to do with me. Just change my heart, so I'll want it too."

CHAPTER  47

$\mathscr{R}$OXY SMILED AS SHE TURNED HER headlights on and pulled out of the parking lot at Madame Zouvier's Dance Studio. She'd just informed her dance coach that she was coming back. The woman had embraced her with absolute joy and asked her if she would dance in the June recital.

Roxy nibbled on her lip. Was she really up to dancing in front of an audience again? Wouldn't she feel just as self-conscious, just as paranoid, as she had the last few times she'd performed? Would word have gotten out about her and Bill Hemphill?

Could she really get on stage and perform?

Then she smiled again. Yes. She could do it, because Sonny wanted to see her dance.

She glanced in her rearview mirror and noticed that the car behind was following her too closely, its headlights too bright. She'd had that same feeling—that someone was tailing her—on her way to the studio tonight.

Uneasy, she turned onto another street. The car turned with her. Quickly, she reached across the passenger seat to lock the door, then locked the one closest to her. She made another turn and watched in her mirror; as the car behind her turned, she saw its color and make.

Bill! Panic-stricken, she stepped on her accelerator and flew home, praying that her father would be there and that she could get safely into the house before Bill caught up with her. Roxy's hands trembled as she raced through town, fearing that he would find some way to keep her from getting there and attack her on a dark street where no one could hear.

Her car skidded to a halt in front of her house. Brooke's and her parents' cars blocked the driveway; she had no choice but to park on the street. As fast as she could, Roxy threw it into park and leaped out.

But Bill was faster. He grabbed her before she got halfway across the yard, and the potent smell of Scotch on his breath assaulted her as he threw his hand over her mouth and dragged her to the side of the house.

"I'll teach you to threaten me," he said as she struggled to break free. "I'll make you regret that you didn't do this the easy way."

She tried to scream, but her cry became no more than a muffled gurgle as his hand crushed harder against her mouth.

Bill flung her against the side of the garage. "Shut up and do what I tell you," he said, "or every neighbor on this street will be out here in thirty seconds flat. I may go down because of you, sweetheart, but you're going down with me. And when it's all over, it'll be worth it."

Roxy squeezed her eyes shut and fought with all her might.

CHAPTER

48

$\mathcal{N}$ICK FOUND NO PLACE TO PARK, either in front of Brooke's house or in the drive. He frowned, wondering if her family had company. That was all he needed—to have to be cordial as his heart burst to get Brooke alone. As he pulled to the curb at the house next door, he took mental inventory of the cars at the Martins' home. There was only one that didn't belong to the family.

As he got out, Nick prayed that Brooke would agree to talk to him. He didn't know why she would, after he'd broken *Infinity.* But if he could just talk to her . . . calmer, more rationally, maybe she would tell him about her talk with the Lord.

He closed his car door and started toward the house. An odd sound stopped him, one that didn't belong on a quiet residential street. He concentrated—and felt a surge of adrenaline when he identified the sound as the broken, muffled cries coming from the dark shadows beside the garage.

"Stop . . . please . . . No!"

He broke into a run, following the voice until he found Bill grappling with Roxy against the wall.

Something inside Nick snapped, and all the anger and pain and heartache and frustration burst within him as he lunged forward. His fist made shattering contact with Bill's jaw, and the man fell backward as Roxy screamed.

Bill struggled to his feet. Nick grabbed the man's collar and shoved him against the wall, his face inches from Bill's. "Don't you *ever* lay a hand on that girl again!"

"All this White Knight stuff is pretty noble coming from you," Bill spat out, his lip dribbling blood. "You know, you and I aren't so different. You liked them young too, if I remember."

Nick jolted the man's head against the wall again and jerked his face up so that Bill couldn't avoid seeing the fire in Nick's eyes. He threw Bill to his knees, and the man crawled to his feet again— then turned, only to see Roxy's father coming toward him with his own raging intentions.

"Call the police, Alice!" George shouted.

Bill barreled past them toward his car, his eyes luminous.

George started after Bill, but Roxy stopped him. "It's over, Daddy," she said, her sobs punctuating her words. "I don't want everyone to know about this. The Hemphills will just tell more lies, and it'll get out of hand, and we'll spend the next ten years fighting them. Nick stopped him before he did anything."

"That man should be in jail," Nick said, his shoulders rising and falling with each heavy breath. His eyes met Brooke's as she ran out of the house. "You have to report this," he said.

Brooke took a tentative step toward him. "Thank God you were here," she whispered.

Nick wiped the cold sweat from his face, then looked down at his feet, his heart pained with regret. "I came over to tell you how sorry I am about the sculpture, and there he was . . ."

George Martin tapped Nick's shoulder, and Nick turned to face the man who had once wanted to kill him—the man who had believed for nearly a decade that he'd stolen his daughter's virtue as shamelessly as Bill had tried to steal Roxy's. Holding Roxy protectively under one arm, George extended his right hand to Nick. "I think I've been wrong about a few things," he said quietly. "I owe you an—"

"You don't owe me anything, not after the trouble you folks have had over the years because of me," Nick cut in, his eyes misting with emotion.

"Well, maybe I was wrong about that too."

Brooke's eyes filled with tears as Nick took her father's hand and shook it in both of his. When her family had gone back inside to call the police, Nick fell back against the side of the house and raked both hands through his hair. He looked at Brooke, the moonlight casting curved slivers of light in his weary eyes.

"Nick, there's something I have to tell you," she whispered. "When I was at your house tonight, I started reading your Bible. And before you came home, I prayed, and . . . I gave my life to Christ."

Nick closed his eyes, wondering if he'd heard right. Sweet relief began to gently ease its way into his heart.

"Tonight when you came home and said those things and broke the sculpture, I would have thought my life was over, if I hadn't prayed that earlier. And I came home and prayed some more, and I know that God knows what's best for me. I know that whatever He has planned, it's better than anything I could have come up with. So it's okay that you don't want to be more than friends and colleagues. If we weren't meant to be—"

Before she could finish, he pulled her into his arms and clung to her with all his might. "He did have it planned," he whispered as tears rose in his throat. "We are meant to be. I thought I was being obedient, listening to Him about how we were different. But we're not different, Brooke. We're the same."

She pulled back and looked at him. "Those goals and beliefs and values? Is that what you mean?"

"Yes. It was all about God, Brooke. I want to be obedient."

"I do too. But I'll need help. I don't know much about God."

"I'll teach you." He crushed her against him again, then whispered, "Let's not wait and play the dating game and pretend we don't know what we want, Brooke. Will you marry me?"

Brooke pressed her forehead against his mouth and closed her eyes, savoring the words she had longed so many times to hear. "Yes, I'll marry you," she whispered.

His kiss was everything she had expected, more than she had dreamed. Bright light glowed in her grateful heart as she thanked her God for giving her such joy.

CHAPTER

*T*HE WHITE LIMOUSINE DRIVEN BY the pastor pulled to the front entrance of the new Hayden Bible Church, parting the hundreds of townspeople who had gathered there for the unveiling of the windows.

Nick's hand tightened over Brooke's, and she looked up at him with wonder and awe in her emerald eyes. "Nick, look at all these people," she whispered. "They actually came."

"They came as much out of gratitude as curiosity," the pastor said. "I've been making phone calls myself, making sure everyone in town realizes the sacrifices you two made for those windows."

Nick leaned over and gazed, awestruck, at the cars he recognized in the parking lot.

"Let's just hope they like them, or we'll be tarred and feathered by sundown."

Horace chuckled. "I've seen the windows. I don't think that's likely."

A cheer rose from the crowd as Brooke and Nick got out of the car, hands clasped tightly. They stood still for a moment, utterly amazed at the emotional welcome they received, but finally the pastor gestured for them to cut through the crowd and enter the finished church.

They went in, shaking hands as they went, and found that the inside held even more people than were outside. The room resounded with a loud roar that crescendoed as they made their way through to the pulpit.

Brooke felt a heady feeling of disbelief as she climbed the wine-colored steps. She glanced anxiously up at the windows, now covered in sheets that would drop to the floor at the assigned moment. Would the church members really like them when they saw them? Would they understand them?

Nick nudged her lightly and gestured toward a cluster of people standing near the platform. Roxy and Sonny were standing arm in arm, beaming proudly up at them, and her parents stood next to them, their pride evident on their faces. And then she saw Mrs. Marcello and the Castori clan, all waving at Nick as if to show everyone in the room that he was one of them.

The mayor stepped to the podium and quieted the crowd, and they saw the captive, anxious faces turn to listen. He began to speak about the reasons for the renovation, the steps involved in reconstructing the church, the church growth it would accommodate. Brooke's mind wandered, and she glanced over the proud faces, one by one, and asked herself if these had, indeed, been the same people who had condemned her and run her out of town. Had they also been the ones who gossiped after she and Nick got married in the empty, unfinished church?

But they were also the ones who had given donations out of their personal, individual funds to make up the balance of what they needed to complete the windows.

Abby Hemphill was conspicuously absent, but Brooke had expected that. So much had gone wrong in the woman's life in the past year. Bill, her son, had been arrested the night of his attack on Roxy, but had been released the next day because Roxy had refused to press the issue. But Bill had still wound up in jail the day after his baby was born, when he'd driven drunk and rammed his car into the glass front of a gas station, injuring the young woman in the car with him—a young woman who wasn't his wife. The scandal had created an uncrossable chasm in Mrs. Hemphill's family, and she had ultimately left her husband and her immaculate house and taken a condo in downtown St. Louis.

"But these two weren't daunted by the lack of funds available for a project they so believed in," the pastor was saying, and Brooke moved her gaze back to him. "They made supreme gestures of sacrifice to get the money to build the windows for a town and a church that had been less than gracious to them. I consider this a real act of love for the Lord. But in gratitude for that love, the town of Hayden has a love offering to give to them in return. A belated wedding gift, if they want to consider it that."

Brooke looked up at Nick, who seemed as confused as she as the crowd roared with delight, and she wondered if everyone in Hayden except she and Nick had been let in on the secret. The pastor stepped toward them. "We'll need you to step outside for a moment, if you don't mind."

Brooke and Nick looked at each other, and as the crowd parted, they stepped through and made their way to the door.

As they stepped out into the sunlight, they saw the gift they had never expected. Nick's grandfather's Duesenberg sat in the parking lot, as shiny and perfect as the day he had sold it.

Nick's face went slack, and Brooke burst into tears.

"The Finance Committee agreed to match, out of the church budget, whatever the members themselves could raise," the pastor said, laughing with delight at the shock on their faces. "And boy, did they come up with it. It meant a lot to all of us to get the Duesy back for you."

Tears filled Brooke's eyes, and she turned back to the crowd as another wave of applause swept over them. Nick drew her against him, his own poignant, eloquent expression touching her heart as he pulled Brooke with him to the microphone. "Thank you," he said, his voice cracking with emotion. "I can't tell you ..." His voice broke, and he took a moment to control himself. "... how much this means to me."

The crowd erupted in applause. He waited a moment as it died down, and finally he swallowed and nodded to Brooke that the moment of truth had come. "So now, if you're ready, I guess it's time to see what all the fuss is about."

He leaned down, cupped Brooke's chin, and dropped a kiss on her lips. "I love you," he whispered.

"I love you," she said. "Let's do it."

Together they reached for the single rope that would release the veils all the way around the church, and the crowd grew still with anticipation.

They pulled, and the sheets billowed to the ground, revealing a panorama of some of the most poignant stories in the Bible—all of them about the covenant-keeping God who worked in each of their lives.

For a moment, not one of all the hundreds of people present made a sound as they gazed up, their eyes circling the room, quietly experiencing the poetry of the windows.

Brooke's mouth went dry, and she shot Nick a panicked look. His frown told her he was as bewildered as she by the absolute silence.

Then suddenly, near the front, someone began to clap.

Then everyone was clapping, and Brooke saw other faces wet with tears, and children pointing overhead and asking questions of their parents, and elderly people nodding in affirmation. And it was as if each person there embraced the windows; as if they had been put there to speak directly to them.

Nick pulled Brooke into his arms and kissed her before God and the world, beneath the halo of beauty they had created with their own hands. And as she held him close, Brooke knew that the rest of her life with Nick would be as intense as the work they produced together, as emotional as the visions they shared, as all-encompassing as the windows that skirted the ceiling of the church for all the world to celebrate. Because God was guiding them, together . . .

Down the same lighted path.

Author's Afterword

*D*on't you hate it when things change? I sure do. And at this writing, I'm looking ahead to a spiritual time of change. You see, my pastor, Dr. Frank Pollard, announced this week that he will be retiring in just a few months.

As I sat in my pew and listened to that announcement, I found myself struck with grief, as if a family member were saying good-bye. Selfishly, I mourned the fact that such a stable, humble, precious part of my spiritual life would be moving on. I mourned for myself and wanted to cling and cry and ask him not to go. I wanted to run to him and ask, "What about *me?*" But I couldn't speak at all, so I swallowed back my tears and decided to speak to him another time when I could be less selfish and think, instead, of all that God has in store for us as our church turns this corner.

I didn't realize how important this man was to my life, since his work in this megachurch made it impossible for frequent one-on-one contact with him. He had his hands full with eight thousand sheep. But over ten years ago, when I joined his church as a broken, grieving, divorced mother of two, Frank Pollard's flock embraced me and drew me in. His philosophy was that church should be a healing place, not an execution chamber. He said time and time again that when hurting people came to our church we would send an ambulance and not a firing squad. In the triage of that wonderful place, my wounds were bound and my broken heart was healed. I was able to rediscover Christ there because he smiled at me from the faces of the members and he touched me through their hands. And through Frank Pollard's two weekly messages, I grew in my walk in the Lord. His prayers and those of his flock unleashed God's power on my life as I gave my career—my last holdout—to the Lord.

So if my books have ministered to you, then you owe Frank Pollard too.

But this is not about one man. This is about the power of the church. I often receive letters from Christians who aren't plugged in and don't have that support system, that accountability, that love. Some belong to dead churches where that support and ministry don't really exist. They praise God alone from barren places and don't know the joy of assembling together with other believers, belonging to a family to whom they can turn in times of joy and stress and devastation. They don't know the joy of being challenged by a preacher who calls them to a closer walk with Jesus.

For those, I pray that God will lead them to a new church, one where the Holy Spirit is evident at the front door, where his power is at work in the ministries of that church, where they can be engaged and active, and experience the joy of riding in that ambulance that goes to the hurting world, and tells them that healing can be found in Jesus Christ, and that he's waiting to give it to them, if only they'll give themselves to him.

God was so good to give Frank Pollard to our church as a minister of his love. May each of you find a shepherd like him, to lead you toward the Great Shepherd.

—Terri Blackstock

About the Author

*T*erri Blackstock is an award-winning novelist who has written for several major publishers including Harper-Collins, Dell, Harlequin, and Silhouette. Published under two pseudonyms, her books have sold over 3.5 million copies worldwide.

With her success in secular publishing at its peak, Blackstock had what she calls "a spiritual awakening." A Christian since the age of fourteen, she realized she had not been using her gift as God intended. It was at that point that she recommitted her life to Christ, gave up her secular career, and made the decision to write only books that would point her readers to him.

"I wanted to be able to tell the truth in my stories," she said, "and not just be politically correct. It doesn't matter how many readers I have if I can't tell them what I know about the roots of their problems and the solutions that have literally saved my own life."

Her books are about flawed Christians in crisis and God's provisions for their mistakes and wrong choices. She claims to be extremely qualified to write such books, since she's had years of personal experience.

A native of nowhere, since she was raised in the Air Force, Blackstock makes Mississippi her home. She and her husband are the parents of three children—a blended family which she considers one more of God's provisions.

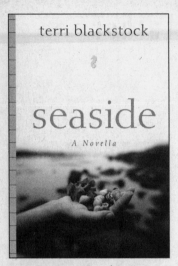

terri blackstock

seaside

A Novella

Seaside

Terri Blackstock

Seaside is a novella of the heart—poignant, gentle, true, offering an eloquent reminder that life is too precious a gift to be unwrapped in haste.

Sarah Rivers has it all: successful husband, healthy kids, beautiful home, meaningful church work.

Corinne, Sarah's sister, struggles to get by. From Web site development to jewelry sales, none of the pies she has her thumb stuck in contains a plum worth pulling.

No wonder Corinne envies Sarah. What she doesn't know is how jealous Sarah is of her. And what neither of them realizes is how their frantic drive for achievement is speeding them headlong past the things that matter most in life.

So when their mother, Maggie, purchases plane tickets for them to join her in a vacation on the Gulf of Mexico, they almost decline the offer. But circumstances force the issue, and the sisters soon find themselves first thrown together, then ultimately *drawn* together, in one memorable week in a cabin called "Seaside."

As Maggie, a professional photographer, sets out to capture on film the faces and moods of her daughters, more than film develops. A picture emerges of possibilities that come only by slowing down and savoring the simple treasures of the moment. It takes a mother's love and honesty to teach her two daughters a wiser, uncluttered way of life—one that can bring peace to their hearts and healing to their relationship. And though the lesson comes on wings of grief, the sadness is tempered with faith, restoration, and a joy that comes from the hand of God.

Hardcover: 0-310-23318-6

Pick up a copy today at your favorite bookstore!

ZONDERVAN™

GRAND RAPIDS, MICHIGAN 49530
www.zondervan.com

Best-selling books with Beverly LaHaye

Softcover 0-310-23519-7

Softcover 0-310-24296-7

Hardcover 0-310-23319-4

Check out these great books from Terri Blackstock, too!

Second Chances Series

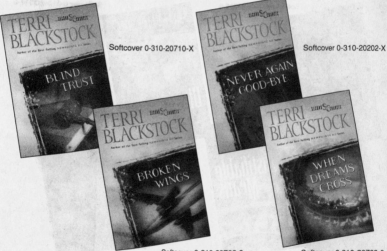

Softcover 0-310-20710-X

Softcover 0-310-20202-X

Softcover 0-310-20708-8

Softcover 0-310-20709-6

Pick up a copy today at your favorite bookstore!

ZONDERVAN™

GRAND RAPIDS, MICHIGAN 49530

www.zondervan.com

Other favorites from Terri Blackstock...

Softcover 0-310-21757-1

Softcover 0-310-21759-8

Softcover 0-31(

Softcover 0-310-20(

Pick up

FICTION BLACK-STOCK
Blackstock, Terri,
Emerald windows /

EAST ATLANTA

Atlanta-Fulton Public Library